To Jen and
Jeff,
I hope you
enjoy!

Return to
Cayman

ERIC DOUGLAS

Copyright © 2015 Eric Douglas
All rights reserved.
ISBN: 1512035874
ISBN-13: 978-1512035872

DEDICATION

Thank you Beverly for supporting me, believing me, and kicking me in the tail when I didn't believe in myself. It's all for you.

CONTENTS

ACKNOWLEDGMENTS

I would like to thank my review committee. I couldn't do it without you all: Beverly Douglas, Bonnie Blackwell, Jon Rusho, Bill Gardner, Charlie Morgan, Suzanne Garrett, Greg Holt, Lois Douglas, Gail Withrow, Danny Boyd, Sandy Sondrol, Steve Barnett, Pam Collins, Dan and Betty Orr, Eric Hexdalll, Keith Sahm and Deveron Milne.

Cover design by Brenda Pinnell
Cover photo courtesy of Sunset House, Grand Cayman
.

CHAPTER 1

The air smelled fresh and new, scrubbed clean by a brief afternoon thunderstorm. Now that the clouds had moved back to sea, the sun was bright and strong. That would bring the humidity back, but it wasn't there yet. A passing storm made the landing at Owen Roberts International Airport on Grand Cayman a lively one with rising air and cross winds, but it was nothing the pilots hadn't experienced dozens of times before. They skillfully brought the passenger jet to the tarmac.

The palm trees outside the airport made Mike Scott smile. It had been 10 years since he had been there, much too long in his mind. He had planned to come back sooner, but his career had other ideas. An international photojournalist, Mike rushed from trouble spot to trouble spot. Even the easier days and simpler stories often had a way of getting interesting. And he wouldn't have it any other way.

"Hey man, you just gonna stand there all day? Let's go!" Mike heard a familiar voice call out. He smiled to see his friend Kelly sitting outside baggage claim in a new crossover SUV. Kelly was, of course, sitting in the right hand side of the car.

"What happened to my jeep? Don't tell me you wrecked it?"

"Your jeep? Yours? You sold me that jeep 15 years ago when you left the island. I finally had to retire it. It was just too old," Kelly said with a grin.

"I know, but the times we had in it…" Mike grinned as he loaded his suitcase and dive gear into the hatchback area of the small SUV. Mike climbed in the left-hand front seat and took stock of the car. "I guess this one's comfortable, but it's not like the old jeep."

"Are you done complaining?" Kelly asked. "Can we go now?"

"You in a hurry for some reason?"

"Let's think about it for a second. We're on a beautiful Caribbean island with amazing water surrounding it and cool rum drinks all over the place and you want to hang out in the airport parking lot."

"And more importantly, Tanya's waiting for us," Mike said with a grin.

"And she'll kill me if I don't get you to the party," Kelly said, laughing as he put the car in gear and pulled out into traffic.

Tanya was Kelly's wife. A Russian marine biologist, she and Kelly had been together forever, but they were having a party for their 10th anniversary. When Mike got the call to hold the date, he had finally cleared his own calendar and made plans to return to Grand Cayman. He had been there when the pair first met, he was there for Kelly's marriage proposal and the wedding, so he wasn't about to miss this. It promised to be the party of the year.

Grand Cayman always held a special place in Mike's heart. It was there he had spent a couple years working as a photopro after college before he decided he preferred to photograph people. And later, it was on Grand Cayman that he and his friend Kelly had stopped a greedy land developer from tearing up the coral reef to build a new cruise ship dock.

In just a few minutes, Mike and Kelly were in downtown George Town, passing by the waterfront. Things were quiet, no cruise ships were there, although Mike knew they still regularly made George Town a port-of-call. They would off-load thousands of passengers a day to shop in the stores along the water front and take water excursions to dive or snorkel close to the main harbor. Sometimes there were as many as three or four cruise ships anchored in the harbor, ferrying passengers to shore.

Mike and Kelly passed through town quickly and headed out South Church Street toward their ultimate destination. When Mike made plans to come to the anniversary party, Tanya had told him not to worry about getting a room. They were taking care of that. When Mike was last on the island, the end result of the turmoil was that Kelly was able to buy Sunset House. It was an iconic dive resort they had both worked at, back in the day. Now, he could run it the way he wanted. The way they had talked about all those years ago when Kelly, Mike, and Tanya were young dive instructors full of fire and dreams.

Pulling in, Mike could tell that things were going well. The hotel was on a narrow strip of land, between the road and the ocean. Turning into the parking lot and going down the slight hill, everything opened up. It was compact, but that was the way the guests liked it. The bar, the restaurant and the dive shop, along with the shore entry to a world-class house-reef, were in easy reach. Everything was spit and polished and looked well-cared for. The resort was full with people milling around, but something seemed different. Climbing out of Kelly's SUV, Mike immediately recognized several people. There were dive staff members he remembered from when he was on the island and younger dive leaders he knew from his last visit.

"You shut the whole place down, didn't you?" Mike asked, genuinely amazed at what his friend had done.

"Yep. Everyone here's our guest, not a guest of the hotel. We own this place for the week!" Kelly said. "But don't think you can tear anything up. I know the owners."

Kelly and Tanya originally bought Sunset House with the help of investors, but had quickly been able to purchase the resort outright. Kelly did it the hard way, but he had gone from itinerant dive instructor to businessman and resort owner.

"Hey, I can't promise anything when you pack this many cowboys into one place," Mike said while he grabbed his bags from the back. Before he had a chance to carry his bags anywhere, a resort staff member lifted his dive bag onto his back and started heading for a room. Mike stood bewildered for a minute.

"I said everyone here is our guest, but the resort staff is going to take good care of you. Especially you."

Before Mike could ask what that meant, he heard footsteps coming up fast behind him. He turned to see who was running at him and was nearly tackled.

"Michael! You're here!" It was Tanya, pronouncing his name with her still-lingering Russian accent as 'ME Kal'. "The party can finally get started!"

Mike turned and gave Tanya a hug.

"What do you mean the party can finally get started? You can't be waiting on me. There's always a party in My Bar."

Tanya turned to Kelly. "You haven't told him yet?"

"Told me what?"

"We couldn't start the party without the Best Man!"

"What're you guys talking about? You got married 10 years ago."

"We're going to renew our vows. Our wedding was pretty small, so this time we are going to do it the way we want with all of our friends. And since you've been with us along the way, you're going to share in this one, too!" Kelly said.

CHAPTER 2

Jay walked through the doors of the Cayman Islands Department of the Environment, stepping from the heat and humidity of the day into the almost-too-cold air-conditioned offices. The Department of the Environment was part of the Ministry for Financial Services, Commerce and Environment, a combination that might seem odd somewhere else, but the environment and the tourism it brought in were key to the financial sustainability of the island.

The Cayman Islands: Grand Cayman, Little Cayman, and Cayman Brac were world-renowned for scuba diving. Three relatively tiny islands just south of Cuba, they attracted divers and vacationers from all over the world. Some came to the island to visit the elegant resorts on Seven Mile Beach and dive as part of their stay. Others came there to do nothing but dive as much as they could. Of course, the cruise ship passengers dived or snorkeled on their day excursions, too. That amount of pressure made protecting the majestic coral reefs, beaches, and marine life a continual balancing act for the staff at the DoE. And that preservation was what Jay had in mind.

At six feet tall, Jay had the looks and bearing of a movie star and he used it to his advantage. An American, he came from money, but he had also been successful building his own software company and he wanted to use his money and influence for the good of the oceans.

"Can I help you, sir?"

"Hi there, ummm," Jay quickly glanced down to see the woman's name plate on her desk. "Hi, Trina. I'm Jay. I have an appointment to see the director. I'm Jaylend Taylor."

"Good to see you, Jay. I'm sorry, Mr. Taylor. I'll let the director know you are here."

Trina stood and walked to the closed door of her boss's office. She was slender and blonde. Jay noted she had the accent and look of an eastern European. Pretty, with shoulder-length blonde hair.

"The director will see you now. Go on in," she said, holding the door open and giving him a smile. Jay barely gave her another glance as he entered the office. He was focused on this meeting. And he was used to that reaction from women.

"Welcome, Mr. Taylor," the older Cayman native said from behind his desk as Jay entered the room.

Jay took a moment to survey the room. He had done his homework and *knew* the man he was meeting, even though it was the first time they had come face to face. They had, of course, communicated by email for a while before he made the trip to Grand Cayman as well. Nothing happened without email exchanges anymore. "Thank you for taking the time to meet with me, Mr. Travers. It is an honor."

Travers was in his late 50s, with gray hair at his temples. He was slight of build and fit, with the dark skin of someone born on the island. Jay knew the minister had been educated in the United States, but had returned home to serve his country. He had worked his way up through the governmental ranks, leading a distinguished career of honesty and integrity. His predecessor in the office of the Department of the Environment had been less-so and when Travers took over nearly 10 years ago, he had cleaned house and put the department on the right track. Jay knew Travers wasn't an environmentalist who put preserving the environment before everything else, but the man had a solid reputation of caring for the island. He hoped it was all true.

The office was large and well decorated, but not opulent. Teak furniture filled the room with a solid teak desk as the centerpiece. There were two comfortable leather chairs facing it. The walls were covered with photos of Travers with dignitaries and celebrities. Beyond that, it looked like the office of someone who worked. Not a director who let others work for him.

"I hope you'll forgive me for getting right to business, but I have a very busy day. I know of your software company. In fact, we use some of your products here in our office, but I'm not sure what you need," Travers said. "How can I help you?"

"Honestly, Mr. Travers, it is how I can help you. As you said, I've been fortunate and successful with my company. It has given me the ability to do whatever I want. I could come here to Grand Cayman and enjoy all the luxuries you have to offer and never work another day in my life if I didn't want to. But that's not the sort of person I am." Jay leaned forward in his chair. "I want to set up a coral reef monitoring system around the entire island. It will be a way to monitor every reef we have and to make sure that no one place is under too much pressure from visitors. We could use it to help the dive operations choose where to dive and to let dive sites take a break and recover."

Jay went on to explain that he would place sensors all around the island, tracking visits from dive boats and gathering information on how many divers were on each boat. If any one site got too many visitors in a year, they could shift to a different site. He also proposed to perform an environmental survey on every dive site on the island to determine if any of those sites were already in peril.

"Mr. Taylor, that sounds like a very ambitious plan, and I appreciate you bringing it to me. We already have scientists monitoring the reefs around the island, but nothing quite as elaborate as you have proposed. I don't know how we could pay for it, though. It sounds very expensive."

"That's the best part of the offer I'm making. You won't have to pay anything for it. I'll pay for everything. I've been diving here many, many times and I love this island like I was born here. This is my way of giving back," Jay explained. He sat back in his chair to wait for Travers to think about what he had just said.

Travers was silent for a moment, studying his visitor.

"Mr. Taylor, you have given me a lot to consider. I will have to take this to the Minister, and I'm sure there will be things I haven't considered, but this is truly exciting. I will also want our scientists to look your proposal over and make sure it fits into our plan. I'll want you to meet with Tanya Demechev so she can show you what we've been doing. Her research may be able to provide a baseline in several locations around the island. It isn't quite as comprehensive as what you're suggesting, but I'm sure it will be useful. "

"I understand completely," Jay said standing and handing Travers a written copy of the proposal. "I look forward to hearing from you after you have had a chance to talk this over with the Minister and your staff. I'm sure Miss Demechev's research will be useful as a starting point for what I propose to do."

Jay left the director's office smiling. Things were going his way.

CHAPTER 3

"Keep Cayman Pure!"

"Make Cayman Green!"

"Not about money, about the environment!"

A small group of protesters marched in a circle around a young man on a bullhorn in front of the Department of the Environment as Jay walked past. *When will these simpletons ever learn? That's not the way to get things done. Money is the key to everything*, he thought as he stepped around them.

The young man in the middle of the circle continued to bark out his chants. He was just over six feet tall with a barrel chest, brown curly hair and fair skin. His accent belied his American roots. He was clearly the organizer of the protest. His marchers represented a mixture of young men and women, white and black, who appeared to be both Caymanian and from outside as well.

"We need to stop the destruction of coral reefs and the environment for the sake of greed and the convenience of tourists," the young man shouted while his marchers waved their signs and marched in a circle. "Grand Cayman can be a shining beacon for the world to see. Not just a playground for the rich and famous!"

"Mister, do you hear me? Don't buy into the stories they tell you!" the young man shouted at two men crossing the street. "We need to focus on the island's environment!"

It just so happened the two men crossing the street were Mike and Kelly. Mike paused to listen to the young man for a minute. It was the morning after Mike's arrival, and they were headed out to make a dive.

"What're you doing, Mike?" Kelly asked.

"Oh, it's the journalist in me. I can't pass up a good protest," Mike said with a grin. "I've covered them all over the world."

"This one isn't likely to change the government or overthrow any dictators," Kelly said, gesturing to the small group. "Come on. We need to take care of business and then meet Tanya. She's organizing the dive today on her research site and you know she wants to share it with you, too."

"You'd be surprised what a small group can accomplish when it sets its mind to it," the protest group's leader said, approaching Mike and Kelly before Mike got a chance to respond to his friend. "You two don't seem like the average cruise ship tourists to me."

"What makes you say that?" Mike asked, curious at the young man's approach.

"Well, first, the tourists don't make it this far into town. They only have a few hours on land so they barely make it off of Harbour Drive or they're off on a whirlwind excursion somewhere. You two are walking with a purpose, but not in a hurry."

"Impressive," Mike said. "Go on."

"You're both dressed for the island." The protester looked the men up and down. Both Mike and Kelly were wearing sandals, shorts and, polo shirts. "But you aren't wearing cheesy t-shirts."

"Not bad, kid," Kelly said. "You pay attention."

"It's my job," the protester said, offering his hand. "I'm Bill. Bill Gardner."

"You're obviously an American. What're you doing down here?" Mike was genuinely curious.

"Trying to save the coral reefs. This place is ground zero for economic environmental devastation. We need to do anything we can to stop it," Bill said. "I'm here for a few weeks to shake some things up and see what I can accomplish."

"Believe it or not, some of us on the island are doing what we can to keep the 'economic environmental devastation' to a minimum," Kelly said, giving those three words air quotes with his fingers.

"I get that you're working to keep things from getting too bad," Bill said. "But I want to turn back the clock and make it better. The banking industry on this island controls the Department of the Environment. It's all tied together. If they won't listen to us about saving the environment, we have to put a strangle hold on the economics and tourism until they do."

"You planning to do that with your huge protest here?" Kelly asked. He had seen more than his fair share of college kids on Spring Break coming down to party and pretend to be activists. He wasn't buying Bill's spiel.

"This's just to let them know we're watching. I have other plans already in the works," Bill said matter-of-factly.

"Where are you from?" Mike asked, changing the angle of the questioning. He was a little alarmed at what the young man just said, but didn't want to press it too hard.

"West Virginia," Bill said, turning to face Mike, his attitude obvious. "And please don't tell me you know someone in Richmond."

"That's funny, Bill. And don't worry, I know where West Virginia is. It's my home, too. I grew up there and went to Marshall University," Mike said.

"You're kidding! I just graduated from Marshall," Bill said, his demeanor changing instantly. His superior tone and stance relaxed. "Hey, wait a minute, I recognize you. You were on campus recently. You were involved in that big mess with the anthropology department and the Adena burial mound. It was in all the papers. I think I even saw you on campus once or twice afterward. Your name is Mike, right?"

"Yep, that was me," Mike agreed. "I stayed around and did a couple of guest lectures in the school of journalism."

"Man, it's a small world," Bill said, looking back over his shoulder at his small group of protesters. "Well, look guys, you aren't the people I'm here to influence, and it seems like my people are losing focus when I'm not there to cheer them on. I need to get back to it."

"Do what you have to do, Bill. Just stay out of trouble," Mike said, grinning. "Oh, and Go Herd!"

"Go Herd, Mike! See you around." Bill trotted back to his group and got them moving again.

"These kids come here with their ideals, but they don't have any idea what it takes to make the world go around," Kelly said.

"I know, but remember when we used to be that idealistic? We were going to save the world before lunch and still have time for the parties," Mike agreed.

"I'm still trying to save the world, mostly because of Tanya. If it weren't for her, I'll admit I would be focused on running the business and trying to live my life," Kelly said. "Not nearly as many parties as there used to be."

"You got that right."

"And speaking of Tanya, we have to get a move on. We have to reserve those chairs and tables for the party and then she really wants to show you her latest project."

"Good point. The last thing we want to do is make her upset this week," Mike said, laughing at his friend. They began walking a little faster toward their destination. Tanya was a caring person, but she also had a bit of a temper.

"That kid said he recognized you from some story? I thought you were supposed to be writing the stories, not making them," Kelly said as they crossed the street.

"Ever since that mess here 10 years ago, it seems like I've been more and more involved in the stories I've been sent to cover," Mike said with a grin as they walked away.

CHAPTER 4

The last time Mike had been on Grand Cayman, a dive with Tanya had tipped Mike off to the actions of a greedy developer who was tearing up sections of the coral reef surrounding the island in search of a shipwreck full of treasure. At the time, Tanya was an independent researcher who had a small project for the Department of the Environment. The developer found out about Tanya's discovery and torched her lab, destroying all of her records. Once it was all over, however, Tanya was tasked with coordinating the underwater conservation efforts around all three Cayman Islands: Grand Cayman, Little Cayman, and Cayman Brac. That series of events had been a terrible time for Mike, Kelly, and Tanya. Kelly almost lost his life, but like many challenges, with some teamwork and effort, it had worked out well for all three of them in the end.

Today's dive was similar to Tanya's earlier projects. They were completing surveys to check the status of the coral growth, taking photographs and measuring new growth. This time, they would be diving right in the middle of the main harbor in George Town to see the progress the island had made restoring the coral reefs in that heavily trafficked area.

Tanya was standing on the stern of a dive boat, staring at a clipboard and impatiently making notes, when Mike and Kelly came trotting up to the end of the dock. They had loaded their gear on the boat earlier and agreed with Tanya that they would meet her for the dive after their business was done.

"It's about time. You're late," Tanya said, looking directly at Kelly. She was smiling, but there was an edge to her voice.

"Sorry, babe," Kelly said, giving his wife a hug and a kiss. "It's all Mike's fault."

With that, Kelly let go of his wife and quickly moved to the side to talk to the boat's captain. As soon as Mike's feet were on board, the crew began throwing off lines to move the boat away from the dock.

"What am I going to do with you two?" Tanya asked Mike. "You can't even show up for the boat on time."

"Well, ummm, you see it's…" Mike stumbled until he looked Tanya in the eyes and realized she was still smiling, but this time the edge was gone.

"Oh, Michael, it is okay. It is so good to see you two together again," she said and hugged Mike. "Pashli," Tanya said in Russian, all business again. "Let's go!" She turned and left Mike standing by himself.

Tanya had three two-man teams of divers on board. Four, if you counted Mike and Kelly, although they were more sightseers than scientists. An avid underwater photographer since his days as a photo pro on the island, Mike had brought his camera housing along on this trip. Whenever he could, Mike still liked to get in the water and do some diving. He often planned an extra day on a trip, when he could afford the time, to make a dive or two, although the extra luggage required for the housing for his digital camera was a burden. The last time Mike dived with Tanya in Cayman, she had coerced him into bringing his camera along for a possible magazine story on her work. This time, she hadn't said a word about any publicity. But Mike knew she wouldn't mind if he shared his photos with her.

The boat captain took them just a few minutes ride into the harbor. The day before, when Mike arrived, there hadn't been any cruise ships in the harbor. Today, two gleaming white ships sat just offshore, delivering their passengers to the shops along the waterfront with ferry boats. Mike noted a third cruise ship was approaching the island, as well. Modern cruise ships were massive, holding thousands of passengers and nearly as many crew members. They were essentially floating cities and were larger than World War II battleships.

The purpose of this dive was to look at the effects the massive ships had on the reefs in the harbor area. They were also assessing the improvements made by rules the Department of the Environment had put into place. As they geared up for the dive, Mike noted Tanya wasn't getting ready.

"Tanya, aren't you joining us, today?"

"No. You and Kelly enjoy this dive. I'm going to stay topside and coordinate the real working divers," Tanya said. "This is the curse of being in charge. I don't get to dive as much as I used to."

"Don't I know that," Kelly said, shaking his head and checking over his gear. "I don't get in the water nearly as much as I'd like. But since you're here, I get an excuse to play!"

"Glad I could serve some purpose," Mike said with a laugh.

"Of course. I don't know how long it's been since you've been in the water. I need an experienced instructor to watch you. And I can't spare any of my people," Tanya said.

"Is she kidding?" Mike asked, turning to look at Kelly.

"Honestly, there are times I have no idea. And I've been married to her for ten years. Come on, let's get in the water before she decides we need to be more productive on this dive."

Mike and Kelly stood and moved to the stern of the dive boat. They pulled their dive fins on their feet at the swim step and did a final check of their gear. Just before Mike stepped off the boat, he heard a high pitched whining sound over his head. He glanced up and saw a small drone coming out across the water. He shook his head. The things were everywhere anymore. Everyone was getting into the act.

Mike took his giant stride out into the water. After a quick signal to the boat's divemaster that they were okay, the dive buddies turned and descended to the reef 20 feet below them.

Mike smiled as the warm Caribbean water washed over his head. He felt totally at ease taking a breath from his regulator. He equalized his ears to the increasing pressure and allowed himself to sink slowly toward the reef. It opened up in front of him, an explosion of color and small reef fish. Mike could see brain coral, staghorn, and elkhorn coral and even some fire coral at a quick glance.

Taking a closer look, Mike realized everything wasn't perfect, however. The reef inside the harbor had taken a beating over the years as boats indiscriminately dropped anchors or large ships brushed against corals as they made their way in, either from negligence or from faulty and outdated charts. Accidental discharges from visiting vessels and storm water runoff had clouded the water as well, reducing the sunlight that fed the coral.

The divable reefs just outside the harbor had seen better days as well. Visiting cruise ship passengers often got off the boats, took a short ride to the closest dive shop that catered to cruise ship passengers, and got right back on a smaller boat. They never went more than a half mile from their cruise ship before they were underwater. That much diving from that many divers led to its own pressure. Errant fin kicks from rusty, inexperienced divers, hand touches and other wear and tear made it difficult for the coral to thrive.

Realizing the problem, and the threat to Grand Cayman's survival as a tourist destination, the Department of the Environment enacted rules restricting the use of some reefs to relieve that pressure and created a system to rotate dive sites between dive operators all at Tanya's suggestion. Her researchers were documenting the recovery they were seeing for a report on this pilot project.

While the reefs didn't look "virgin" by any stretch of the imagination, Mike could see signs of new growth and recovery. That made him smile. His friends were doing some good.

Mike was content to follow Kelly on the dive. It had been a while since he had dived this area and he knew Kelly would show him the best spots. Mike had his camera with him, his digital SLR camera, in a specially made housing that would allow him to take it anywhere he wanted. And deeper than he wanted to go. And really, he was simply taking photos because he wanted to. He wasn't working. He wouldn't know what to do with his hands if he weren't shooting.

Kelly led them at an easy pace, allowing Mike to pause and take photos and explore as he wanted. The area they were diving was known for coral swim-throughs and Kelly led Mike to several of them. Mike was certified as a cave diver so being in tight spaces with a roof over his head wasn't new for him. Still, it gave him a moment's pause when Kelly led him into a long, narrow tube underneath and through the coral. It took a moment for his eyes to adjust to the gloom. Small openings in the reef above them allowed light into the swim-through, keeping it from being completely dark, but those sky lights were much too small for a diver to fit through.

Before they began the dive, Kelly told Mike that he planned to take him through a special swim-through that they didn't share with visiting tourist divers. They might take tourists through swim-throughs that traveled for 15 or 20 feet, short enough for the diver to see the other end, but that was all. This part of the dive was something the dive pros on the island kept to themselves.

When exploring an underground cave, divers tie off a line behind them so they could find their way back out. More than one diver paid the ultimate price for not doing so. In a coral swim-through, there was no turning around. You simply followed it to the other end... even if you couldn't see it.

Once Mike's eyes adjusted, and he turned on his external flash units to light up the swim-through properly, Mike began photographing the coral tube. It wasn't as colorful as the coral outside, since the sunlight was dramatically reduced, but the formations inside were in better shape. There were larger reef fish and soft corals as well.

Mike's exhaled breaths pooled on the roof of the swim-through as he swam along, looking like mercury wiggling above his head, disturbed by even the slightest ripples in the water. The pathway was narrow, making them swim single-file.

Mike noticed the light growing dimmer in front of Kelly. They had reached a section devoid of skylights. Kelly turned abruptly to his left, following the path laid out through the ancient bones of the dead coral in front of them. Mike lost sight of him for a moment as he approached the elbow in the tunnel. For a moment, Mike was alone.

Making the turn, Mike came face to face with a prehistoric creature. A Goliath grouper sat calmly in Mike's way, not blinking and barely moving in the current-less tunnel. In spite of his experience and knowledge, in spite of himself, Mike startled at the sight. The massive fish's gray-green scales were rough and thick and covered with dark black spots and dark green patches. It had huge lips lining its mouth that stayed ever-so-slightly open and its large eyes were set back on either side of its face. The fish's body was built like a triangle, wider at the bottom and narrow at the top with two pectoral fins that barely budged to keep the Goliath in position.

That's an ancient one, Mike thought as he got his breathing back under control. *Must go 1,000 pounds.* Mike could almost hear Kelly laughing ahead of him. Grouper tend to hang out in the same place and enjoy their solitude. Mike was sure Kelly knew the enormous fish would be hanging out in the tunnel. His only satisfaction was knowing the grouper was probably as unhappy at seeing Mike, and Kelly before him, as Mike was with running into him in a blind, dark alley.

Good thing they don't bite.

Ever the photographer, Mike paused for a few minutes to photograph the gentle giant in front of him. The fish barely acknowledged him as Mike moved in close to fill the frame with the animal. When he was done, Mike moved to the side of the narrow passageway and watched the Goliath slowly back into a small alcove in the coral. Mike made his way past and could see light up ahead. The grouper must have been blocking the light at the end of the tunnel. Mike saw the silhouette of a diver at the entrance and knew Kelly was waiting for him. When Mike got close enough, he could see the laughter in his old friend's eyes. Kelly gestured to the camera and signaled like he knew Mike would want to photograph the Goliath grouper. Mike smiled back and gestured toward his friend, in a way that left no doubt of his feelings about the gag Kelly played on him.

They were only in the tunnel for a few minutes, but Mike instantly felt better coming back out into the light. In his years of diving, he had spent hours underwater in caves, but the feeling was the same regardless. There was always a vague sense of relief when he could see the sun again and knew he could make a direct ascent to the surface. That made the shadow that passed over the two divers that much more disconcerting. They looked up as one and saw what obscured the sun. A massive cruise ship, the one they saw from the distance approaching the harbor, had arrived. Where they hovered, less than 20 feet underwater, they felt like they could almost touch the hull of the massive ship, its gray anti-fouling paint clean below the surface. The ship came to a stop, like it had reached its final destination.

Mike looked at Kelly and realized something was wrong. Behind the mask and regulator mostly obscuring his face, Mike could tell Kelly was angry, but he didn't know why. Kelly gave Mike the signal that they needed to move. They began swimming in the same general direction as the massive ship, heading back toward their dive boat. Kelly took off swimming. Mike did his best to follow, but the large camera in his hands made that a little more difficult.

CHAPTER 5

Tanya was deep in her reports, sitting on the swaying boat and feeling mildly nauseous. A swaying boat at anchor made her feel that way, especially when she was looking down and trying to read. The divers were bringing her consistent numbers and their efforts really seemed to be paying off. She just had to figure out the best way to present it to the Department of the Environment so they continued to support her work and spread their efforts to more dive sites around the island. They had told her if she was able to fix things, or at least improve them, in the harbor, she could improve things anywhere.

Fish populations were up. Coral growth and regrowth were up. There was a greater diversity of coral and fish species, too. Not just more numbers of a few fish, but more types of fish. They still had to figure out the best way to deal with the invasive lionfish, but the lionfish rodeos seemed to be keeping them at bay for now. Several restaurants on the island had added lionfish entrees to their menus and the local divers and fishermen were doing their best to keep the eateries supplied. That was the one case where Tanya agreed, and fully supported, overfishing. "Eat 'em to beat 'em" was a motto crossing the Caribbean.

Tanya *felt* something coming up behind her before she saw it. She turned to see a massive cruise ship approaching the harbor. But it was out of position. The ship needed to be 100 yards to its port—the north. It was too far to the south and right on top of the coral reef they were tracking. A feeling of dread came over Tanya. It was right where Mike and Kelly were diving, too.

The radio. Tanya sprinted for the boat's pilot house. The captain had been dozing in the sun, waiting on the divers to return and was startled to see Tanya come flying up and more startled to see the massive white hull looming in front of him.

"We have to pull the anchor and move!" the boat captain shouted at Tanya. "Dat ting gonna run us down!"

"We can't move, Biko. We still have divers in the water. Send out the recall. Get them up here, now!" Tanya barked. "I'm gonna call that captain and tell him he's in the wrong spot."

Biko, the boat captain, knew Tanya was right and ran to the diveboat's stern to activate the diver recall system. The boat had an underwater buzzer that gave off a high-pitched squeal when activated. The divers had long-since been briefed to surface and return to the boat when they heard that noise. It could only mean there was a problem. Tanya grabbed the VHF radio and tuned it to the frequency she knew the harbormaster used to guide cruise ships into position.

"*Island Paradise, Island Paradise*, this is the *Bubble Blower*," Tanya said, identifying the ship she was calling followed by the boat she was calling from. The name was written on the massive ship's bow towering above her. "*Island Paradise*, you are out of position. There are divers in the water beneath you and you are on top of protected coral reef. Repeat. You are out of position, *Island Paradise*. This is an emergency!"

"*Bubble Blower*, this is a restricted frequency. You do not have authorization to broadcast here," the harbor master replied immediately. "I show the ship is in perfect position, right where it should be."

"Rex, it's Tanya. That ship is in the wrong spot, and I have divers in the water right below it. You know I'm out here. I told you I was coming out an hour ago. I'm sitting right where I always am. If you're on that ship, look down!"

"Tanya, I don't know why you are trying to cause trouble today, but I'm going to order you off this channel once and for all. You do not have authorization to be on here. Once this is done, I'll order an investigation into your actions today. Now clear this channel!"

Tanya slammed the radio microphone down in frustration and turned to the boat captain.

"Is there any chance we're in the wrong position?"

"None, ma'am," Biko replied over his shoulder as he scanned the water for the returning divers. "We're tied off on the only mooring ball on this site. The same one we use every time."

Two divers broke the surface just behind the boat. They started to ask what the problem was, but immediately figured it out when they saw the cruise ship. Two more teams of research divers in the water and Mike and Kelly were still unaccounted for.

*****

Mike stared upward in horror as the cruise ship's anchor and chain began crashing into water. They were directly beneath it. He looked around at Kelly and saw his friend gesture frantically for him to follow and then Kelly began swimming as hard as he could. Mike took off. He doubted he could outrun the falling steel, but he wasn't one to give up either.

A roaring sound filled Mike's ears. He glanced backward without meaning to, his body reacting to the sound. When he looked back Kelly was gone.

Mike began swimming again as hard as he could, racing against the inevitable.

Where did Kelly go?

And then he saw bubbles coming from an opening in the reef below him. Back into the coral swim-through. The skylight opening was just big enough, but it was going to be close. Mike pushed his camera ahead of him and tried to make himself as streamlined as possible as he dove for the opening. He felt the gloom surround him as he made a final push forward, the adrenaline rushing through his body urging him forward.

And then it hit. The massive anchor chain dropped onto the coral with the force of a bomb blast. The water transmitted the energy of the anchor's collision with the reef. Mike tumbled in the water as everything grew suddenly dark. He was turned upside down and slammed against the jagged coral. Debris fell all around him. His mask was knocked from his face and he lost his regulator.

Mike was in trouble.

*****

21

"*Island Paradise*! You just dropped anchor on my divers and a reef. What are you doing?" Tanya screamed into the VHF radio microphone. "Are you insane? I've got people in the water!"

The force of the anchor chain hitting the water rocked the small dive boat, throwing Tanya, Captain Biko and the team of divers that had made it on board to the deck. As soon as she climbed back to her feet, she was back on the radio. She switched the radio to Channel 16, the emergency channel.

"All vessels, all vessels. MayDay, MayDay MayDay! We have an emergency. The cruise ship *Island Paradise* just dropped anchor on divers in the water. I need help. Six divers are missing. There may be injuries. Please respond!"

"Miss Tanya, the divers are surfacing. I've got two buddy teams on the surface," Biko called out. He was pointing to the two groups of divers and scanning the surface for the third team.

"Who is it? Doesn't matter. Get them on board. And keep an eye out for the last group," Tanya said as she raced for the boat's stern, to help the divers on board. She quickly realized who was on the surface. It was her two teams of science divers. Her people were safe. But that left Kelly and Mike still down there.

"I need help!" one diver called out while he towed his partner to the boat. "Kim's unconscious!"

Without hesitation, Tanya grabbed a rescue float and dove into the water headfirst. She was there in mere moments and grabbed the stricken diver. With the strong kicks of an experienced swimmer she began towing the young woman to the boat, letting the other diver care for himself. As she swam, she checked the diver's breathing and shouted at her to see if she was able to respond at all.

"Kim, Kim! Are you still with me? Come on, Kim, wake up!" she yelled to the girl, just inches from her face.

As they reached the swim step of the boat, Kim began to stir. Tanya handed the girl off to the boat captain and the other divers on board and began helping the diver's buddy out of his gear.

"Phil, what happened?" she asked.

"We heard the recall alarm and started heading back. And then we heard the anchor falling. It was like a wall of water knocked us over and slammed us against the reef. I didn't realize Kim was out until I started to swim for the surface and she didn't follow. I grabbed her and brought her up."

"You did good, Phil. You probably saved her life," Tanya said, treading water at the back of the boat. "Did you see Kelly? Or Mike?"

"Not at all. No idea where they went."

"Give me your mask," Tanya ordered the young man. "I'm going to see if I can find them."

Knowing the others on board would take care of the injured diver and bring everyone on board, she had time to think about her husband and friend.

Tanya hadn't paused to put on fins so she couldn't swim down very far, but fear and worry allowed her to swim down 10 feet to look around. Visibility was bad as the anchor and chain kicked up sand, tore coral loose, and threw everything every which way. She surfaced quickly.

"Any sign of them?" Tanya called out to the divers on the boat.

"Nothing yet, Tanya."

The first dive boat to respond to Tanya's Mayday call over the radio slowed as it approached the scene. The boat and crew was from *Off The Wall Divers*, a different dive shop from the one she and Kelly owned. In an emergency none of that mattered. All the divers on the island knew each other and most had worked together at one time or another. If not, they had partied together. They were a community and were there to help each other out if one was in trouble. That was what it meant to be a Cayman cowboy. They looked out for each other.

*****

Blind and without any air, it took Mike a moment to pull himself together. Then his training kicked in and he reached out for his regulator. It was still attached, so it couldn't go far away. He quickly found the second stage mouthpiece and put it in his mouth. With the last bit of air in his lungs he blew out the water and then took a cautious breath in. Air never tasted sweeter, even the dried and filtered air from a scuba tank, than when you were deprived of it.

Mike looked around. Without his mask, everything was blurry. He could only see shapes, but he could see light filtering down from the broken coral above him.

Now where did my mask run off to? He'd had it until he was slammed against the wall. He reached up and touched his face. It was tender and he thought he could see some blood in the water. *That's gonna leave a mark.*

Searching around him with his hands, he found his mask below him and shook it in the water to clear the debris from it. He quickly placed it against his face and pulled the strap in place, exhaling through his nose to clear the water from in front of his eyes. The lens in front of one of his eyes was cracked, but it held and he could see. Through the gloom and mayhem surrounding him he took stock of his situation. The skylight opening he had just come through was blocked. He thought he could make out part of the anchor chain in the rubble.

That's about as close as it gets. Time to find Kelly and get out of here.

*****

"Tanya, I heard Kelly say something about showing Mike the 'swim-through'," Biko called to Tanya who was still treading water.

"Jon," Tanya yelled to the divemaster from *Off The Wall Divers.* "Kelly and Mike might be stuck in the swim-through. Do you know it? From the looks of it, the anchor chain dropped right on top of that area."

"We'll get 'em, Tanya. Kelly still owes me money," Jon said with a smile that didn't make it to his eyes. "I'll be underwater in 30 seconds."

Jon Rusho and Higgy Higginbottom grabbed their gear as they jumped in the water, settling straps into place as they fell. They didn't hesitate or resurface. As soon as they hit the water, they began swimming for the bottom, clearing water from their masks as they kicked.

*****

Mike looked around him. A war photographer, he'd been in war zones and seen bombed out buildings before. This reminded him of every one of those times. Except, this was the first time he combined that experience with being underwater. He was in a small "room" in the tunnel, but the hole he had bolted through was gone. Rock and steel lay over his head. To his left, there was rubble and it looked like the tunnel had collapsed. To his right, things still seemed to be stable.

The question in his mind, though, was *Where is Kelly?* If his friend was on the other side of that pile of rubble to his left, or worse underneath it, he couldn't just leave him. And then again, his air supply was limited. He couldn't stay down forever.

They had been nearing the end of their dive, and it had been a relatively shallow one, so he still had air, but there were still physical limits. Mike checked his pressure gauge. He had 1000 PSI in his tank. At that depth, he could probably last another 20 minutes or so. *Twenty minutes to find Kelly and swim out of this mess. Not a lot of time.*

Mike paused for a moment and stared at the rubble pile looking for any sign of bubbles rising through the rock that might signal Kelly was buried underneath. *If Kelly isn't breathing anymore...* he thought. Mike tried to be still and slow his own breathing. It was dark, but his eyes were slowly adjusting to the dim light.

Okay, time to get out of here. Kelly is probably on the surface waiting for me.

As Mike turned to swim away from the rubble pile and out the other end of the tunnel, he hoped, he was startled to see a diver swimming toward him out of the darkness. Kelly.

Mike smiled for a moment, relieved his friend was alive. Until he saw the look on Kelly's face. Kelly gave him the Okay handsignal and Mike replied with the same signal. Question asked and answered. Then Kelly gestured back down the tunnel and then moved his hand on a chopping motion, across the tunnel.

Blocked.

The two men were trapped in what was left of the swim-through. They had survived the falling anchor and chain, but now they might run out of air less than 30 feet underwater.

*****

Jon and Higgy swam as quickly as they could to the reef below them. They paused for a moment to look at the devastation caused by the massive cruise ship anchor chain lying on the surface. Higgy shook his head, overwhelmed by the sight of the destruction, but Jon grabbed his arm and gave him a signal. They needed to swim and look. *We'll worry about the reef later,* Jon thought.

Higgy pointed at the reef and shrugged his shoulders. *Where?*

Jon gestured at the anchor chain and indicated he wanted to follow it where it lay on the reef. He wanted to see if it opened up a path inside the tunnel. If Mike and Kelly were in the swim-through and could get out on their own, he knew they would. Jon was concerned about places where the tunnel had collapsed.

Jon took one side of the chain and Higgy took the other. It wasn't long before they found the first place where the tunnel had collapsed beneath the weight of the chain. All either of them could see was broken down coral. The first collapse was only five feet wide but then the roof of the tunnel was stronger and had held up to the direct assault from the steel chain. Thirty feet farther along the chain, they found another tunnel collapse. After waiting a moment to see if they could see bubbles rising, Jon realized what they needed to do.

Turning, he signaled to Higgy that they needed to go back along the length of the chain where it was resting on the coral reef. He reasoned that beyond the last collapse, where the chain was no longer lying on the reef, Mike and Kelly could swim out on their own. If they were underneath a collapse, there wasn't much the rescuers could do. He wanted to see if he could find any sign of them between the collapses.

*****

On the surface, more boats began to arrive, including one carrying the harbormaster who yelled at Tanya earlier. Now that he could see the scene for himself, he realized she was right all along. Calls went out to the Department of the Environment and other government offices. Before long, there were too many people in the area. And none of them were helping the situation as far as Tanya was concerned. She climbed back on board to coordinate the rescue efforts.

"Miss Tanya, the harbormaster wants you to come to his boat. He wants you to give a statement about the accident," Captain Biko said, standing a few feet away from Tanya. He knew how she would react to the *order*.

Tanya never turned to look at the captain, a man she had considered her friend for many years. She knew he was just relaying a message. Barely above a growl, she replied.

"Tell the harbormaster to get stuffed. I'll give him a statement when they bring Kelly and Mike back to the surface. If they aren't all right, he definitely isn't going to want to hear what I have to say."

Tanya knew if the man had listened to her when she called to report a problem they wouldn't be searching for two missing divers. If he had listened, the cruise ship anchor would not have torn up more than 1000 feet of coral reef that was making a recovery. Now it was rubble.

More divers appeared from local dive operations, willing to help out however they could. They jumped in the water to help search for any signs, and Tanya coordinated their efforts from the surface.

"Tanya, Tanya!" a voice called out to her right.

"What is it, Jon? Did you find them?" Tanya asked the first diver who had jumped in the water to help. Her heart was in her throat. She wanted them found, but dreaded that they might be too late.

"I'm not sure, but I have an idea. Tell the cruise ship to raise the anchor chain. I see some bubbles rising from underneath it. They're coming from a spot between two collapsed sections of a swim-through. The guys might be stuck in the middle and their bubbles are leaking out. I can't tell with the chain in the way.

"Got it. Go get 'em, Jon," Tanya said. "Bring Kelly home." It felt good to have something to do. She turned and ran the few steps to the radio microphone.

*****

Mike and Kelly rested on the bottom of their underwater cage, their exhaled breaths collecting on the ceiling. They had looked all over, but couldn't find a way out of the tunnel. They were going to have to wait to be rescued. To give the people on the surface time to find them, they both did their best to relax and conserve their air. They made themselves comfortable and waited, doing their best not to watch their pressure gauges as the displays counted down to zero. Kelly pulled out a small, erasable underwater slate and began writing a note. Just in case. He wanted Tanya to know his last thoughts were of her. Mike had friends and people he knew would miss him, but he wasn't carrying a slate and there was no "one special person" that he would write to anyway.

Mike could feel the air from his regulator becoming harder to draw. His tank was getting low. He knew Kelly had just a bit more air left in his tank than he did, but the last thing he would do was tell his friend, in case Kelly would try to sacrifice his own life for Mike's. Mike glanced down at his dive computer. It showed less than 50 PSI left in his tank. Probably just a few more breaths.

Mike thought about his legacy. He had told stories and won awards. He had made a difference in thousands of lives. He knew that. But, he had never settled down and had a family of his own. He was loved by friends. And he had a few relationships that meant something over the years, but he could never take the step and settle down. His career was always more important to him than family. If he died today, he knew his magazine would run a lengthy piece about him and his work. But, he wondered, does any of that really matter?

Kelly heard the scraping sound first. Mike was lost in his thoughts, and probably beginning to lose consciousness as he was breathing as shallowly as he could. Kelly looked up at the ceiling of the tunnel. Through a small hole, both divers had noted the smooth steel of the anchor chain sitting directly on top of them. Now, it was moving. But slowly.

Someone was coming to get them. Would they be in time?

Mike looked at Kelly and gave him a signal. He slashed his hand across throat. He was out of air.

*****

Jon and Higgy waited underwater, hovering inches above the trashed reef, while the cruise ship began to pull up on the anchor chain. It was a slow process. Each link in the chain weighed hundreds of pounds.

The first thing Jon noticed was a rush of air bubbles exploding from underneath the chain as soon as it budged. The massive steel link had corked the hole. As soon as it moved, the air was released like bubbles from a shaken soda bottle. Jon's guess was right, but now he hoped he was in time.

The chain's rise was agonizingly slow, but finally it was six inches off the coral, then nine. Jon slid his hand through the opening. He was relieved to feel a hand grab his. Someone was still alive.

Jon immediately pulled his back-up regulator loose and snaked it down through the hole. He heard the sound of someone taking a breath from his regulator. And then another. Jon signaled to Higgy to take his gear off. The man quickly did it and then made a free ascent to the surface. Jon moved Higgy's gear into position, shoving both regulators down through the hole.

*****

"Tanya, they're still alive!" Higgy shouted when he broke the surface.

"You saw them?" Tanya shouted back, barely containing her joy. "They're okay?"

"No, but someone grabbed Jon's hand. They're breathing off my scuba gear."

"So, someone is alive, but you can't be sure if they both are," Tanya said. It wasn't a question. Fear returned to her heart. She had to know.

Tanya sat down on a bench and began pulling on a scuba unit. It wasn't hers, but that didn't matter. She had to be on the bottom. She had to know what was going on.

"Miss Tanya, that's not a good idea," Biko said, resting a hand on her shoulder. "You need to stay here. Trust the others."

"Biko, I can't. I have to know!" The sound of hysteria began to enter Tanya's voice. She had been calm and directed until this point, but she couldn't stand by not knowing.

"Tanya, it's okay. They're both okay!" It was Jon. He had come to the surface without his dive gear as well. Two other divers had made it to the bottom and were staying with Mike and Kelly. Kelly had passed his erasable slate through the opening and Jon knew he had to let Tanya know what it said. He read it from the water.

"Both still alive. Tunnel blocked, both ends. Tell Tanya I love her. Stay on surface."

The divers on the boats were all quiet for a moment. And then the cheering began. Tanya slumped backward in the shoulder harness of the scuba gear, allowing it to hold her up on the seat. They were both alive. She began to cry.

CHAPTER 6

The afternoon sun was the same as it was the day before. The wind blew steadily and the sea air smelled the same. But for Mike and Kelly, everything seemed to be just a touch clearer, brighter and better. Being trapped underwater will do that to you. For the rest of the guests at Sunset House, gathered around the bar and on the patio at My Bar, things were a bit quieter. Nearly losing two friends will do that to you, too.

It took nearly an hour to get Mike and Kelly out of their watery prison. Divers on the surface used lift bags to float coral rubble out of the way while keeping the men trapped below supplied with air. Once they were free, the Department of the Environment would begin an investigation into how the accident happened in the first place. But that wasn't on top of anyone's mind yet.

The two divers spent nearly two hours underwater. The shallow depth kept them out of danger for decompression sickness, the bends, but they were exhausted from the ordeal anyway. When they were finally rescued, Tanya insisted both men go to The Cayman Islands Hospital for evaluation. Just in case. The hospital had a hyperbaric chamber and was well-versed in treating injured divers.

Watching the sun set into the ocean, the air and a cold Caybrew Ironshore Bock never seemed sweeter than it did at that moment.

"That was a close one, my friend," Mike said, staring out at the water. The orange sun was reflecting off the ocean and up into the clouds, showing where Sunset House earned its name. He couldn't take his eyes off it. "I've been in close scrapes before, but for a moment there, I thought it might be my last."

"I don't know that I've been in as many close scrapes as you, but I never gave up hope. The last time I almost died in the water, you and Tanya were there. And you didn't let it happen. Same thing this time," Kelly said referring to the time a hired assassin had kidnapped him and placed him in a diving bell with no air supply.

Once the sun finally dipped below the surface, Mike looked over at his friend seated on the other side of the My Bar patio table.

"I don't know that I had much of anything to do with saving you this time. I'm still surprised Tanya wasn't underwater pulling out rocks with her bare hands," Mike joked, laughing for the first time.

"I told her to stay on the surface."

"Like that's ever stopped her."

Before Kelly could respond, Tanya approached the table with Jon, one of the divers who found them and coordinated the rescue efforts from underwater.

"I see you two are back where you should be," Jon said with a laugh. "Sitting at My Bar drinking a beer."

"And you need to join us," Mike said, rising to shake the Jon's hand. "Thanks for being there, man."

"You'd do it for me. I know that. Cowboys take care of each other," Jon said, picking up a plastic cup and pouring himself a beer from the pitcher on the table. "But I will join you for a beer or three."

"Where've you been, babe?" Kelly asked Tanya. She had been with him at the hospital and wouldn't leave his side, but after everything calmed down, she had to run into George Town to meet with her bosses.

"Life goes on, even when *you* are sitting at the bar," Tanya answered with an easy smile. "I still have work to do. And now I have even more work to do. Director Travers from the DoE has asked me to head up a coral reef restoration effort. There will be a full investigation into how this all happened, but we're going to get started immediately trying to repair the reef. There's some bigwig, outside investor guy who was already here on the island pitching a system to monitor the reefs, but he's offering to help pay for the repair efforts. At least until they convince the cruise line to pay up."

"How do you repair the reef?" Jon asked.

"Glad you asked, Jon. We're going to need your help and the help of just about every diver on the island. It's going to take a lot of diving. We'll have to clear away all of the rubble and determine which pieces of coral are still living and viable. Then we'll nurse it back to health and anchor it back down to the reef. From there, we hope and pray that it begins growing again. The first step, though, is to clear off the sand and torn-up rock so it doesn't choke off the coral that wasn't disrupted."

"Let me know what we need to do. I'm sure all the operators around here will jump in and help. You can count on Off The Wall Divers."

"Thanks. This's going to be a long process. A couple of my divers are out there right now surveying the area. I expect it will be next year some time before we're finished."

"Any idea how it happened?" Mike asked.

"Nothing yet. The harbormaster was on board the cruise ship, just like he was supposed to be, and their navigation computers showed everything as normal and that they were exactly where they were supposed to be. Except, obviously, they weren't," Tanya said as she slid a deck chair up beside Kelly and put her hand on his arm.

"What could cause a ship that size to be that far off?" Kelly asked.

"Everything on those ships is controlled by computers and GPS systems. Of course, you have to rely on people to make good decisions, too. Not sure why the computer would read that badly, but someone should have visually confirmed the location before letting go of the anchor. That should be the harbormaster's job," Mike said.

"You'd think so."

The group grew quiet for a moment. Mike watched Kelly and Tanya hold hands and thought about how close they came to not making it out of the tunnel. Before he could think about it too much, though, they were interrupted by more new arrivals. Tanya's divers were there to give her a report on the reef. And they had a surprise for Mike.

"We found this in the tunnel. I'm guessing you dropped it when the sky fell," the older diver said, holding up Mike's camera in its housing.

"Wow! Thank you, guys," Mike said taking the camera. "That's great. I was afraid it was underneath the coral when the roof collapsed. It looks like everything is okay."

"One of your strobes didn't make it, but the camera itself looks fine. No water inside the housing that I could see."

Mike released the seals on the housing and pulled his camera out. It was dry inside, much to his relief. One of the external flash units—strobes— had taken a bad hit and would never work again, but the one on the other side was fine and the glass view port didn't seem scratched either.

Mike turned on the camera to check his photos in the LCD screen.

"With everything that happened, I forgot about you leading me into a face to face with that big grouper," Mike said looking over at Kelly with a smirk. "I owe you for that one."

"He didn't scare you did he?"

"Well not nearly as much as what happened a few minutes later. But I did get a couple of nice photos of him. That is one big, beautiful fish."

"I'm glad you got photos of him, Mike," the second diver who surveyed the reef said. "Unfortunately, he didn't make it. He was killed in the collapse."

"Oh, no. Not Bubba," Tanya exclaimed. "He was a big puppy dog. Had to be 50 years old. And now he's gone. I can't believe it."

"Bubba was a great fish. Everyone around here knew him. He definitely had a personality," Jon said. "That really sucks."

"One more thing someone is going to have to pay for," Tanya said with an angry glint in her eye.

CHAPTER 7

Life continued on for Tanya, even with the preparations for the upcoming celebration and the near loss of her husband. The previous day's events on the coral reef were the reason behind this hastily called meeting and she had no choice but to attend, even if there was no place she wanted to be more than in bed beside her husband.

Crossing the street from the parking lot to the Department of the Environment offices, Tanya heard a high-pitched buzzing sound over her head. It sounded like it was coming close, she ducked purely on instinct. She quickly scanned the skies to see what had buzzed past her, but she didn't see anything in the air. The skies were clear.

"Great. Now I'm hearing noises and seeing things. This week is supposed to be a relaxing celebration. And I'm more stressed than before," she muttered as she entered the air conditioned offices.

"Zdrastvoitya, Ekatarina," Tanya said to the young woman working the desk at the Department of Environment. "Hello."

"Priviet, Tatyana," Trina said in reply. "Hi." Trina stood and gave Tanya a hug. "I was so sorry to hear about Kelly, but glad he got out okay."

"Spasiba, Trina," Tanya said. "Thank you."

Tanya was Russian and Trina was from Ukraine, but many Ukrainians spoke Russian as well. Tanya had lived in Cayman a long time and had long since grown comfortable speaking English all the time, but she knew Trina hadn't been away from home as long. It made the younger woman happy to hear her native language.

"The others are already here and waiting on you. Go on in," Trina said to Tanya as she released the hug and turned to open the office door. They were meeting in a conference room beside Director Travers' office.

Entering the room, Tanya saw Director Travers and a couple other officials from the Department of the Environment that she knew. There was also one man she didn't know. He was good looking, with perfectly-coifed hair; something Tanya thought was fairly ridiculous in a place like Cayman. The heat, wind, and humidity wreaked havoc on hair. And so did time in the water. Most people on the island who worked outside kept their hair cut short. Or let it grow into dreadlocks, but no one kept their hair *perfect*.

The only open chair in the room was next to *perfect hair*. Director Travers quickly introduced Tanya to Jay and the meeting began.

"Tanya, since you are our expert on the condition of the coral formations around the island, and happened to be on site yesterday when the terrible accident occurred, please give us an update on the situation," Director Travers said.

Tanya quickly launched into a description of the accident and her role in trying to prevent the cruise ship from dropping its anchor and chain on the reef.

"I appreciate you are giving us the background on the situation, but I'd really like to hear about the coral reef itself. I'm sure there will be an investigation into the circumstances of the accident itself," Jay said, dismissively, looking from her to Director Travers.

"I… I'm sorry Mr. ummm, Taylor. I was just trying to make sure everyone understood the situation. You do understand that my husband almost died in the incident, so it's a little raw for me," Tanya said, doing her best not to glare at the interruption, and failing.

"We all understand the dire situation you experienced yesterday and I am sure I speak for everyone at how glad we are that Kelly and the other man made it out alive," Director Travers said. "Mr. Taylor is in a bit of a hurry, so if you could jump to the situation on the reef, maybe that would be best and we can come back to the circumstances of the accident later. We will definitely need your statement for the investigation."

"Tanya, please forgive my abruptness," Jay said, with an air about him that said he was anything but sorry. "I understand you're very close to this.

And that's why I would like to help you and the Department of the Environment out. Maybe it will help if I step in for a minute."

Jay stood and addressed the others in the room. Tanya stared for a minute and then, realizing she had lost the floor, simply listened. Jay quickly reminded everyone of the coral reef monitoring system he had proposed, doing his best to acknowledge the work Tanya and her staff had done as the foundation for his work.

He showed them one of the sensors he planned to place all around the island. It was four inches square and about two inches thick with wires coming from all four sides, making it look like a boxy octopus. Jay explained that the sensors worked together to gather data and analyze motion. When they were in place, they would create a ring around the island that would send back real-time data telemetrically to his proprietary software. He would be able to monitor growth, destruction, and progress on the reef along with sunlight, salinity, currents and wave action. All of that would allow him to determine the factors that led to the positive growth. He explained that his sensors were even able to detect motion from passing boats along with underwater vibrations and impacts.

"It seems awfully small to be able to do all of that," Tanya said. She was used to seeing single sensors for water motion or salinity that were about the same size.

"These units are a marvel of microcircuitry. Each one is limited on its own, but together they form a network, almost like the neural network in your brain, giving each sensor the ability to gather more data than it could individually, making the ring greater than the sum of its parts."

And then Jay bridged the conversation to the purpose of the meeting.

"In light of the tragic circumstances yesterday, I've established a fund at the Cayman Islands Bank and Trust of $1 million dollars specifically for use in restoring the coral in the harbor area destroyed by the cruise ship," Jay finished. The men in the room clapped their hands while Tanya sat silently. As things quieted down, Tanya raised her hand.

"Yes, Tanya, what is it?" Jay asked with an edge to his voice.

"This all sounds like an amazing offer for the island. Your passive reef monitoring system will be useful and your generous offer to help restore the harbor is beyond question. I'm just wondering why we need money at all. I'm sure we will go after the cruise ship line to pay for the restoration. Right, Director Travers?" Tanya asked.

"You are correct, Tanya. We have already been in contact with the cruise line, and they are willing to make amends as best they can. We all realize this will be a long-term project, of course," Travers said.

"Well, if you don't need all of my money, I'll be happy to take it back, of course," Jay said with a broad laugh. "But consider it a gift to the environment of this island. It may take a while for the check from the cruise company to clear, but this way you will be able to begin the important work immediately, instead of waiting."

The officials in the room began to stand and offer their goodbyes to Jay. Tanya realized they had already accepted his offer without question.

"Mr. Taylor, umm Jay, I guess this is a go, so contact my office and I'll give you the information you need to get started on placing your monitoring system," Tanya shouted above the sounds of the officials leaving.

"Thank you, Tanya," Jay said turning from shaking one man's hand. "But don't worry about it. I've already planned each location for the monitoring units. My team has determined the key location for each sensor to be able to encircle the island efficiently. We've been planning and researching this for a while before we brought it to you. I like to be thorough. And don't you have a party to plan? It must be even more poignant now that you almost lost your husband. Don't worry about a thing. I've got everything under control."

The meeting broke up quickly, leaving Tanya still standing in the conference room. She wasn't sure what to do next. Hearing a sound behind her, Tanya turned with a start. It was Director Travers standing quietly, watching her.

"Did I just lose my job? Have I been replaced?" Tanya asked her boss.

"Not at all, Tanya dear. Everything is as it should be. You are still in charge of the island's environmental program," Travers said. The older man stepped up close to Tanya. "Mr. Taylor has some interesting ideas for our island. His technology can help us out, but of course, we have to watch what goes on here with our best interests at heart. And I believe we should question every person's intentions."

"Are you saying you don't trust Jay?" Tanya sneered the name a bit.

Travers smiled. "I'm not sure I trust anyone, but I have no reason not to trust Mr. Taylor. Your role in this project will be oversight. He may not like it, but we'll make sure he explains everything he does to your satisfaction. I don't have a lot of choice in allowing this project. It came to me with blessings from above. He is a very rich, powerful man who has connections. But no one said I had to give him carte blanche, either."

"Thank you."

"I do believe he is correct, though. You do have a party to plan. And I plan to be there for it."

Travers left Tanya alone to collect her thoughts.

CHAPTER 8

Bill Gardner sat hunched over a cup of coffee in an open air coffee shop. He was in paradise, but he really didn't feel like celebrating. Despite endless hours of planning and hard work, nothing was changing. But it had to. He knew it. If a place like Grand Cayman couldn't see the importance of protecting the environment from the greedy, he didn't think the rest of the world stood a chance.

"Bill, what are we going to do next?"

"Huh, what? Sorry, Sherri. I got lost in my thoughts there," Bill said, looking up at one of the two young women across the table from him. They were both a couple years younger than he was, still in college.

"I asked what we're going to do next? Do you want to stage another protest?" Sherri asked again. The petite blonde had her long hair tied back in a pony tail.

"I want to go snorkeling," the other girl, Miranda, said.

"How will that help save the environment?" Sherri asked her sister. The two girls were both blonde and pretty. Their physical similarities led the two girls to take opposite sides of just about every argument.

"Well, it probably won't do anything to help the coral reefs around here, but it'll give me a better idea of what we're fighting to save. And this is my spring break, too. I want to have a little fun. It can't be all about marching around in circles, being ignored by everyone as they walk past," Miranda said reasonably.

"You just don't get it, do you? I knew it was a mistake bringing you along," Sherri began.

"Hold on, Sherri. Miranda's right. We do need to see the ocean and the coral reef. Besides, it will be good for my blog to have photos of what things look like around here. We'll just have to find a place that isn't torn up," Bill agreed.

"Did the cruise ship tear up that much?" Miranda asked, a bit bewildered. "I saw the story on the news last night."

"It tore up a thousand feet or so," Sherri said shaking her head. "Bill means that all of the reefs around here are suffering."

"Actually, it could go both ways. If we could find some reef in good shape and get close enough to the places that were torn up by the cruise ship, we could show them side by side. Then people would have to listen," Bill said, thinking things through as he talked.

"What do you think caused it? The cruise ship to drop its anchor on top of the reef, I mean." Sherri asked.

"Don't really know. I heard them say that the cruise ship captain and the harbormaster both confirmed the ship was in the correct spot. Obviously, it wasn't," Bill said, staring out at the water near the café.

"What would cause that?" the sisters said at the same time. For all their differences, they tended to do that.

"It would be possible to hack into the ship's computer controls and tell its onboard computer that it was off by just a little bit. Enough to make a difference in a small port like this, but not enough for anyone to notice when they were out at sea. Someone with the right skills could do it pretty easily," Bill explained.

"That's what you do, right?" Miranda asked. "You studied computer science in school. I heard a couple other people say you were a hacker, too."

"I'm a gray hat hacker. That means I use my skills for good, although there are times that others might not see it that way. I help companies protect their information and that sort of thing. Sometimes that takes breaking into a system to see where its weaknesses are before you can fix them," Bill said, with a grin.

"It seems to me that the cruise ship tearing up the reef might actually be good for the island. Some reef got destroyed. That's bad. But more people will pay attention to the problem now. I'm sure it made national news back home, too," Sherri said, standing up. "It's almost like this was supposed to happen while we were here."

"Almost like someone planned it," Bill said standing up. "Let's go see if we can't get some masks and snorkels. I have my camera with me. Let's get some pictures of you two on the reef. Then we'll see if we can't get out to see the torn up reef. I think this is going to work out perfectly."

CHAPTER 9

"In some ways, it feels like we just did this. In others, it seems like ages ago," Mike said as he stood on the deck of the gently swaying boat, looking out at the cobalt blue water of George Town Harbor. Everything about the situation felt the same as it had 24 hours earlier, and totally different at the same time.

They were out on the *Bubble Blower* again, just like the day before, with Captain Biko at the helm. It was a smaller group on board. Just Mike and Kelly along with Herb and Phil, two of Tanya's divers. Tanya was on the surface to coordinate the divers' findings.

On the other hand, the area they were in was officially off-limits to boat traffic. Even the cruise ships were as far away from the area as possible. And Mike and Kelly were returning to the same exact spot where they would have died, if not for Jon and Higgy and the other divers who found them and brought them air. The act of going back to a place where both men questioned if they would ever see the sun again was a bit daunting, but neither one was prepared to not face their memories either. They knew they had to get back in the water and even more importantly, they knew they had to dive on the site of their near miss and face it. If not, it would haunt them both.

Just as importantly, Mike was suddenly back on the clock. The story about the grounding had made the news in the United States. Mike's editor at *First Account* magazine knew he was on vacation in Grand Cayman so she had called Mike to see if he knew anything more than the official word and got the shock of her life. She had almost lost an award-winning photographer in a silly mishap. She worried about him when he was in war zones, but not on a dive vacation.

Once the editor caught her breath, she wanted the story. It couldn't have worked out better that Mike had *before* photographs taken minutes before the anchor chain came crashing down. All he needed now were *after* photos. Those combined with his first-person account of the accident were sure to make headlines and score another coup for the magazine and maybe an award for Mike, although he certainly didn't chase them. It wasn't the first time he had stumbled into a story that turned out to be unique. He suspected his editor was beginning to expect it of him.

Mike stretched for a moment, working out the kinks from the day. *If nothing else, I was pretty tense yesterday,* he thought with a smirk. *Okay, tense is an understatement.*

"Is that your buddy over there?" Kelly asked from behind Mike.

"What? Where?" Mike was momentarily confused as he turned to look at his friend and then back out across the water to see where Kelly was pointing.

"Over there by the rocks. Those snorkelers," Kelly said, continuing to point. He could see two young women and a man wearing masks, snorkels, and fins splashing around in the shallow water near the rocks. They would occasionally dive under the water for a minute. The man had a camera.

"My buddy?" Mike asked, confused.

"Okay, I'll admit a lot has happened since then, but if you don't remember him, I'm taking you to the hospital to get your head examined. The protester guy we met yesterday morning. You all went to the same college," Kelly prodded his friend.

"Oh yeah! Now I remember. It does look like him," Mike agreed.

"He was an environmentalist, wasn't he? I wonder what he's doing out here?" Kelly said while they continued to watch.

"Well, first, he's playing in the water with two young women. It doesn't take a lot to figure that one out. Second, he probably wants the same thing we do. Photos of the damage. He's an environmentalist and the grounding and destruction is an environmental disaster. Exactly what he's campaigning against," Mike said, turning to look at Kelly. "You ready?"

And then Mike realized he was the only one on the boat who wasn't ready. Everyone else was in their dive gear and waiting for him.

"Oh. Sorry guys," Mike said, shaking his head. He quickly sat down on the boat bench and slid his arms into the BCD harness that held his air tank and regulator in place. The two research divers moved to the boat's stern and stepped out into the warm clear water quickly and efficiently. Tanya was acting as the boat's divemaster and handed each of the divers their equipment: a slate and ruler for taking notes and measurements for Phil and a camera for Herb.

And then it was Mike and Kelly's turn. While neither of them dived as much as they used to, both were experienced divers and they moved on muscle memory, buckling their equipment in place and shuffling to the stern before settling their masks in place and pulling their fins on their feet.

"You guys come back safe this time, okay?" Tanya asked. Her tone sounded light, but the look in her eyes told a different story. They were all three remembering the events of 24 hours before and none of them could forget those awful emotions.

"I promise we'll be careful, Tanya," Mike said.

"You better."

"Mike, I think we need to get in the water now," Kelly said, hearing the tone in his wife's voice. "Or we may never again." Kelly stole a quick kiss from Tanya and then put his regulator in his mouth to cut off any further discussion.

"Roger that."

The two men quickly stepped out from the boat and fell into the warm Caribbean water. A quick bob to the surface to signal that they were okay, and for Mike to grab his camera from Tanya, and then they were off. Neither man was in a hurry, though. They allowed themselves to sink slowly toward the bottom, as compared to swimming for the reef. The *aerial* perspective allowed them to look the area to grasp the scope of the damage. Mike immediately began photographing what he saw.

The Cayman sun was bright and hot, penetrating through the clear water, bringing out the colors in the shallow reef.

Like many disasters, natural and man-made, the destruction caused by the massive ship's anchor and chain left contradictions. Where the steel actually came down, the coral was pulverized. Within inches, though, things were close to normal, only being disturbed by the collision or covered by silt and sand. A few feet away from the impact spot, the reef looked completely normal. There was no sign of a problem at all. Even spots between the chain links had some semblance of normalcy, mixed into the middle of total destruction. In Mike's mind, it was like a tornado scene, in miniature, where a massive twister picked up and destroyed one home while leaving the one immediately beside it untouched.

Surveying a devastated coral reef wasn't the way Mike had planned on spending this vacation, but at least he was diving. And he knew he was never truly happy without a camera in his hand. Even if he hadn't been directly involved in the situation, he would still have wanted to dive it, photograph it and tell the story.

Lost in his own thoughts, and taking photographs as he moved slowly along the shallow reef, Mike didn't realize where he was until he almost ran into Kelly. His friend was hovering in place, waiting for Mike to look up. Mike sculled backward with his free hand and gave Kelly a questioning look. And then he gave the Okay signal divers use to ask a question and also reply when everything is okay.

Kelly signaled he was Okay and then pointed at the reef below them. It took Mike a second to recognize the spot since he had only briefly looked at it from above and that was before the anchor chain crashed down. It was also before other divers had pulled broken pieces of coral away from the hole to get him and Kelly out. Kelly was pointing to the opening to what almost became their underwater tomb.

A flood of emotions raced through Mike's mind. He almost died right there. It wasn't the first time he had come close to dying. He had been in war zones and seen terror attacks up close and personal as an international news photographer. But this was different. In a war zone, you prepare yourself mentally for the possibility you might not come back. He had been in a happy mood, having fun with friends until everything came crashing down, both literally and figuratively.

Mike wasn't sure about all the stories about your life flashing in front of your eyes and that sort of thing, but nearly dying this time had bothered him more than previous close calls. Living life on the road chasing from one news story to the next hadn't left much time for relationships and much less of a chance that one would amount to much.

Shaking his head and pulling himself back to the moment, Mike moved in closer with his camera and photographed the scene. He swam down and stuck his head through the hole in the reef. It took his eyes a moment to adjust to the shadows, but then the tunnel began to look strangely familiar.

In reality, they were only stuck in there for a short time, but in the moment it had seemed like forever. Even after their friends found them and gave them air, lowering their anxiety, the waiting for freedom had given them a lot of time to notice their surroundings.

Backing away from the hole in the roof of the tunnel, Mike made eye contact with Kelly. His friend shook his head and smiled. Then Kelly held up an underwater erasable slate. "Want to go in?" the slate read.

Mike took the slate, cleared it and replied, "No thanks. Spent enough time down there."

Kelly took the slate back and answered with a single word. "Agreed."

Mike saw Tanya's research divers in the water ahead of them. They were taking careful measurements of the amount of devastation. It would be up to Tanya and her team to put the teams together to begin repairing the reef itself so it could begin growing again. Mike photographed the scientists at work for his story. He would also share everything with Tanya when they got back to the hotel. He would only be around a few more days, but he wanted to help out however he could.

Mike glanced at his dive computer and realized they had been underwater close to 45 minutes. *Time flies when you're thinking about dying,* Mike thought. The reef was shallow and they were in no danger of running low on air, but Mike and Kelly turned and began heading back toward the boat anyway. Neither man wanted to push it.

Nearing the end of the rubble field, Mike noticed something out of the corner of his eye. Something that didn't fit. In nature, there are few naturally occurring straight lines.

Mike moved closer to pick up the square flat box. It fit in the palm of his hand. The box had a rubberized cover on it, but the cover was torn. From its position on the reef, it must have been hit by the anchor chain itself. There were wires sticking out of three sides and two more hanging loosely from the fourth side. The plastic box inside was broken so Mike guessed it wasn't functional any longer. He could see what appeared to be circuits and computer chips. As an underwater photographer, he knew all too well that electronics didn't mix well with salt water. If the physical trauma didn't destroy the device, it was ruined moments later by the Caribbean Sea.

Mike showed the device to Kelly, but all he got was a shrug in return. Mike stuck it in the pocket of his BCD and then made a slow ascent to the surface. He smiled to himself as his head broke the surface and he felt himself relax. In spite of the perfect diving conditions, he knew he was tense the entire dive. Kelly was right behind him as they made their way back to *Bubble Blower.*

"I was wondering when you two were going to get back here," Tanya said, smiling but just as relieved as they were.

"We kept waiting for another cruise ship to pull in, but it never came," Mike said, grinning.

"I think we've had enough of that for a while, don't you?" Tanya replied.

Mike climbed the ladder to the boat and handed Captain Biko his fins.

"How was the dive?" the captain asked.

"The dive was good, but the damage isn't pretty," Kelly said behind him.

The two divers went on to describe what they saw. Tanya's two science divers were already on board as well and they all talked about the amount of damage they saw. It was localized, but it was severe. And the damage caused by the silt and sand on the other coral was starting to show as well.

"We're already organizing teams to get out here," Tanya said. "I've been on the phone with every dive operation on the island recruiting divers since you went underwater. We'll need plenty of help cleaning the broken pieces off of the coral that's still living. And then we'll sort through it all to see what of the broken stuff can be salvaged and reattached."

"Glad you made good use of your time. It's not like you spent any time underwater," Mike said with a laugh. "But you're saying you can actually keep some of the coral alive?"

"Yes, there are techniques where we can take broken pieces of coral and reattach them to substrate and keep them growing," Tanya explained. Several times over the last few years, ships ran aground, tearing up the coral. Groups of scientists had developed a system to recover the larger pieces and keep them growing in coral nurseries. Once they were strong enough and beginning to grow on their own, they could be *replanted* on reefs. Since it took years for coral to grow just a few inches, any opportunity to save some growth kept them ahead of the game.

"That's great. I'll work that into my story," Mike said as he pulled off his gear. "Oh, hey. You know anything about this?"

Mike pulled the electronic device from the pocket of his dive gear and held it up to the sun.

"Where'd you get that?" Tanya asked.

"Found it on the dive," Kelly answered. "From the damage to it, it looks like it was hit by the anchor chain. It's pretty messed up."

"What is it?" Mike asked.

"Well, it looks like one of the reef sensors an outside group is planning to place around the island to monitor growth and changes. But it doesn't make sense that it was down there yesterday," Tanya explained.

"Why not?" Kelly and Mike asked together.

"They just got permission from the Cayman government to put them in the water this morning," Tanya answered.

"Maybe they were testing it out and put it in the harbor before they asked permission," Mike said, offering an explanation.

"Anything's possible, I guess, although the guy doing it, Jaylend Taylor, didn't mention anything about it at the meeting," Tanya said. "There was a lot going on, though. I'll take it with me and ask him the next time I see him."

Mike was handing Tanya the broken sensor device when everyone on the boat looked up at the high-pitched whining sound over their heads. A remote controlled drone flew over their heads, streaking across George Town Harbor.

"Someone sure is having fun with their new toy," Mike said, watching it fly. "I've seen or heard that thing a couple times since I got here."

"Me, too," Kelly said. "But I haven't seen the pilot yet."

"Could be anywhere around here."

CHAPTER 10

That evening they were doing their best to return things to the scheduled events. They were having a party at My Bar for all of their friends. Things started out a little subdued. Everyone in attendance was a diver and a fan of the ocean. Even the ones who didn't identify themselves as *environmentalists* thought of the ocean and the reef as *theirs*. Seeing it damaged had upset a lot of people.

The smells of island food, with some curry thrown in for good measure, and with the rum punch flowing, everyone eventually loosened up and started having fun. And that, of course, led to good-natured ribbing of Mike for nearly dying in the middle of the party and ruining everything. He said he would try harder next time. Try harder at what, he didn't say. Cayman cowboys might have each other's backs, but that didn't mean they couldn't have some fun at each other's expense, too. Mike took it all in stride. He enjoyed the fact that even though he had been gone from the island for years, they still treated him like family. Laughing and dancing continued into the evening to the sounds of a steel drum band Kelly brought in for the party.

Out of breath, Mike dropped into a plastic chair on the My Bar patio overlooking the ocean and smiled. The sun was down, Sunset House's trademark sunset having passed with much cheering and discussion about the "green flash." If conditions were just right, many believed you saw a brief flash of green light as the sun disappeared below the horizon over the water. It was supposed to bring good luck. No one at the party was completely confident whether they saw it or not. All Mike could see now were dive boats at anchor just off the shore and the vastness of the ocean at night. He could sense the latter more than see it, of course. In general, that sensation was a comfort to him. Whenever he was struggling or had seen too much of the world, he escaped to the ocean. It worked wonders at salving his wounds. Tonight, though, the combination of the party, friends, and the ocean wasn't doing the trick. He couldn't put a finger on the problem, but something was out of sorts. Was it nearly dying? Maybe. He wasn't sure.

Tickling at Mike's consciousness was a discordant ringing that conflicted with the steel drums and dancing. It finally brought him back to the present to realize a mobile phone was ringing on the table. It wasn't his, but he quickly realized it belonged to Tanya. She was out dancing with Kelly and had left it on the table. Mike picked it up and answered it, concerned it might be important.

"Hello?" Mike said, placing his finger in his other ear, trying to hear over the party sounds.

"I'm sorry I must have the wrong number. I'm trying to ring up Miss Tanya Demechev," the voice said. Mike could detect a Cayman accent from the caller. That wasn't surprising, of course, but it confirmed to Mike that the call might be work-related.

"Hold on one moment. She stepped away from her phone," Mike said, moving out onto the dance floor with his hand covering the mobile's microphone. He finally dodged and danced his way to Tanya and Kelly.

"Tanya, you have a call!" Mike shouted above the noise.

"What?"

"On your phone. You have a call!" Mike shouted as the music ended, leaving him standing there pointing at the phone and shouting while everything else was quiet.

"You don't have to yell," Tanya said with a laugh, taking her phone from him and moving away from the party.

"Always the way it goes," Mike said with a grin, looking at Kelly. "Everything is so loud you have to shout until you start talking about some *rash* and everything gets quiet."

"Man, I really don't want to hear about your rash," Kelly said with a chuckle as they walked to the table. A server brought two rum punches to the table as soon as they sat down.

A few moments later Tanya returned, visibly upset.

"What's up, babe?" Kelly asked.

"I knew everything was going too easy. Everyone was accepting responsibility for the grounding and we were all going to work together like one big happy family," Tanya said reaching for Kelly's drink, but stopping. She grabbed a glass of water from another table.

"What are you talking about?"

"Director Travers just called. The cruise ship captain, through the lawyers with the cruise line, is not accepting responsibility any longer. He's blaming the harbormaster. The harbormaster, of course, is blaming the cruise ship captain, me and everyone else who was in the water," Tanya explained. "The national police have begun an investigation into the incident. We've all been asked to come in tomorrow and make statements."

"Sure. I'll be happy to do whatever I can, of course, but obviously we didn't see all that much," Mike said. "And once the anchor chain came crashing down, I didn't see much of anything."

"I know and I told Director Travers that, but he asked that you come in anyway. Frankly, he suggested that if you don't come in on your own, you might be forced to," Tanya explained. "I'm really sorry about this, Mike. It's the first time we've seen you in years and now you are in the middle of a controversy."

"Eh, you know me. I love some excitement in my life," Mike said shrugging.

"I know. It's just…" Tanya started to get choked up. She picked up her phone and walked off saying "I have some calls to make."

"Is she all right?" Mike asked Kelly.

"Just frustrated, I guess. She'll pull it together. I'm guessing this investigation will delay their recovery efforts on the reef. And if the cruise line isn't paying for the damages, we'll have to see where the money comes from," Kelly said, watching his wife walk away. He was concerned about her, too, but knew enough to give her some space. Her Russian temper was legendary.

"I hadn't thought of that," Mike said. "Didn't she say someone set up a fund to begin the cleanup?"

"She did, but for some reason, she didn't seem happy about it. Not sure what's going on there, but she might not have any choice now. I'm just guessing, but what if the police won't let them begin the clean up until everything is settled?"

"That could be really bad," Mike agreed. "Tanya has told me and everyone who will listen that this work has to be done quickly or more of the reef will die."

"Let me go talk to Tanya and find out what's going on," Kelly said standing. "And we'll need to find out what time the police want to see us tomorrow. I'm sure it will be the crack of dawn. They just don't understand a good party."

"Okay. Let me know. I think I'm going to turn in anyway. I'm not feeling like a party right now."

CHAPTER 11

Jay stood on the balcony of his penthouse luxury suite on Seven-Mile Beach looking out at the ocean. The gentle breeze from the warm Caribbean water pushed his perfectly-styled brown hair around, making him even more appealing. His plans were coming together, even better than he had originally hoped. The government people had accepted his offer to help, happy to take the money he offered to help out with the clean up in the harbor. And from there, it was a simple step for them to approve his coral reef monitoring system. Yes, it was all coming together.

"Jay, you need to come inside. Matt needs you," a woman's voice said behind him, sounding hopeful. It was Trina from the Department of the Environment.

After a few moments, without a word to Trina, Jay turned and walked back inside. The suite was opulent and large with two bedrooms and a large living area in the middle. Each bedroom had its own bathroom suite and there was a third for the common area. Jay remembered the early days when he and Matt had been struggling to start their software company, sharing a one-room flat where the heater worked occasionally and the hot water never did.

Matt sat at a long dining table off to one side of the living area. He had papers spread around and two laptops open and active in front of him. A computer server rack rested on the floor beside him with wires connecting the laptops and other peripheral units. Matt, short for Matthias, was everything that Jay was not. A Belgian by birth, Matt had the brains to equal Jay's looks. He stood 5'7" when he actually stood up straight, which wasn't often. He had the pudgy, thinning-haired look that most people pictured when they thought of computer geniuses. He and Jay met in school at Massachusetts Institute of Technology. Jay himself was no slouch, or he wouldn't have been at MIT in the first place, but he immediately knew that Matt had him beat by leaps and bounds. They formed an unlikely friendship, much of it fostered by Jay, who saw the potential his new ally presented. For Matt, the friendship provided him with social openings and introductions he never would have had on his own. Neither man took their friendship for more than a convenient arrangement. It was a partnership that worked out well for both of them.

In what had become a common story in the Internet age, in the style of Bill Gates or Steve Jobs, the pair had an idea for a piece of software. They struggled during the development phase, enduring setbacks and hardships, only to have it succeed beyond their wildest dreams six months after the launch. A year after that, they sold the company to a software giant for just shy of 10 figures and then walked away. They were in their mid-20s and rich. They spent their time traveling and living the high life, focusing on nothing but taking their millions and turning them into even more millions. Both men floundered for a bit, each going their own ways, until Jay had another idea and turned to his old partner. In some ways, both of them needed the project. It gave them a mission and a purpose and felt good to be *working* again.

Trina followed Jay into the room, a few steps behind, scurrying after him. Jay walked to Matt's table.

"What is it?"

"We're getting some glitchy data back from the sensors that are already in place."

"Is it a problem with the equipment?"

"I don't know yet. Definitely not with the hardware," Matt said, pulling off his glasses and cleaning them with the tail of his shirt. "It may be something with the firmware on the units. Or it may just be caused by not having the full network on line."

"Will you be able to fix it? If it is a problem, of course."

"When they're all online and running, I'll be able to adjust them all at one time, just like a network with remote peripherals. It won't be a problem."

"So what did you need? I trust you with this part of the project," Jay said, mildly annoyed at being summoned but realizing the need to stroke his friend's ego a bit. While Jay understood the network and programming his friend did, he was smart enough to realize he couldn't pull this project off without Matt. Jay's strength was project management and managing people. He understood how to get people to do what he wanted them to do.

"What's the timeline for getting the rest of the sensors in place? That'll tell me how long I have until I can fix the problem, or get everything online," Matt replied. He knew his role and he knew Jay's tactics. He mostly ignored the compliment.

"They tell me two more days. The crew's working quickly, but having to place them in specific spots, rather than just throwing them overboard is taking some time," Jay said. "We didn't plan on that one sensor getting hit by the cruise ship anchor chain."

"I know. It's all my fault. I had to adjust the sensor placements because of that. You've been grumbling about it ever since."

"I'm pushing them to get the work done as quickly as they can."

"Why are you in such a rush to get the sensors in place?" Trina asked, still standing behind Jay. Her blonde hair and high cheek bones, the classic Eastern European look, would have been striking anywhere in the world, even in a room full of fashion models. Not uncommon for women with her looks, though, Trina had been tossed from one powerful man to another who wanted her for a trophy instead of a partner.

"That's none of your business," Jay said. He turned slowly, not really facing her. "You just need to do as you're told and make sure you tell us what is going on in the Department of the Environment."

"Yes, Jay. Sorry."

"Let me check in with the guys on the boat again. I'll let you know how many more they have to go and when they expect to have everything finished. Is that what you need?"

"That'll do it. Thanks," Matt agreed.

Jay nodded and turned to walk away, almost running into Trina. She jumped out of the way and nearly fell, stumbling against a couch. Jay didn't say a word to her. He just shook his head and walked away, pulling his phone from his pocket to make a call.

"He shouldn't treat you like that," Matt said to Trina with a mixture of pity and adoration. Trina barely noticed.

"He's just busy. I know he doesn't mean it. He just gets so focused on what he's working on that he forgets to be nice. I know he loves me. I get upset sometimes when he ignores me, but then I remember he's working to save the oceans and I forgive him. He needs me and needs my help."

"If you say so. I know how Jay is. I've worked with him for a long time. I'll bet there is someone else out there who would treat you better. Treat you like you deserve. A woman like you should be treated like a queen. That's how I would treat you."

"I'm sorry. What was that?" Trina asked. She had been watching Jay talk on the phone, ready to jump and get him whatever he needed.

"Nothing. I didn't say anything. You look really nice tonight."

"Okay, Matt. Thanks. You're so sweet," Trina said. She walked over and gave Matt a kiss on the cheek and a hug. And then scurried across the room toward Jay when she noticed him glance in her direction and raise his hand to get her attention.

CHAPTER 12

The next morning, Mike and Kelly were first up on the interview list with the Cayman prosecutors. Tanya joined them, but she wasn't going to be called to testify until later that morning. Everyone involved knew what her role had been and expected Tanya's testimony to be particularly important. As Tanya found out more about the hearing, she learned that the cruise ship officials and the ship's captain had changed their story. The captain had originally accepted responsibility, but after talking to his home office, and getting away from the island with his ship, he laid the blame squarely on the harbormaster. When a large vessel approaches a major harbor, a local harbormaster boards the ship and guides it to the appropriate dock space or anchorage. Faced with the potential blame for the accident, the harbormaster was trying to blame everyone else, including Tanya.

The Cayman court wanted to hear from Mike and Kelly mostly about the shock and trauma of being nearly killed in the accident. Since the cruise ship line was pulling back from accepting responsibility, the island prosecutors were going after the company from every angle, they explained. Attempted manslaughter was on the table as far as they were concerned.

When they got to the courthouse, the three of them were glad they had taken the time to make themselves presentable. They found themselves in a setting far more formal than a deposition in a lawyer's office or an interview with the police. A panel of judges was present, along with other witnesses and lawyers and the media. The courtroom was nearly full.

Mike was the first to take the stand.

"Please identify yourself for the court," the prosecutor said with a tone that left no room for doubt about who was in charge. The man was in his mid-30s and dark-skinned from a life in the islands. He had a bearing that said he was an up-and-comer in the legal system. This wasn't an office newbie, but the lead prosecutor for the Cayman Islands government.

"My name is Michael Scott."

"Are you presently a resident of the Cayman Islands?"

"No sir. I lived here for a few years, but I'm just a visitor now."

"Can you tell me your current occupation?"

It took Mike a few minutes to explain that he was a photojournalist for *First Account* magazine. He wanted to establish his own credentials and experience so he talked about some of his better-known stories and the awards he had won, including his Pulitzer prize for photojournalism.

"Mr. Scott, can you please describe for us why you were diving on the morning of the cruise ship grounding incident?"

"Primarily to have some fun," Mike said.

"Mr. Scott, I would appreciate it if you took these proceedings seriously. This is a court of law."

"My apologies, but that was an honest answer. I've been friends with Kelly Anderson and Tanya Demechev for many years. As you know, Tanya works for the Cayman Islands Department of the Environment. She invited me to see the progress she and her team were making helping the coral in the harbor area to recover from the previous wear and tear. I was there to have fun and see a beautiful, recovering reef. No other agenda than that."

"So you weren't planning to write an article or publish photographs from your dives?"

"Not at the time."

"Would you please elaborate?"

"I had no plans to write an article at that time, but since the incident, my magazine has asked me to send them photos from before the grounding as well as some I took the day after the grounding to show the before and after. A few times during my career, I've been on vacation and stumbled on a story of international interest. One notable story came from this island 10 years ago."

"Yes, Mr. Scott, we are well aware of your involvement with the situation surrounding Gray Walker and his efforts to steal money from the island to build a cruise ship dock. That is why I find it interesting you were involved with another incident on the island that involved a cruise ship. Do you have some problem with the cruise line industry?"

"Are you suggesting I had something to do with this?" Mike asked, caught off-guard. "Considering I almost died in the process that would be pretty poor planning on my part."

"There have been instances where people were caught by their own bomb blasts, for example."

Mike stared at the prosecutor for a moment. And then he turned to the panel of judges.

"Your honors, I believe I have been invited to these proceedings under false pretenses. I was told I was giving my account of the incident from two days ago that almost took my life and the life of Kelly Anderson. The idea that I had something to do with this is completely unfounded. If I am under suspicion for something, I believe I must ask for legal counsel. That is my right. If necessary, I would like to speak to the US consulate."

The crowd in the room had been quiet while listening to the prosecutor, but everyone erupted into shouts when Mike was finished. The judges called the prosecutor to the bench for a conference.

Mike didn't see Tanya stand and move toward the courtroom's exit. He was too busy watching the men in front of him to see what would happen next.

*****

Tanya realized things weren't going the way any of them expected so she decided to get some of her research logs to show that the dive had been planned long before Mike's arrival on the island and that it was a legitimate trip. She'd had teams of divers in the water conducting research when the anchor chain fell. She didn't know where this conspiracy theory had come from, but was determined to cut it off before it went any further.

"Leaving so soon, Miss Demechev?"

Tanya was startled to hear someone speak to her. She was focused on getting to the office. It took her a moment to realize who it was.

"Oh, hi, Mr. Taylor. "I'll be back, I just want to get some documents for the court to consider."

"That makes sense," Jay said. He had been inside the court room. "I'm as surprised as you are by the prosecutor's line of questioning."

"I can't believe he'd do this," Tanya said. "It's funny, I hadn't thought we were going to need your money for the cleanup and restoration, but now it seems like you've saved the day. The cruise line is going to fight this tooth and nail. Who knows when we'll see any money from them."

"You're very welcome. Saving and preserving the reef is very important to me."

"Thank you, I appreciate that. Sorry, but I really need to get moving," she said as she moved toward the exit.

"I understand. Do what you need to do."

"Hey, one quick question," Tanya said. She paused and turned back. "We were taking stock of the damage yesterday and found a device underwater that looked like one of your sensors. It was damaged by the anchor chain. Did you have any of them in place early?"

"Oh, that's amazing," Jay said, with a broad smile. "What a coincidence, we were testing a couple of the devices before we were given permission to implement the project. We wanted to see if they worked the way we expected. We picked them all back up when we were done, but one fell overboard. We didn't realize it until we got back to the dock. Incredible that it fell off right where the anchor chain fell."

"You're right. That's an amazing coincidence."

"Do you think I could get the device back from you?"

"It's at my office with my research. I'll bring it to you shortly."

*****

After a few minutes, the court reconvened. This time, however, the prosecutor stayed seated and the lead judge on the panel took over. She was a petite woman, with fine features and short gray hair. Her dark eyes and posture left no doubt in Mike's mind that she was in charge.

"Mr. Scott," she began quietly, but firmly. "You are absolutely within your rights to call your Consulate and be represented at these proceedings. To be frank, I do not believe that will be necessary, however. I am well aware of your involvement in our earlier problem, and I know of your role in helping the island government clean out the men who were using the island for their personal gain. I was the prosecutor in that earlier situation and know very well the sort of man you are. I hope you will accept my apology for the implication that you had anything to do with this unfortunate situation."

"Thank you, your honor."

"The prosecutor has heard stories of a blogger on the island, who is a visitor, who has posted some reports and photographs that have implied there is a greater problem here. The blogger also suggested the grounding might have been a good thing. I've seen the blog posts as well, but I am certain they did not come from you. The writing and photographs are amateur in my estimation and not something you would have had any part in. I have instructed the prosecutor to let me handle the questioning from this point forward."

"Thank you again, your honor. For the moment, I will answer your questions. I'll let you know if I feel the need to have a representative from my government here with me."

"That will be fine, Mr. Scott. Now, if you would please describe the situation that led you to be diving on the morning two days ago when the cruise ship dropped its anchor and what happened next."

It took Mike about 10 minutes to give his version of the events, describing how he and Kelly were trapped underwater and rescued by the other divers from several dive operations. When Mike was finished, the judge seemed satisfied with his story and recessed the court for a half an hour. Kelly would be up next.

CHAPTER 13

"Wow! That wasn't how I expected that to go at all," Mike said when he stepped onto the street in front of the judicial building in George Town. To clear their heads, they began walking down Albert Panton Street and then onto Cardinal Avenue, heading toward the harbor. The both knew they needed to stretch their legs and they instinctively headed toward the water.

"You and me both, brother," Kelly agreed. "Do you want to call the consulate, just in case?"

"I don't think so. The judge who took over seems to be playing it pretty straight. Not sure what got into the prosecutor, though. I mean, where would he come up with an idea like that?"

"The judge said something about some blogger writing about the incident," Kelly said.

"Yeah, but that seems a little thin. I mean, how do you make the leap from a blog post to accusing someone who nearly died in the incident of setting it up. If anything, if I were the prosecutor, I would be more surprised you and I weren't bitter and angry and accusing everyone around us of trying to kill us."

"So you're saying he should be looking at us because we aren't throwing temper tantrums?" Kelly asked with a laugh. In the back of his mind, he wanted to see the cool, calm, and collected Mike Scott really pitch a hissy fit.

"What? You don't think I could do it?"

"No, not really. You've probably already looked at the incident from every angle and decided you can see everyone's point of view."

"You say that like it's a problem…" Mike's voice trailed off and then he changed the subject. "Where did Tanya take off to?"

"She ran to her office to pick up some stuff about her research. She thought it would come in handy in case they kept pressing the idea that we were somehow involved. Or that you were anyway."

"Well, I'm glad I didn't need it after all. I'm guessing she didn't realize I would be done so quickly after the judge took over."

"Yeah, I'm surprised she isn't back yet. She left before the judge stepped in so she doesn't know anything that's going on. I'm sure she expects to get back and see you in handcuffs. I'm sure she'll be here any minute."

"Why do I get the feeling you would like that? Kelly?" Mike said his friend's name louder when he realized he had lost his attention. "What are you looking at?"

"The judge said some blogger was talking about the grounding like it was a good thing. I think I've figured out who that was," Kelly said. He was pointing at the water's edge.

Mike followed his friend's gesture and saw the protester they met the morning of the accident, Bill Gardner.

"Well, we did see him yesterday out snorkeling with those two girls. They could have been taking photos of the damage. But he didn't strike me as the kind of guy who would cause something like that. I'm not even sure how you would do it. I mean, a cruise ship is one big, complex machine. How would you move it 100 feet to one side without anyone noticing?"

"I don't know, but I think we should go check him out. I'm just mad enough at almost dying, and then getting sandbagged in court, that someone is going to have to take responsibility for it," Kelly said. He was already moving toward the young environmentalist.

Bill Gardner was standing beside the water's edge in the harbor with an electronic device in his hands. The young man was staring out at the water and didn't see Mike and Kelly approach from the side.

"What are you doing?" Kelly asked. He had worked himself up and was feeling confrontational.

"Wha? Huh? Oh, hi guys," Bill said, glancing over to see who interrupted him and then returning his attention to the water. "Flying a drone. I want to get some aerial photos of the damage from the cruise ship for my blog."

"That's exactly what we want to talk to you about," Kelly said, moving between Bill and the water so the younger man would have no choice but to look at him.

"Do you mind?" Bill said with exasperation. He had to concentrate on the flying machine.

"Yes, I do, actually," Kelly said. He took a step closer to Bill. "I really do mind."

"Hold on, guys," Mike said, stepping between the two men. "Bill, we'd like to talk to you for a few minutes. Can you land your drone, please?"

Bill glanced at Mike and then back to Kelly. With a huff, he piloted the drone back to the walkway where they were standing and shut it off.

"So what's this about? I'm not flying in restricted air space here and neither one of you guys is a cop anyway. Why do you care if I'm flying a drone?"

"The drone isn't important. The grounding is," Kelly started as the heat returned to his voice.

"Kelly, let me handle this. Bill, we were called into court this morning to give our statements about the grounding accident and how we barely escaped."

"Yeah, I heard about that. So?"

"When we got there, the prosecutor basically accused me of staging the whole thing," Mike said. He went on to describe the events in the courtroom from just a few minutes before.

"Did you write the blog posts saying the grounding was a good thing?" Kelly asked when Mike finished up.

"Well, not in so many words, but I did say that this accident could work out for the best. That people will pay attention to the problem instead of just ignoring it. The last thing I want is to destroy a coral reef, though."

"I think you need to explain that to the judge, then," Kelly said, reaching out to grab Bill's arm.

"Hold on, Kelly. Even if Bill had wanted the cruise ship to drop its anchor, we don't have any proof that he could have done it. I'm not sure how it would even be done. Someone would have to get inside the ship's computers and fool everyone on board into thinking they were somewhere they weren't."

"I shouldn't say this, but you guys'll find out anyway. That's what I do for a living. I'm called a gray-hat hacker. That means I hack into secure computer systems to help people find weaknesses and then fix them," Bill said. He looked down at his feet. "So, I probably could have done it."

"See! I'm taking him to meet the judge."

"Hold on, Kelly. Bill? What would it take to get inside the ship's computers?"

"The easiest way to do it would be from on board, of course. But a ship like that is in constant communication with its home office through satellite uplinks. That's how they get their Internet and everything," Bill explained. "So, you could probably do it by getting close enough to hack into their secure network, using some sort of remote device."

"Like what?"

"If I were going to do it, there are network control boxes not much bigger than a pack of cigarettes," Bill explained. He forgot he was on the edge of getting in trouble as he worked through the technical problem. "I'd attach it to a drone and fly it close to the ship. The hacker could connect to the wifi network and then hack into the secure systems."

"So you're going to stand there and tell me you could do something like that with a drone, like the one you were just flying?" Kelly said. "I've heard enough!"

*****

Tanya was mad. This week was supposed to be a celebration. It was supposed to be a special time. Friends were there. Family was coming in. It was supposed to be a party, a joyous time, yet nothing was working out that way. She was mad.

"I can't believe that prosecutor," she grumbled as she stormed into her office a few blocks from the court house. She had decided to drive instead of just walking because she didn't want to work up a sweat hurrying back and forth. It hadn't ended up being much faster, but at least she stayed cool in the air conditioning. The car was brand new, a present from Kelly. He wanted her to be comfortable in the island heat. It had every electronic feature available from GPS to computer controls, Bluetooth and even wifi.

She sat down in her office chair for a moment and took a deep breath. The emotions and frustrations of the morning, and the last several days, almost caught up with her then, but she gripped the edges of her desk hard until she got things back under control. This was not the time. Later, yes. But not right now.

Tanya wanted to bring along records showing the work they had been doing, in that exact location and establish a pattern. The implication that Mike had set things up completely floored her.

It was totally baseless, but that spineless idiot prosecutor… Calm down, she told herself. *You need to focus. Later.*

She printed off several more work sheets that would show what they had done and what their plans for the area were. Of course, that frustrated her even more. They had great plans for that area, and now those plans were out the window. She was going to have to shift gears completely and work on a coral restoration project. That meant her plans for several other projects around the island were going to get put on hold while she devoted all of her energy and manpower to cleaning up the grounding site.

"At least we'll have Jay's money. That'll help," Tanya said as she gathered up the documents from the printer. "Oh yeah. I almost forgot."

She ran into the next office, a make-shift storage room, and grabbed the damaged sensor unit Mike and Kelly brought back from the dive. Might as well take it to Jay back at the courthouse, she reasoned. He seemed to be well-connected. If things went south with the prosecutor, he would be a good person to have on their side.

Grabbing her papers and the sensor, Tanya took off for her car. As soon as she got back outside, the humidity hit her hard. It had bothered her more than usual lately. She jumped in the car and cranked the air conditioning onto high before she began making her way back to the judicial building.

Tanya paused for a moment before turning right onto Harbour Drive, the street that ran along the harbor front. She was praying the waterfront area wouldn't be too crowded in town today, but she didn't think there were any cruise ships in port. If that was the case, the George Town waterfront would be nearly deserted and the only way a local would willingly drive through that part of town. The presence or absence of cruise ships had nothing to do with the grounding. Some days there were none and other days three or four.

Contrary to her native Russia, turning right onto a street meant she had to cross it. Drivers in Cayman followed the British rules, driving on the left side of the road. That placed her closest to the water. Tanya glanced out across the harbor. She would have preferred to be out on the cobalt blue water than in the courtroom, but this was one of the days she didn't get her wish.

George Town Harbor was small, relative to the amount of boat and tourist traffic it saw regularly. Formally known as Hog Sty Bay, the harbor was a small slip of water indenting the island. Cruise ship terminals were positioned on either side of the bay where ferries brought passengers to disembark for their day trips and excursions. Boats of all sizes and descriptions tied up on the docks that lined the harbor. A small coral head jutting up out of the water. A low fence ringed the harbor, keeping pedestrians on the walkway. The water rippled in shades of blue green as the white sand led up to a tiny beach at the very end of the bay. The harbor itself was regularly dredged out, though, keeping it deep enough for private yachts of the rich and famous.

*****

Before Kelly got a chance to do or say anything else, he was distracted by the sounds of car horns honking and tires squealing. He looked around to see what was going on. It was Tanya in her car headed back to court. Her car lurched from side to side, the engine revving up and then shutting down. Every light on the car blinked on and off and the windshield wipers were flailing back and forth furiously. All the car's windows rolled halfway down and then all the way up.

"What's going on?" he asked, mostly to himself. No one in earshot had any ideas. Kelly stood frozen to the ground, confused and afraid, although he didn't know why.

*****

Without warning, Tanya's car stopped. Cold. It just shut off. Almost immediately, the heat inside the car began rising since the air conditioning was off and no air was moving. There was no pedestrian traffic from tourists, but islanders were attempting to move through George Town and the car following her barely stopped in time. Tanya stared at the car for a moment, confused.

"I do *not* need this right now," she said as she turned the key off and slid the transmission into Park. She switched the key forward again. Nothing. Again. And then the car jumped to life. She was even more confused. Everything seemed to be normal.

"Come on, baby," Tanya purred. "Get me to the courthouse."

Fifty feet further down the road, Tanya's horn began honking. The windshield wipers started flipping back and forth and the lights began flashing. The engine began revving up. It wound up so far, it began to scream. The wheel spun in Tanya's hands. The car moved on its own, as if it was possessed.

*****

In less than a second, Tanya's car broke through the fence and plunged engine first into the water. As the car left the ground, Mike and Kelly saw fear in Tanya's eyes. Both men took off running.

CHAPTER 14

Tanya would have screamed if her brain had been able to process what was happening fast enough. One moment, she was focused on getting back to the courthouse and the next her car was acting as if it wanted to kill her. The moment after that, she was slamming forward against her seat belt and her car was sinking. It didn't make enough sense to even be real.

But it was.

In the back of her head, Tanya wondered why the air bag hadn't deployed, but she was glad of it in this case. She didn't really need to be knocked senseless by the safety device at this moment. Tanya heard the car radio was still playing. The electrical system hadn't shorted out yet. She pushed the buttons to lower the car windows. Nothing happened.

Tanya tried to unbuckle her seat belt, but it was jammed. Nothing was working right. She realized her feet were wet. Water was beginning to enter the passenger cabin. The car's windows were rolled all the way up. The air pressure inside would keep the water out, even once the car submerged. It also made it harder to equalize the water pressure outside the car with the air pressure inside making it virtually impossible to open the car door.

The car had been floating on the surface, but without warning, the weight of the engine pulled the car forward and the car sank to the bottom of the harbor 10 feet below. The car radio went silent as they salt water shorted out the electrical system.

A skilled freediver and scuba diver, with thousands of hours diving, Tanya knew how to handle herself underwater. She had been in emergency situations before, rescuing divers who ran out of air or otherwise got themselves into trouble on a dive many times. Still, she could feel the panic beginning to rise. She tried every trick she knew to keep calm, but considering the situation, it was getting harder by the second. The human body's reaction to danger was fight or flight. Flight wasn't an option for Tanya since she couldn't get out of the seatbelt. Or out of the car. But there was no question Tanya planned to fight.

Tanya closed her eyes to focus and calm herself. She said a quick prayer and wished Kelly were there. She remembered a time 10 years before when a madman had kidnapped Kelly and placed him alive in a diving bell with no air supply. Mike was there and the two of them rescued Kelly. That was the day he had proposed. He'd said later that he promised himself that if he made it out, he would be with her forever. She needed him.

A banging noise on the car window startled her. She opened her eyes and saw Kelly there in the driver's side window. He was stripped to his waist, trying to open the car door and banging on the window.

Tanya immediately started struggling with her seat belt again. Kelly was there to save her. It was going to be okay.

Mike swam up to the passenger side of the car to see if he would have better luck on that side of the car. Both men had run down the dock, pulling off clothes and then jumped in the water. After just a few seconds, they both had to surface to get a breath of air.

"We're going to have to break the windows!" Mike shouted as his head cleared the surface, using the last bit of air in his lungs. He gulped in air as quickly as he could.

"Any suggestions?" Kelly asked. "We've got to get her out of there!"

"I don't know. I'll find something."

"I'm going back down," Kelly said. He took a deep breath, tried to still himself for half a second and then ducked his head underwater. He wasn't going to leave Tanya alone.

Both men hoped bystanders had seen the car go into the water and called for help.

Mike was about to swim back down to the car when he heard someone call his name. "Mike!"

Mike turned to see Bill standing on the dock, panting from his run.

"What do you need? How can I help?"

"We need something to break the car window. She's stuck inside!"

Mike inverted and swam down to the car. Tanya wasn't going to die if he had anything to say about it.

Without a mask, Mike couldn't see clearly. The car stirred up the sand and silt on the bottom of the harbor, too. Going back to the same window, Mike looked inside at Tanya. The water was up to her waist. That was good news. They would be able to open the car doors when the pressure equalized. And then Mike realized the second problem. She was still buckled in. Seat belt material was designed to be tough enough that it wouldn't break. Even if they got the door open, they were going to have to cut her out or she would still drown.

Mike looked into the floor of the car and in the back seat. He saw what they were going to need. But how to tell Tanya? It would have to wait. His body was screaming at him. He needed air. Mike bolted for the surface. Kelly came up right behind him.

"We've got to get her out!" Kelly screamed. He started to swim back down immediately.

Mike realized panic was beginning to set in and grabbed his friend's arm. "Kelly, stop! You're not going to help her that way."

It took a second for Kelly's eyes to focus on Mike.

"Don't stop me, man. I've got to get back to her."

"Kelly, listen. There's dive gear in the back seat of her car. She's got a dive knife on her BCD. That'll cut the seat belt. She's got to get out of the belt before we get her out of the car. Make her understand," Mike shouted. "Now go!"

Without a word, Kelly took a quick breath and swam back down. Mike looked around and saw a crowd gathering. He heard sirens in the distance but it was going to take them another minute or two to get there. He didn't think Tanya would last that long. He inverted and swam back to the bottom.

Instead of stopping at the car, though, Mike swam to the bottom and began feeling around. His hand found what he was looking for. A piece of coral about the size of a baseball. He returned to the window and slammed it against the glass. It bounced off. Mike grabbed the car with his free hand to give himself more leverage and then hit the window again. And again. Nothing. The rock began to crumble in his hand. This wasn't going to work.

Surfacing again, Mike heard Bill yell his name again.

"Is help here?" Mike asked, spinning to look at the young environmentalist. He found him on the dock.

"Not yet. Try this!" Bill tossed a hammer he found on the dock to Mike.

Out of breath and surprised by the move, Mike missed it as the hammer flew past him. Without hesitation, Mike dove back underwater and flailed around with his arms. On the third stroke, his hand brushed the hammer handle. He grabbed it and settled it in his hand. He hadn't prepared this time, but it didn't matter. He had to get the window open. He had to get Tanya out of the car.

Glancing inside, Mike realized the water was up to Tanya's neck. She wasn't going to last much longer. Mike swung the hammer with every ounce of energy he had left in his body. The hammer head bounced off, but he saw the glass crack. He prepared himself and swung again. Getting the window out of the way was only going to be half the problem. Tanya hadn't been able to reach the dive knife and get herself free.

Crash! The window shattered with the second blow from the hammer, filling the car almost immediately. Mike pulled on the car door handle, but the door was locked and wouldn't budge. He slipped through the window and reached into the back seat to grab the scuba gear. His hand hit the small dive knife and he released it from its sheath. He knew Tanya carried a small serrated edge blade on her BCD to cut fishing line and other debris from the reef.

With slashing motions, Mike began cutting at the belt holding Tanya in place. In the edge of his own consciousness, he heard pounding and realized Kelly was slamming his hands onto the driver's side glass. With his free hand, Mike was able to unlock the car door from inside. As soon as he did, Kelly began opening the door. Mike wasn't sure if it moved slowly because of the water pressure holding it back, or if he was beginning to lose consciousness.

With another slash, the belt broke and Kelly pulled Tanya free from the car. She was unconscious. He immediately towed her to the surface. That left Mike to get himself out.

Mike started to back out of the car, back through the window he had pulled himself through, but his air-deprived brain quickly realized that wasn't going to work. He began pulling himself forward, across the passenger seat and through the open car door. He was free, but he wasn't sure he was going to have the strength to get to the surface. He wasn't even sure which way that was. Just before he lost consciousness, Mike felt strong hands grab his arm.

Mike came to on the dock, surrounded by rescuers from the Cayman Island Fire Service. He was receiving oxygen through a mask, but other than that, he seemed okay. He sat up in time to see other rescuers loading Tanya onto a stretcher. They were taking her to the Cayman Islands Hospital, but she appeared to be conscious. Kelly was with her. Everything was going to be all right.

Mike allowed a female paramedic to lean him back while she completed her examination. Looking up in the sky, Mike could just make out a drone hovering above them. It seemed to pause for a second, and then it flew away.

CHAPTER 15

Mike stared out at the water, slouched in his chair listlessly, the sound of the gentle Caribbean waves lapping at the dock in front of him. He hadn't bothered to clean up or take a shower. He changed into shorts and a t-shirt to get out of his wet court clothes, but that was it. His dark curly hair was a mess. He was drinking water. The party atmosphere of the last few days was gone. His near miss from a few days before had been unsettling, but the friends and divers had laughed it off. This was different.

It wasn't the first time Mike had come close to dying, not even that week. But to see Tanya in trouble had shaken him and the rest of the crew assembled to celebrate Kelly and Tanya's ten year anniversary was too much.

Kelly was at the hospital with Tanya. They were checking her out, but all reports from the hospital were positive. She was banged up and bruised, but otherwise okay. She lost consciousness in the water, but not long enough to make anyone overly concerned. Still, they were being cautious. Kelly's last message had been that they expected to be back home in an hour or so. That, of course, had relieved everyone, but until Tanya was with them and they could hug her and see her smile, the mood wouldn't lift.

"Mr. Scott?"

Mike turned to see who was speaking to him, and it took him a moment to realize who it was.

"What can I do for you, Bill?"

It was Bill Gardner, the environmental protester they were talking to just before the accident happened. The last thing Mike felt like doing was talking to the young man, or even *doing* something for him, but it was a standard response. He really didn't feel like discussing whether Bill had anything to do with the cruise ship grounding, either. When the judge heard what happened, the court proceedings were postponed until further notice.

"I've been thinking about what happened and I think something's going on here," Bill said, pulling up a plastic chair to the table.

"What do you mean?"

"I saw what you saw. I saw your friend's car go out of control and go into the water. I think it happened on purpose," Bill said carefully. "I heard she's going to be okay. That's a huge relief."

"Her name is Tanya. Tell me what's on your mind," Mike said, sitting straight up for the first time.

"Okay, Tanya's car is pretty new, right? It looked like it has all the bells and whistles. What I saw looked like someone jacked into the computer control systems on the car and ran it off the dock and into the water."

"You've got my attention. Tell me more." Mike had been confused about what had happened, seeming to be so random, but it didn't sit right with him, either. What the young man was suggesting made sense in a strange way.

"When the car seized up at first, it was really strange. I think that was when someone hacked in. They weren't expert at it so they were checking controls and making sure they had the car. Then, it seemed to settle down for a moment, right up until it went crazy and went into the water."

"I agree it looked pretty strange. But how do you know this?"

"It's what I do. I mean, I'm a computer guy. I work in information security," Bill said.

"Do you know who did this?"

"Not a clue. But I think there's a way to find out," Bill said. He continued explaining what it would take to control a car remotely for the next few minutes.

"So, it's possible to take over a car remotely. You would just have to know the car's information, right?"

"Sure. The times I've heard of it, it was used to shut down the engine. Like a low-jack system where the police shut down a stolen car."

"I don't think low-jack works here," Mike said, trying to wrap his head around what he was hearing.

"That's just an example. There are other ways. They could do it with the VIN number, but that would be harder. It would be easiest if they had some sort of control unit in the car, I guess. I'm not sure how they did it, but that's what it seemed like to me. I noticed a drone flying around. They could use that to get close to the car and patch into it. That would make things easier," Bill said.

"You mean like the drone you were flying?"

"Well, yeah, but I didn't do it. Do you think I would be sitting here if I had just tried to kill your friend?"

"You're saying someone intentionally did this. They were trying to kill Tanya," Mike said, ignoring the question, his fire coming back. Now he was mad. "That's a really stupid way to kill someone. In broad daylight with all those people around."

"Sounds like someone was reacting. Tanya was supposed to testify about the cruise ship grounding. Maybe the two things are connected."

"Wait. Would it be possible to fudge the GPS on the cruise ship the same way?"

"Sure. It's all computer controlled. The cruise ship is a lot more complex, and I'm sure they have better security, but you never know. It's amazing the weak systems big companies have," Bill agreed. "That's how I earn my living. And really, they wouldn't have to do all that much. It's not like they took control of the ship and plowed it into the dock. They just had to tell the GPS system it was off a little bit. Put the ship 100 feet to one side. In the grander scheme of things, taking of the car was probably harder. Especially if they did it at the last minute."

"The court of inquiry caught us all off-guard. We got the call last night and then had to show up first thing this morning. No one had time to prepare anything," Mike agreed.

"So, if I'm right, whoever did all of this was reacting rather than following through with their plan."

"My question is, what's their plan? Why kill Tanya?" Mike asked.

"I couldn't even begin to answer that question. But something is definitely going on here."

"You're right, something is going on here and I don't like it!" It was Kelly approaching the table where Mike and Bill were sitting. They had their backs to the dive resort and hadn't seen Kelly and Tanya arrive.

"Hey, man, I'm glad you're back. We've got something to tell you," Mike said, seeing his friends, but not hearing the tone in Kelly's voice.

"I can see that, but I don't think I want to hear what you have to say. What are you doing with this creep? He's the reason Tanya almost died today!" Kelly turned to face Bill. He reached forward and grabbed the younger man by the shirt, lifting him up from his chair. Bill wasn't a small man, but Kelly had indignation and anger on his side.

Mike leapt forward, grabbing Kelly's arms. "Kelly, stop it! Bill's here offering to help. He didn't hurt Tanya. If anything he helped save her life. He found the hammer I used to break open the window."

At first Kelly didn't let go, but he did relax slightly. He stared at Bill without either one of them making a sound.

"Kelly, let the man go and listen to Mike. You know Mike would never hurt either one of us or steer us wrong. If Mike says we need to listen, we need to listen," Tanya said, placing her hand on Kelly's arm gently and speaking softly. Her husband was tired and stressed. He wasn't thinking clearly. She knew that and knew the only way to get through to him was to be gentle. Kelly looked at his wife, looked at Mike and then let go. His shoulders slumped and Mike thought for a minute Kelly was going to collapse. Mike put his hand on Kelly's back and helped his friend sit down in a chair. He signaled the waitress to bring them a round of Cayman Island Brewing's best. A crowd of friends staying at the resort for the celebration had gathered seeing Tanya's return, but they mostly stood around quietly, unsure what was going on with Kelly's outburst. These friends had been around through hurricanes. Kelly and Tanya had helped almost every one of them out at one time or another. If Kelly had said the word, and Tanya had agreed, they would have picked Bill up and thrown him in the ocean. Possibly with lead weights around his ankles.

When everyone had a drink, Mike addressed the divers and friends gathered around.

"Friends, this week of celebration has been tough and not like the endless party any of us expected when we received our invitations. When I look around at the faces gathered here I see the very best of what it means to be a Cayman cowboy. Some ugly people took that name from us for a while. They were the coke runners and the money launderers who used the banking system on this island with its international connections to hide drug money and other spoils of crime. But we've taken that name back and returned it to what it is supposed to mean. Being a Cayman cowboy means sticking together through thick and thin. It means watching your buddy's back and knowing he will watch yours," Mike said, warming the crowd up a bit. "I want to introduce you to someone. He's not one of us. He's not a cowboy in that sense of the word. He's not from here. He's not done his time here. His name is Bill Gardner."

Mike gestured at the young man still sitting at the table. The divers gathered around and looked Bill over, but didn't say much. A few sipped their beers and one or two fidgeted nervously, but they were willing to give Mike a chance and hear him out. As long as it didn't take too much time. Mike went on to explain what Bill had done and how he had helped them out. He paused to take a drink from his beer and let what he was saying to sink in. Mike could have convinced Kelly one-on-one and that would have been the end of the situation, but he knew he was going to need the help of everyone else around them and he wanted them all to be convinced.

"Mike, I know Bill went to Marshall like you did, and you want to like him for that. I get it. But that kid is half your age. Who knows what they teach people at your old school now. You're going to have to convince me that your new friend here isn't behind all of the trouble we've seen this week," Kelly said, still angry, but his voice was calm now. "I've had some time to think about everything that's happened while I sat in the hospital. The computer system on the ship was off. Tanya's car went crazy. We've seen drones flying all over the place. It is all tied together. I don't know how, but I know it is. And like you said, we saw Bill here flying a drone right before Tanya's car went nuts."

Mike turned to face Kelly directly, but he spoke loud enough for everyone to hear.

"You're right. I'm sure something's going on. But you need to remember that Bill landed his drone and turned it off before Tanya's car went crazy. He did all of that before Tanya came into sight. Yes, he wrote about the ship grounding, but if he had something to do with that, why try to kill Tanya? Why not just take credit for the grounding and make his big statement? He didn't have anything to do with it. I'm sure of it," Mike said and then he turned back to the crowd. "Bill came here of his own free will to tell me what he thought was happening. We've been discussing it and I am convinced there's a plot as well. Someone is behind this."

"Who did it?" a diver asked. "I'll take him over the wall without any air."

The crowd chuckled for a moment, but Mike could see a couple of them would be more than willing to carry out the threat.

"You guys know me and you know my history. We need to get to the bottom of whatever is going on. I plan to do that and I'll need your help. I'll need the help of everyone here to make it happen. So, what do you say, cowboys? Are you with me?"

Mike raised his beer bottle up in a salute and waited. There was some nervous shuffling, but no one moved. And then Tanya did.

"Mike, you're as amazing as ever. I hope you are with us every time we need a calm, reasoned voice. Bill, I want to thank you for helping out today. I want to thank you for being there today and being here right now. I see good in you and I'm willing to trust you." Tanya moved forward and hugged the young man, breaking the spell that held the divers in check.

CHAPTER 16

Jay paced back and forth through his hotel penthouse. This was the critical moment. Every project had one. You prepared to the best of your ability but then had to see if it would fly on its own. Of course, Jay never left anything to chance. So far he had a spotless record, too. He had never failed.

"Was all that really necessary?" Matt asked, looking up from his computer. He had been staring intently at the monitors on the table where he still sat. His body ached from sitting still for so long, but pacing wasn't in his job description. And staring at the computers gave him something to do, unlike Jay who handled the messy human components.

"What's that? What did you say?" Jay asked, focusing on Matt. He had been lost in thought.

"Was all that in the harbor today really necessary? It seemed pretty dramatic without a lot of payoff to me," Matt said. He might be the quieter, shyer one of their partnership, but that didn't mean he was afraid of Jay. "I'm not worried about getting someone out of our way. We've done that before. I just don't see how killing that woman would have helped. Even if it had been successful."

Jay stared at his partner for a moment, debating the best way to respond. For Jay to call Matt a friend would have been an exaggeration, but they did need each other and he knew that. They had both discovered that fact after they sold their company and attempted to go their separate ways. Neither one seemed to be able to function without the other. Jay valued Matt's contribution and even Matt's ability to ask cutting questions from time to time. He often made Jay think through the next several steps and prepare for problems he hadn't seen. Jay never *liked* to be questioned, but he recognized the necessity of it.

"You're right. We didn't manage to kill Tanya, but really that was never my ultimate goal and it wouldn't have helped anything. We didn't need her dead to pull off what we are about to do. We just needed to slow things down with the courts and that nosy judge. In two days, I won't care who Tanya talks to, because our plans will be so far along no one will be able to stop us. But interference right now would foul things up," Jay explained. He was doing his best to sound patient. He mostly failed. "What we did need was for everyone to worry about her and take a recess. In some ways, I think it worked out to our advantage that she wasn't killed. There would certainly be a bigger investigation if she had died in her car. They would have removed the car from the water immediately and begun looking at everything. This way, I was able to get back what was mine without anyone noticing."

"You got our unit out of the car? You got lucky it wasn't totally destroyed, just damaged. Lucky the inner workings were compartmentalized."

"I had one of our people on scene before they raised the car from the bottom to make sure the sensor disappeared. The woman probably isn't even out of the hospital yet and I've covered our tracks."

"What about the other complication?" Matt asked.

"I thought you said he wasn't anyone to worry about," Jay asked.

"I told you he was a computer guy from a small college in West Virginia. I never said he wasn't good at what he does," Matt said. He stood and stretched for the first time in what felt like hours. "Don't let your pride in our alma mater go to your head. Most of the best and brightest go to the top schools in the country, but not all of them. You never know where native talent is going to come from."

"Talented or not, there's no way for Tanya and her people to connect with your hacker. If they were talking, it might be a problem, but they aren't. It's that simple," Jay said dismissively. He was tired of this discussion. "Now, I need you to get back to work and make sure everything is up and running. The boat crew expects to finish placing the sensor remote units in a few hours. I want to get the system online immediately. Once that happens, it really won't matter who is talking to whom."

"Understood," Matt said as he resumed his seat. "I'm running a system diagnostic right now. Everything is coming up just fine now that there are more units in the water. Our earlier problems have gone away. When the last pieces are in place, we'll be able to flip the switch quickly. I'm just saying we don't want to ignore potential problems. I wasn't happy to see Bill on the island when he arrived. It was a little suspicious."

"Your concerns are noted, but you let me worry about that. I've got your friend covered. I handle the human element, remember," Jay said with a smile that almost seemed sincere. "I've got friends keeping an eye out to make sure he doesn't cause any problems."

CHAPTER 17

Once everyone settled back down and the assembled cowboys filtered off, Mike, Tanya, Kelly, and Bill sat back down at the table, with a few other friends, to discuss what Mike and Bill had been talking about. Bill gave them a quick synopsis of what they discovered and what they thought happened to Tanya's car.

"I don't mean to sound critical of your theory, but I see some holes in it," Kelly said. He was doing his best to accept Bill into the discussion. His wife and best friend had, but it took him a little longer to forget his earlier feelings.

"It's just a theory. It's based on some good observations and educated guesses, but until someone comes forward and tells us exactly what is going on or publishes a white paper on 'Tools and Techniques for Moving a Cruise Ship and Commandeering a Car', it will be a theory," Bill answered, scrunching his fingers down to mark the air quotes around his fictional title.

"But, it does make sense," Mike threw in. "It explains what's happened. Of course, it doesn't explain *why* it happened."

"It does dot the i's and cross the t's, I'll give you that," Kelly agreed. "You said for someone to take control of Tanya's car, they would have to have some sort of sensor on it, right? That would take some planning. They would have to decide to kill her, get a sensor onto her car and then set it up to take over. It just seems pretty far-fetched."

"You're right about that and I don't have any explanation for it. If I was going to kill Tanya by sending her car into the harbor, that's what I would need," Bill agreed. "I'm telling you what's technically possible. Not the why."

"Okay, let me ask you something," Tanya said, speaking up for the first time. "First, I'm going to ignore the whole 'If I was going to kill Tanya' bit, but what would a sensor look like?"

"Sorry. I didn't mean it like that," Bill said. His face flushed with embarrassment. He took a sip of his beer to recover his thoughts for a moment. "Honestly, it could be anything. I've seen sensors about the size of a deck of cards with the technology inside them to do what we're talking about. Remember, it doesn't have to have a brain, just a micro controller and a bluetooth or wifi chip. We think whoever did this turned the sensor on and controlled your car using a drone. Basically, the drone and the sensor unit in your car become repeaters for someone sitting at a computer somewhere. If we had the sensor, we should be able to trace it backward to whoever controlled it. That is, of course, if the salt water hasn't ruined it. It would need to be shielded and sealed to protect it from the ocean."

"Yes, I know. That's how you would do it if you were trying to kill me," Tanya said with a grin.

"Well, um, I, um…"

"It's okay, Bill. She's playing with you," Mike interrupted. "So, I guess we need to get to the car and find something that doesn't belong there."

"Pretty much a needle in a haystack," Kelly said. "They could hide it anywhere. It'll be tough to find."

"True, but I don't know how else we are going to track it backward," Mike agreed.

"Hold on, guys. I may have something," Tanya said. "Bill, would the sensor unit have to be designed specifically to control a car?"

"No, not really. It would have to have the appropriate microcontrollers and interfaces to communicate with remote devices, but it wouldn't have to be set up just for your car."

"What are you thinking about, honey?" Kelly asked.

"When I was leaving the courthouse to get the documents to defend you guys, I was stopped by Jaylend Taylor. He asked me a few questions. As I was leaving, he asked me to bring him the sensor unit you guys found on the cruise ship grounding site. He said they lost it when they were doing some testing, before they pitched the idea to the Department of the Environment," Tanya explained.

"What's this?" Bill asked.

Tanya gave him a quick overview of what the sensor units were supposed to do and where Mike and Kelly found the unit underwater.

"Do you think that could have been used to take over my car?"

"I'll need to see it and take it apart, but it definitely sounds like it would have the technology inside to connect to your car and let someone outside assume control. They would have to be connected to the sensor device, of course."

"So, what you're saying is, just having it in the car wouldn't allow someone to take control of the car. They would have to be connected to the sensor and from there they could hijack the car," Mike said.

"Sounds like I want to have a long talk with this Jay person. He just moved to the top of the suspect list for people who tried to kill my wife."

"You're right about that," Mike agreed. "At the same time, it makes me wonder what he's doing that he would want to kill Tanya in the first place. I mean, it's not like he came here to kill Tanya. Was she getting too close to something and they needed to get rid of her? Tanya, what did you say Jay is doing?"

"He got permission to place a ring of those sensors all around the island to set up a coral reef monitoring network. I don't know how far along he is. I can't imagine he's done much. I mean, he just got permission yesterday," Tanya said, shaking her head. "Wow, was that really just yesterday? A lot's happened since then."

"There's even more guessing going on here than there was before, but it all does seem to make sense. Jay seems to be up to something, and it must be big enough that killing you wasn't out of the question. It sure seems like more than coral reef monitoring to me," Mike said.

"We need to call the police," Bill said.

"And tell them what, exactly?" Kelly asked. "Don't get me wrong. I'm with you, but until we have some more evidence, they'll laugh at us. The island police are actually pretty good, but wild theories about espionage and computer drones aren't going to go very far."

"We need to take a look at one of those sensors and figure out what he's doing with them," Mike agreed. "And I have an idea how to do it."

CHAPTER 18

The foursome, Mike, Kelly, Tanya, and Bill, grabbed a Sunset House van and headed to the Cayman police impound yard. Kelly made a couple phone calls and confirmed the police had pulled Tanya's car out of the harbor almost immediately after they left for the hospital. They couldn't leave the car submerged. Oil and gasoline had begun leaking from the car immediately and fouling the harbor. It had taken two police divers to connect cables to the car and make sure everything was secure. From there it was a relatively simple exercise in pulling the car to the surface and out of the water. Of course, they had to move it slowly to allow the water to drain from the car before the tow truck was able to lift it onto the dock.

The impound yard was located in the island's interior, away from the tourist area. Grand Cayman was like any other place in the world that catered largely to tourists. The areas where visitors frequented were kept well apart from the places necessary to doing business. The island's interior held some low-income housing and a landfill among other things. The police impound yard was adjacent to a scrap metal recycling center. More than likely, when the police were done with Tanya's car, and their insurance company had written it off, the car would simply move to the scrap metal yard for crushing to be sold off the island and turned into something new.

It was getting dark when they arrived at the impound yard. The drive from the resort was mostly quiet, all of them lost in their own thoughts. The day and the week had been extremely eventful. And not in the way any of them had planned. Bill's life hadn't been in danger, but he knew his new friends had other things on their minds so he kept quiet and mulled things over, trying to figure out what was going on.

The guard was reluctant to allow them to enter at first, but Kelly was well-known around the island and he convinced the old man they were there to look for a few personal items from the car. Obviously, Tanya hadn't been able to take her things with her when she left the car. After a few minutes of discussion, they were allowed inside. Kelly followed the guard's directions to the end of a row, closest to the office. The yard wasn't big, but there were several dozen cars stored there for one reason or another having been abandoned or used in a crime.

The van's headlights lit Tanya's car as they approached from the passenger side. They heard Tanya draw a sharp breath when she saw the car for the first time since hitting the water. The jagged glass in the passenger door frame showed where Mike was finally able to break out the glass and get her free.

"Babe? Are you okay?" Kelly asked, putting his hand on Tanya's leg. "Maybe it wasn't such a great idea for you to come. You can just stay in the car."

Tanya was quiet for a minute. Finally she said, "I'll be okay. It just caught me off guard. Let's do this."

They opened the van doors and got out, taking their time approaching the car.

"Tanya, do you remember where you placed the sensor when you got in the car? The one Jay asked you to get?" Mike asked. He knew this was tough for Tanya and wanted to keep things moving. She closed her eyes to recall her actions from the morning.

"I tossed everything in the back seat, behind my seat when I was getting in the car. I still had dive gear back there so I had to push it out of the way, to make room for my computer and for the dive log spreadsheets I printed off. I put the sensor unit on top of everything and then got in the car." She opened her eyes again.

"That's great, Tanya," Mike said. He turned on a flashlight and opened the rear car door. The dive gear was still there in the seat. It was right where he left it when he had entered the car and pulled Tanya's knife to cut her free from the jammed seat belt. The remainder of the backseat was empty except for some soggy papers.

"You hit the water nose first so anything loose would have flown forward. Then when they pulled the car out of the water, they probably dragged it out by the back of the car. It would have been closest to the dock."

Mike got down on his knees and began digging underneath the driver's seat. He was guessing that's where the missing items would have ended up.

"Here's your laptop and some papers." Mike pulled the sodden mess from underneath the seat. The laptop was a complete write-off the moment the car hit the water. It was a work laptop, though, so everything on it was backed up. Tanya used the computer on dive boats and around the water continually so she had long ago learned not to keep anything that couldn't be replaced on them. It was annoying, but not a devastating loss. "I'm not seeing anything. The sensor unit isn't back here."

Bill and Kelly opened the passenger side doors in the front and back and began searching the floorboards and the seats. Water drained from the door panels when they did. The car was already beginning to sour with the stagnant sea water and dying microscopic marine animals that had been trapped inside when it was pulled to the surface.

"Would this sensor thing float, do you think?" Bill asked. He was the only one who hadn't seen it in person.

"No, it was weighted to stay on the bottom," Kelly said. He held up his hands up to represent the device. "It was about this big with tentacles coming out from it."

"Okay. Those tentacles might have been sensors, or they might have been antenna, or both," Bill said. He shined a light underneath the passenger seat from the front to get a look. He had to be careful to avoid the broken safety glass that still lay on the seat.

Tanya stood still for a moment and then she approached the car. She opened the driver's door and bent down to look. Slowly at first, but increasingly fast, she started flashing back to the morning, sitting in that very seat. Kelly was outside the window. Mike was on the other side of the car and both men were trying to save her. At the time she had felt strangely at ease, knowing they were there. Until the water covered her head. At that point, panic had set in. She had forgotten everything that happened next, but now she could see it clearly. Flashes of Mike slamming on the window. Kelly jerking on the car. The glass breaking. Mike coming inside. Sawing at the seat belt. Kelly pulling her loose and covering her mouth with his, a gentle kiss, but also tasting air. She remembered another time, ten years before, when the situation had been reversed and she had kissed Kelly the same way. Giving him life. Now it was his turn. His strong arms wrapping around her and pulling her to the surface. Others there lifting her gently from the water.

She felt a hand on her shoulder, shaking her gently.

"Tanya, are you okay?" Mike asked. Her eyes were closed, but he could tell she was breathing deeply. He knew she was reliving the morning. Tanya's eyes fluttered open. She put her hand on top of Mike's where it rested on her shoulder.

"I am. Thanks. And thanks for being there, this morning," Tanya said quietly.

"You're welcome. Now, why don't you take a break and let me look around in there?"

"I'm fine. I'm not that fragile," Tanya said with a laugh. She realized while she had been flashing back, her hands had continued searching and her eyes looking. Her body had continued functioning while her mind had drifted off. "There's nothing here. The sensor unit is gone."

"Do you think the police took it for some reason?" Bill asked.

"Doubtful," Mike said, shaking his head. "It looks like everything else is here, except for the sensor unit. I would think they would have recovered personal effects and that sort of thing. Frankly, it doesn't look like anything has been disturbed inside the car since they brought it to the impound yard."

"Do you think someone got to the car and took the sensor unit out while it was still underwater? Divers?" Kelly asked.

"That's about all that makes sense to me. It could have come out of the car somehow I guess, but that doesn't seem likely. All of the windows were rolled up and the doors locked tight when the car went down," Mike said, while he thought through the morning. "If it floated it could have come out when I broke out the window, but like Kelly said, it was weighted to stay down. I think someone took it. And they did it before the police had a chance to recover the car."

"I hung around for a little while after they took all of you to the hospital," Bill said. "It probably wasn't a half an hour before the police divers arrived and started hooking the car up to bring it to the surface. I didn't see any other divers get in the water."

"Someone could swim in from the other side of the harbor," Kelly said. "You probably weren't looking in the water, especially in shadows from the dock."

"That would mean that whoever did this planned it out more than we thought. They had divers ready to get in the water to recover the sensor unit as soon as the car went down. They didn't want it found by the police," Mike said. "I'm not a big fan of conspiracy theories, but this is getting bigger by the minute. I think this confirms that someone did this on purpose."

"But probably not enough to take it to the police, yet," Tanya said. "Something being missing isn't proof that someone took it."

"You're right about that," Mike said. "But we can keep looking and it gives us a direction. This Jay guy asked you to put the sensor in your car and it disappeared as soon as you went in the water."

"So, what do we do now?" Bill asked.

"Let me go talk to the guard and see if anyone has been around the car," Kelly said before he walked off. "I gave his cousin a job a few years ago. He'll talk to me."

"Do we go confront Jay?" Bill asked. "I'd really like to get my hands on one of those sensor units to see what they were capable of and see if he even could have sent Tanya's car into the water."

"I agree, but I'm not sure how to make that happen. He's not just going to give us one. Especially if he is dirty. Or, if he did, it wouldn't be one we would need to see," Mike said.

"I've got a better idea," Tanya said. "At the meeting, Jay got permission to place his sensors all around the island. He said they were being used for coral reef monitoring."

"All we have to do is figure out where he put one of the units and bring it up," Bill said.

"Easier said than done. They aren't very big and while Grand Cayman isn't a big island, they could be anywhere," Tanya said. "But that's the idea. We just have to find one."

"I talked to the guard. No one has been around here all day since they brought your car in," Kelly said as he walked back to group.

"That leaves us where we were," Bill said. "Stuck."

"Maybe not. I have an idea how we can find the sensor units," Mike said. "With Kelly and Tanya's network of friends on the island, we've got to be able to find out what boat and crew they're using to put the sensor units in the water."

"I'm sure we can figure that out," Kelly said.

"But even if we know where they are putting the units in the water, finding one will be like looking for a needle in a haystack."

"I have an idea about that, too. I have a friend who has some equipment that might be useful. Let me give him a call and see how quickly he can get it sent down here," Mike said. "Then we'll see what we can find."

CHAPTER 19

Jay stood looking over Matt's shoulder, watching him work. It annoyed Matt almost to distraction, but Jay wasn't concerned about Matt's feelings. This was the crunch time for their project. Everything was about to come online and then they could get to work. This was also when the project was at its most vulnerable. Their sources told them no one in power suspected anything. Trina, their mole inside the Department of the Environment, said no one was talking about any problems at all. The DoE was under the Ministry for Financial Service, Commerce and Environment, and if anyone had raised a flag about their plans, that was where it would happen.

Their apparent success didn't make Jay any less nervous. But it was nervous excitement, not trepidation. It bothered him to turn everything over to Matt, but through many projects he had come to realize where his expertise lay and where he needed to take a hands-off approach. Jay congratulated himself for learning that lesson. He thought of himself as a good manager.

On the other hand, he had his own plan working inside the plan Matt knew about. He might not have the technological skills Matt had, but that didn't mean he was a slouch either. When Matt was finished, Jay would finish up with his own side project. At this point, it wouldn't take much to put it all in gear. Just a few key strokes and everything was in motion.

"Are you going to get that?" Matt asked, looking tired and irritated, turning to face his partner.

"Hmmm, what?" Jay asked, coming back to the present from his thoughts.

"That's the third time your phone has rung and it's driving me up the wall. Of course, you breathing down my neck was almost putting me there anyway. Now go away, answer your phone and leave me alone. I'll tell you when something happens."

Jay realized he had been deeply lost in thought and had the good graces to look embarrassed as he pulled his phone from his pocket. He didn't want Matt to begin to wonder what he had been thinking about. Jay saw who was calling and slid his finger across the screen to answer the phone. He moved the phone to his ear, but said simply. "Hold on a moment." And then he turned back to Matt.

"Sorry about that, old friend. I was watching you work and got lost," he said. "I wish I had your skills."

"Blow it out your ear," Matt said in reply, with a grin just the same. "Go take your phone call and leave me alone for a bit."

"You got it."

Jay quickly walked across the room and out onto the patio, shutting the sliding glass door behind him. Jay could see the blue-green water of George Town Harbor in front of him, with the deeper blues of the Caribbean further out. It was morning and the air was beginning to get warm, but a soft island breeze stirred the air making it comfortable. Palm trees swayed gently, making a rustling sound. *Paradise, if I wasn't working,* Jay thought. And then he returned to his phone call.

"I'm here."

"What took you so long? Is everything going as planned? Is there a problem?" the caller asked.

"Sorry about that," Jay said, turning on his charm. "Everything is going fine. We were just in the middle of something and I couldn't break away."

"I heard your conversation. It didn't sound like a good working relationship to me," the caller said, flatly. "He sounded like he was the one in charge, not you."

"Don't you worry about our working relationship. We've been working together a long time and I know how to handle my friend. He'll do what I need him to. I just have to make him feel important. He'll get the work done."

"He had better. We have a lot riding on this," the voice said.

Jay took a breath before answering the man on the other end of the line. The man was thousands of miles away in Europe and he thought he had something riding on this. He wasn't on the ground where he could get caught. Jay took another deep breath and reminded himself he needed the man and his contacts for now. He had to keep this man in line, the same way he kept Matt working and Trina at her post reporting what happened in the government offices. They were almost ready. Managing people was his job, and what he was really good at.

"Please relax and let us do our job. I know you are used to being in control and having your hand on the pulse of a project, but this time you need to leave it up to me," Jay said, thinking, *We are partners, I don't work for you. And when I've gotten what I need from you, we won't even be partners.* But he didn't say that out loud.

"Please report back to me when you have put things in motion. We will monitor your progress from our end," the caller said.

"I will do my best to send you a message, but the work we are doing will make communications difficult. And possibly traceable. I suggest you monitor your networks. You will see when things begin," Jay said, doing his best to sound respectful, but not feeling it. They had had this conversation more than once before.

"Very well. I will look forward to receiving your message." The phone went dead.

"I don't think he heard a thing I said. Self-important ass," Jay grumbled. He stared at the phone and shook his head. "He doesn't understand what we're doing, so he thinks he can micromanage it. The technology is over his head, but he wants me to think he's in charge."

Jay went back inside and took up his spot, hovering over Matt's shoulder. Waiting for updates about their progress.

CHAPTER 20

Mike stood in the Owen Roberts International Airport, waiting on a flight to arrive. The night before, on their way back from the police impound yard, Mike called his friend Rich Synowiec. He knew Rich would have just what they needed.

Rich was a commercial diver and recreational diving instructor in Huntington, West Virginia. Mike and Rich had been college roommates but had lost touch over the years. Rich had traveled some before taking up commercial diving and opening his own business. Mike's career had gone off in its own direction. Ironically, Mike hadn't been a diver when they were in college, only learning to dive after he graduated. Mike and Rich hadn't dived together until a strange turn of events when Mike returned to their alma mater to give a speech. Those dives led to them solving the mystery of the death of another college classmate and sparking a controversy in the archaeological community about connections between the Adena Indians and the Maya in Mexico. Mike had even stayed in Huntington for a while, doing some guest lecturing at the school. He and Rich fell back into their 25-year-old routines quickly. When Mike called to ask Rich for his help, Rich didn't hesitate for a second. Without asking for details about *why*, Rich agreed to help and get the equipment on the next flight out of Huntington, heading for Grand Cayman. Standing in front of the international packages counter, Mike was fidgeting. He wanted to get back to work. He felt guilty leaving Kelly and Tanya at the hotel. Not that they needed his protection, of course. They were surrounded by dozens of their friends and were as safe as they could be. Still, near misses for both of them made Mike nervous. He wouldn't forgive himself if something happened to them.

"Mike!"

Mike glanced up and looked around. He had been lost in his thoughts. He looked at the chute where packages and over-sized luggage would be processed separately from the regular conveyor belts. There was nothing new there. The package hadn't arrived.

"Michael," a new voice, a feminine one, said.

"I think he's lost it," the first voice said. "I told you he was slipping."

Mike turned to face the people talking to him. He was floored by what he saw. In front of him was his old friend Rich. And Frankie. Mike was confused to see Rich, since his friend said he would get the equipment on a plane, but didn't say anything about hand-delivering it. But Frankie was a completely different situation all-together.

Dr. Francesca DeMarco, Frankie to her friends, was an Italian archaeologist. Mike met her on an assignment for his magazine, sent to cover the discovery of an ancient city that had slipped under the ocean on the Adriatic coast of Italy. Frankie had been in charge of the project and had fought tooth and nail to get her university to allow her to complete the excavation. When fanatics had threatened her life, and Mike's as well, they had worked together to unravel the mystery of Guardians' Keep. Frankie's discovery had changed religious history forever, bringing the Breastplate of Judgment back into the world. It had been lost to history nearly 2000 years before. The breastplate was worn by the Jewish high priest when he went into the Holy of Holies, before the Ark of the Covenant. Mike and Frankie had developed more than a professional relationship while researching the story, but both of their careers had gotten in the way of much more. Frankie's life was filled with the ongoing underwater excavation and speaking tours and writing a book about what she found. And what happened when she put on the breastplate herself. They had seen each other off and on since then, but had finally drifted apart.

Now, Mike was looking directly into Frankie's face. Her dark, straight hair framed her fine features. She was tall at 5'10" and fit from a life of diving and exploration. Her naturally dark Italian complexion reflected a deep tan from working outside in the Italian sun.

"See, I told you he's lost it," Rich said, smiling. "I brought what you asked for. And something you didn't. But something tells me you're not disappointed about it."

"I, ummm, I… what are you doing here?"

"Well, you called and…"

"Not you, Rich," Mike said with an eye roll.

"Is that how you greet an old friend, Michael?" Frankie said, her eyes twinkling. "I hoped you would be happy to see me."

Without another word, Mike grabbed Frankie in his arms and lifted her off her feet in a hug, feeling her firm body against his and smelling her hair. When he set her down, he gave her a kiss as well.

"It's great to see you," Mike said. "You look amazing."

"Don't I get a greeting?" Rich asked, teasing. "But I warn you, if you try to kiss me, I'm getting right back on that airplane."

"You, my friend, have some explaining to do," Mike said, shaking Rich's hand and pulling him into a one-armed hug. His friend was 5'10' with salt and pepper hair.

Mike helped Rich and Frankie gather their things and get loaded up in the car. They were headed back to Sunset House before Mike asked how his friends decided to show up instead of sending a package. And how Frankie came to be there in the first place. He wasn't mad. In fact, he was happier to see Rich and Frankie than he thought he should be, but he was still confused.

"All right, start talking," Mike said. "Either of you."

"I'm not sure you're going to believe me," Rich began.

Mike gave his friend a sideways glance from the driver's seat. "Try me."

"About fifteen minutes before you called, this gorgeous Italian woman walked into my shop. I thought I had died and gone to heaven, but of course she was looking for you," Rich began.

"Oh, Richard, you are so sweet," Frankie smiled from the back seat, her accent making his name sound more like *Reeechard*.

"Go on," Mike said.

"So, this angel walked into my shop and asked for you. I was just explaining to her that you were indeed my so-called friend, but that you had once again left me while you jetted off on an adventure to an exotic locale, leaving me behind in the cold. Both literally and figuratively. The phone rang and it was you. You were in a hurry and really didn't give me a chance to tell you that Francesca was standing there in front of me. You just asked for a piece of equipment and then you got off the phone. I told Francesca that I was going to have to run to the airport to get you a package overnight and, well, one thing led to another and here we are."

"I hope you are not cross with me for coming to visit. And I hope you are not angry with Richard, either. He is only doing what a good friend would do," Frankie said with a smile that said she knew exactly what Mike was feeling. "We both know you and knew you would not have asked for a piece of equipment like that if you weren't involved in something exciting. And we were sure we could be of assistance."

"Okay, I give up," Mike said. "You both have my best interests at heart. I see that now. But Frankie, what were you doing in Huntington, anyway?"

"I came to see you, of course, Michael."

"From Italy?"

"Well, I was in the states giving a lecture and wanted to see my favorite American journalist. It has been too long since I've seen you," Frankie said. "Oh my, please tell me I haven't interrupted something. You aren't here sharing this island with a special friend, are you?"

"No, there's no one special. At least not until now," Mike said. "I'm sure Rich told you I was here for my friends' celebration. But things have gotten pretty serious since I arrived."

Mike quickly caught Rich and Frankie up on the events of the last few days as they drove the rest of the way to the hotel. Getting out of the car in the Sunset House parking lot, Mike finally reached the point where he had decided to call Rich.

"Sounds like you guys've had a pretty hairy week. But how does my metal detector play into it?" Rich asked. The special piece of equipment Mike asked Rich to send him was an underwater metal detector that could be towed behind a boat. While other systems existed, Mike knew Rich had fine tuned and prepped his underwater metal detector to find small metallic objects under difficult circumstances. As a commercial diver, Rich used it to find evidence in the local rivers and lakes for the police. He had recovered guns, knives and other evidence. The system was weighted to be neutrally buoyant underwater, keeping the sensitive search head close to the bottom, while allowing the user to stay dry on the surface, listening to reports. A diver would have to dive down to check out every positive hit, of course, but the metal detector would allow them to search for the control units more quickly and efficiently.

"We need to find one of those sensor units and see if it has the capability to take over a car's computer system and send it into the water," Mike said. "Going straight to this Jay guy would probably spook him, or have him give us one that was set up differently. We need to make the connection without him knowing what's going on."

"So, we've stumbled onto another murder mystery," Rich said.

"Well, attempted murder, but yeah," Mike agreed. "And that's the only reason I'm not overjoyed to see you both. I really don't know what's going on around here and having you guys here means more of my friends are at risk. Neither of you knew what was going on when you decided to come, so if you want to get back out of here, I wouldn't blame you a bit."

"Michael, don't be ridiculous. You stood by me when men were trying to scare me and stop me from discovering one of the most important finds in the world. You didn't shy away from it and I won't either. Remember, I'm not some defenseless woman, either. I can take care of myself," Frankie said, her affectionate smile replaced by steely resolve. "You cannot protect all of your friends from everything. You have to let others help you. You can't keep people out for their own good. Especially when things are this important."

Frankie had hit too close to Mike's thoughts for his comfort, but before he had a chance to reply, Rich said, looking longingly at My Bar, "Yeah, what she said. Now, where can we throw our stuff down? And is that curry in the air? It smells amazing!"

Mike went off to make arrangements for Rich and Frankie to have places to sleep and sent them toward the patio to order lunch. In the meantime, he tossed his friends' bags in his room and moved the case holding the metal detector into the dive shop. By the time he was done setting things up, Rich and Frankie were already seated at a table with his other best friends, Kelly and Tanya. The foursome was laughing and talking like they were old friends when Mike walked up, although he was sure they had never met. The only thing they had in common was him, which told him what they were probably laughing about.

"Ah, leave it to my friends to have fun at my expense," Mike said when he approached the table. "Did you at least order me some lunch?"

"Do you believe the ego on this guy?" Rich said with feigned offense. "He thinks we're talking about him."

"Maybe that's because we are," Tanya said. "Why haven't you told us about Frankie. She's gorgeous, Mike, and every bit of a perfect match for you."

Before Mike got a chance to defend himself, Frankie added her thoughts.

"Tatyana, he is embarrassed by me," Frankie said, pretending to pout.

"All right, all right. When you guys are done roasting me, let me know and we'll get down to the business at hand," Mike said, raising his hands in surrender.

Before anyone else had a chance to comment, the resort's office manager approached the table.

"Kelly, can I talk to you for a minute? We have a little problem," she said.

"What is it, Sheila?"

"It seems the Internet has gone down. We can't connect to anyone off the island," the woman explained.

"That's odd, but it's happened before. Any word from Cayman Telephone and Telegraph when it will be back online?"

"That's just it. They say the entire island is offline. They can't connect to anything off-island, either. I tried calling the United States and it wouldn't connect. The satellite phone got through, but none of the land line phones or Internet-powered phones are getting through."

"The island is completely off line? How does that happen?" Tanya asked.

"Hold on, guys. It looks like the local news is talking about this," Mike said as he gestured to the television above the bar in My Bar. They all moved closer to hear what was going on.

CHAPTER 21

"... island-wide communications blackout. Mobile phones are continuing to work as well as other intra-island communications, but nothing that connects off-island is functioning, except for satellite phones. Anything that relies on the undersea telephone and Internet cables is not working. For now, Grand Cayman is truly an island, cut off from the rest of the world. As a precaution, flights into Owen Roberts International Airport are being diverted away from the island and no flights are being allowed to leave. It is unknown the extent of the communications outage or the effects this will have on international banking or business. Governor Phillips has promised to comment on the situation soon. We will be back with more details when we have them."

*****

Grand Cayman has two major industries: international banking and tourism. Both relied heavily on communications with the United States and Europe. Banks were constantly making wire transfers and communicating with international clients who need to move their money, make deposits, and withdraw money. There are nearly 600 banks on the tiny island, including 43 of the 50 largest banks in the world. That is on an island with a little more than 75 square miles of terrain. The total area for the three Cayman Islands is a little over 100 square miles. All together, the total population is just over 56,000. A little over 32,000 of those are Caymanians, with the rest international ex-pats from all around the world.

Tourism works on both a larger and smaller scale. The amount of money involved in each individual business transaction is much smaller, but there are many more of them. There are dozens of hotels and dive operations on the island, catering to thousands of visitors. And that doesn't include the cruise ship passengers who just stay for a few hours. On top of that are the ancillary and support businesses like restaurants, shops, and stores that supply those hotels and tourists.

Losing connection to the Internet and land line phones meant none of those businesses, large or small, could communicate with their clients. Business ground to a halt almost immediately and the government ordered an investigation into what caused it, while working to get the island back online. No one knew the extent of the outage or how long it would last, although public officials immediately took to the local airwaves saying it was a temporary glitch and they would restore service as quickly as possible.

Ultimately, they had no idea what was going on.

After an hour or so of panic, everyone realized things were still functioning as normal on the island. They still had electricity. They could still listen to local radio and watch local television. They could leave the island by boat, if they needed, and their GPS systems still seemed to be working, although there was no way to confirm it or calibrate their units. They were simply cut off from the rest of the world. Considering that the US Coast Guard made regular stops in Grand Cayman and the US Army had a base a few hundred miles to the north in Guantanamo Bay in Cuba, it wasn't like they were all alone. Everyone quickly calmed down and things returned to mostly normal. It was the islands after all. No one got too excited about anything for long.

Right up until they got *the demand*.

*****

"Please excuse the interruption," the well-groomed news anchor said directly into the camera. She wanted to look serious and concerned, but reassuring at the same time. "We have just received a video from an anonymous source explaining what has happened with international communications on Grand Cayman. They say the video has been sent to international publications and media outlets in the US and Europe as well. It says why we have been cut off and what will happen next. They are claiming to keep the island off-line until their demands are met, but they have not sent us any information on exactly what those demands are. We are being held hostage, virtually. We will show you the video now, so you know what is going on, although I must tell you that we are still working to determine the authenticity of the recording."

The image on the television screen shifted to the image of a masked man, sitting in a chair on a beach with the ocean behind him. He looked casual and comfortable, except for the ski mask over his head and the electronic scrambling that made his voice sound mechanical.

*****

For too long, we have treated our oceans as a dumping ground. We have believed we could do anything to them. Because they were so vast, it just didn't matter. Our fishermen have caught fish on top of fish believing they would miraculously and magically reproduce, even while seeing the size of the fish they caught get smaller and smaller. On top of that, fish are showing up with concentrations of heavy metals so high we've told pregnant women not to eat them. Now, there are fish swimming in our oceans filled with radioactive waste from Fukushima and tons of plastic floating on the surface that we call the Great Pacific Garbage Patch, like it is out of a cartoon. But no one seems to care. It is easier for us to stick our heads in the sand.

Coral reefs are dying around the world. Climate change is just part of the problem. Farm runoff, untreated sewers and other forms of pollution are causing unchecked algae growth unchecked, choking out the sun corals need to grow and prosper. Corals protect our beaches from erosion and storms, providing habitat for small fish to grow. The recent event on this island where a cruise ship dropped its anchor on a coral reef that was beginning to recover is the latest example of how we mistreat the ocean.

Grouper, long considered an icon of the Caribbean, are endangered and populations are struggling because we harvest them during their mating gatherings. Sharks are caught for their fins and thrown back in the water to die.

This is all throwing the oceans out of balance, and we will no longer stand by and accept it.

This place, Grand Cayman, is a temple and we should treat it like one. If we won't take care of this beautiful ocean jewel, what will we save?

And that is why we are holding this island hostage. We want the world to wake up and understand what is at risk. We are in control of this island. And make no mistake, we are firmly in control. Cutting communications is just the first step. No one has been hurt and, except for a few tourists, no one has been inconvenienced. Mark my words, this is just the beginning. We are in complete control and plan to stay that way until the world is willing to come together to change. These are drastic measures, but these are desperate times.

From this moment, you have 72 hours to bring together a group of representatives from every nation in this world. We are sending this same manifesto to news organizations all over the world. We expect to see presidents and prime ministers, kings, queens and dictators. And don't think we won't know what is going on. We are not just here on this tiny island. We are monitoring communications. Don't think we aren't ready to counter anything you might try. We are everywhere.

Lastly, be warned. If the military from any nation should try to intervene by invading the island, there will be consequences. We have the power to erase every computer system on the island. Much of the world's banking and commerce flows through Grand Cayman. On any given day billions of dollars flow through this island. If we choose, we can make it all disappear, throwing the rest of the financial world into chaos and taking the rest of the world with it. Stay away and get to work meeting our demands.

If that body of leaders is not ready to make the changes we ask for, the people of Grand Cayman, and the world, will face more serious consequences.

The Saviors of the Ocean are watching.

CHAPTER 22

"Commissioner, I've gotten the information you requested. There are two people on the island at the moment that we've been able to determine could have set up the information blockade around the island. We've been keeping an eye on them both, just as a matter of security," the police detective explained. The young detective was in charge of the police department's cyber crimes division. He went on to describe Jaylend Taylor and Bill Gardner. When the detective was finished, the police commissioner sat quietly for a moment, his hands steepled in front of him, considering his options.

The police commissioner was Alex March. For many years he had been a detective just like the man in front of him. His own success had led to his eventual promotion to head up the Royal Cayman Islands Police Force. There were times he would have preferred to be out in the field. Like now. A dark-skinned Caymanian who spent much of his time outdoors, he was still strong and fit, but there was some gray around his temples.

"These are the only two *unknowns* on the island who could have done something like this?" March asked.

"Yes, sir. We make it a point to know about hackers who live here or come to visit. None of the Caymanians or ex-pats living here have made any suspicious moves in the last few days. Both of these men are visitors to the island and have both been active. We can't tell what Taylor is doing, but his condo has been pulling large amounts of electricity, common with computer systems. The other, Gardner, has actually been staging environmental protests on the streets."

"Let's talk to both of them and see what they've been up to. Of course, it could be someone from outside the island doing this, but I doubt it," March said.

"I agree, sir. I'll get right on it," the detective said as he turned to go.

"Hold on, Rogers. Give me the address for Taylor," March said while standing. "I think I'll take this one personally. I've heard of him and it is likely he has influential friends. I'd rather I get yelled at for talking to him than you. We'll split this duty."

"I understand, sir," Detective Rogers said, not understanding at all. He had been looking forward to talking to Thomas and stopping this crime himself. "Do you want me or one of my men to go with you? This is cyber crime."

March chuckled at the man's thinly-veiled question. "I may not understand all of the issues with computers and technology, but I think I can still tell when someone is acting suspiciously or is hiding something."

"Yes, sir," Rogers said. "I didn't mean to imply…"

"Don't worry about it. You track down this other one, Gardner. See what he's up to. I'll talk to Taylor and see if I can get a read on him. If he isn't involved, maybe he can help."

CHAPTER 23

The group stood at the My Bar bar for a moment, too stunned to say much of anything. And then everyone started talking at once.

"We're being held hostage?"

"They really think they will get every world leader in one place? Really?"

"How in the world are they doing this?"

"Just think, we must have come in on the last flight to land. If I had known…"

"The guy said he's in control. What else could they do to us?"

"Are you guys sorry you decided to get involved?"

"I don't think they know who they're messing with!"

"The problem is, I don't really disagree with what he said," Tanya said. "Of course, this isn't the way to do it, but everything he said is true."

"I agree completely." It was Bill Gardner. He hadn't been there when the "island kidnapper" made his statement, but as soon as it was done, he had headed for Sunset House to hook up with his new friends. He brought his two young female friends with him this time.

"Are we sure you aren't the mastermind behind this?" Kelly asked suspiciously. "When we first saw you, you were protesting and saying a lot of what he just said. And you've told us you have the computer skills for this."

"We've been through this. I may know how to make it happen, but I promise I don't have the resources to make this happen. To take down an entire island? That's not in my budget," Bill said and laughed. "Not to mention that it goes against every fiber in my being to hold people against their will."

"I'm guessing you might have some thoughts on who is behind this, though?" Mike asked to keep the conversation moving forward and away from Kelly's suspicions.

"I think we were on the right track before," Bill explained. "I never imagined those sensors could do something like this, but it makes sense. Somehow he has hacked the Internet coming to the island and taken it over."

"Remember, he was planning to place those sensors all around the island to monitor coral reef development. Or at least that was his story. What if that part was true and he has ringed the island with those computer gadgets?" Tanya asked. "Could he place a cone of silence around the whole island that way?"

"Actually, that makes a lot of sense. It would be a good way to distribute the load and make it harder to break," Bill said. "And nice 'Get Smart' reference, too. You get bonus points for that."

"I thought the Internet was everywhere. How do you take the whole island off line?" Rich asked.

"Remember when North Korea lost their Internet connection? They only had like four connections to the Internet. They only had about 1500 IP addresses in the whole country. Grand Cayman has more than that, and a lot more IP addresses, but it is still an island and all of those connections have to come in through underwater cables. Remember, the country directly to the north, Cuba, isn't exactly a technological marvel, either. So, those connections have to come from a pretty good distance under the ocean."

"And don't forget, the Cayman Trench is pretty deep as well," Mike threw into the conversation.

"Wouldn't it be easier to just take out the undersea cables when they came to the surface?" Rich asked. "I mean, it would be simpler than this cone of silence. A little C4 goes a long way."

"It probably would be easier, but not if you don't want to come across as a terrorist. I guess he wants to come across as being *reasonable*."

"And when you start blowing things up, it's a lot harder to keep the US military out, at least in the short term," Rich agreed.

"Exactly. So, this guy, the Savior of the Ocean, has lowered a cone of silence around the island and he's blocking signals coming through the undersea cables," Bill finished. "And let's be honest. All the signs point to it being Jay. He has the means to do it and has been present for every key event, or has had connections to them."

"So have you," Kelly said.

"I have the technical skills, but not the means to make it happen. There is a serious investment in technology and manpower that I can't do," Bill argued.

"The most important question, then, is what do we do about it? I mean, we're not going to just sit here and take it," Mike said.

"And it sounds like we have 72 hours to figure it all out," Kelly agreed.

CHAPTER 24

The plan came together quickly. They divided themselves into groups and began to work out what needed to be done. There were three plans of attack.

Kelly, Tanya and Rich, along with a couple other old hands who couldn't stay out of trouble if they had to, were going to take one of the Sunset House dive boats out on the water with Rich's metal detector system to look for the sensors causing the communications breach.

Bill and his two friends, Sherri and Miranda, were going to stay at Sunset House and coordinate the search efforts for the electronic equipment in the water, as well as trying to find a way to override the controls shutting everything down. They were also going to serve as a dispatcher between all three groups using the dive shop's VHF radio system to communicate with the boat. Cell phones were still working, but that was an electronic signal that could be hacked into. They didn't have any way of knowing how extensive the electronic network was or what Jay had his fingers into.

Mike and Frankie headed into town to see if they could find Jay and get a better idea of what he was up to, what they were facing and how to stop him. They wanted to confirm that their suspicions were correct and if he had help to do everything. None of them had any faith that the world leaders were going to come together to bow to his demands. Even if they all agreed to meet, there was no way they could act that quickly. Most countries in the world, including the United States and Great Britain, which were the two major nations with the most to lose when it came to Grand Cayman, had a policy of not negotiating with terrorists. And that was exactly what they had branded Jay. Mike had been involved in the take down of terrorists before as an international photojournalist. He knew how the antiterrorist teams worked and understood what information they would need if it came to a military assault. Mike knew that wasn't out of the question, but he hoped to avoid it if he could. He had seen too many situations like this where assault teams started kicking down doors and throwing grenades and innocent civilians got hurt when the bad guys started shooting back.

"After what happened to Tanya, we're going to need to stay off the grid as much as possible and keep an eye out for drones. If you see one circling overhead, you've been made," Mike said.

"That's not a worry for most of us. The boats aren't built around electronic systems like cars are. There's no way someone could take control of them. The most they could do is shut them down," Tanya said. "And I doubt that's even realistic."

"I'll stay undercover here at the hotel," Bill said. "Of course, they could find me by tracing back into what I'll be doing, but I've played these games before. I won't get caught."

"I believe you know what you're doing, but don't think of this as a video game. Remember what they were willing to do to Tanya. These people are playing for keeps. And that just leaves us," Mike said, gesturing to Frankie. "We'll need to stay off the radar as much as we can, but still get around in town."

"I have just the solution," Kelly said with a grin.

"Do I dare ask?"

"It's possible I wasn't entirely honest with you when I picked you up at the airport. It was going to be a surprise for you, but this seems like as good a time as any."

Grand Cayman was a beautiful and well-developed island. Except where it wasn't. Where the tourists stayed and in George Town, the streets were smooth, clean and well-cared-for. There were other parts of the island where that wasn't the case. The island was essentially a sea mount that rose up from the sea floor more than 2000 feet below the surface. The island itself was just the very tip and was completely made up of coral skeletons from a time when the ocean's surface was higher than today. Much of the island was covered with loose, sandy soil, but in other places the hard calcium skeleton of the ancient coral was exposed to the air making rough and treacherous terrain. For people who found themselves exploring the tiny island from time to time, a vehicle with a higher ground clearance and heavy-duty tires was a must. And having a convertible top to appreciate the air, the view, and the island breezes was even better. Even though most tourists never left Seven-Mile Beach, the rental car companies realized the appeal of vehicles like that and rented convertible, compact SUVs for people to have fun navigating George Town streets.

When Mike lived on the island, he owned a 1977 Jeep CJ5 that was his pride and joy. It was rough, smelled of mildewed wetsuits most of the time, and lacked anything passing for a top to protect him and anyone riding with him from the afternoon thunderstorms that always popped up around the island, dumping sheets of rain for 15 minutes before moving off-shore. When he left the island, he sold the jeep to Kelly and his friend had driven it for years. Ten years before, when Mike last visited the island, he used the old Jeep to avoid his pursuers and rescue Kelly. All it took was remembering how to start the old Jeep without a key and the certain knowledge that Kelly hadn't fixed the starter system.

Kelly led Mike and the rest of the crew to a small garage area behind the main hotel buildings. The nature of the small hotel meant nothing was far away, but creative use of palm trees and other island plants and flowers kept most of the functional parts out of view of the hotel guests. When everyone was standing around the carport, Kelly pulled a tarp from what was obviously a car and revealed the old Jeep was still there. And had, in fact, been restored.

"You're kidding me," Mike said, his feet glued to the ground from surprise. "You still have it? But you said…"

"All I said was I retired it. I never said I got rid of it. This old Jeep went into retirement for some tender, loving care and a complete rebuild," Kelley said with a chuckle.

The CJ5 gleamed like it was new, better than Mike had even seen it. He, of course, had bought it from someone else who was leaving the island, who bought it from someone else before that. He wasn't sure who had brought it to the island originally or how many owners had driven it. It sported a shiny new green paint job over a seamless body. The Jeep was always lifted higher than it came from the factory, but it sported new island tread tires and a bikini top to keep the sun and rain off of passengers. Even though the island required drivers to drive on the left side of the road, and most cars built for that situation had a right-hand drive, the Jeep still had its original left hand steering. Kelly had added some other features to the Jeep, though. It now sported a winch on the front and a radio inside capable of communicating on VHF and CB frequencies. He planned to use it to communicate with the boats on the water and talk to the shop at the same time.

"You kept it all original?" Mike asked.

"Restored to the way it was when it came off the assembly line," Kelly said.

"Then this will be perfect."

"It seems to be a fine Jeep, but what makes this car so special?" Frankie asked.

"This Jeep is from before computers controlled everything on cars. It's got all manual controls and a distributor instead of an electronic ignition. There is nothing anyone can use to take control of this Jeep," Mike explained. "This is definitely going off the grid."

"So no one can do to us what they tried to do to Tanya. Makes sense to me," Frankie agreed.

"And they can't lock you in because it doesn't have doors or windows," Tanya said. "No one will have to break you out if you happen to fall into the water."

"Don't you think people will notice this Jeep?" Bill asked.

"No, there are lots of Jeeps still around along with the newer convertible SUVs. It'll blend in nicely," Kelly explained.

"Well gang, I think it's time to get this show on the road. The clock is ticking and something tells me we don't have as much time as we think we do," Mike said, taking the Jeep keys from Kelly. "Let's all stay safe and stay in touch. Check in as often as you can. I don't want anyone getting in trouble."

"Mike, trouble seems to follow you. And I don't think any of us would have it any other way," Frankie said jumping into the passenger side of the jeep and putting on her seat belt. "It's going to be a bumpy ride, right?"

"I think you've got a keeper with this one, Mike," Tanya said smiling, looking at Frankie. "She's got spunk."

"Spasiba, Tatyana," Frankie said in Russian. Her smile showing that she felt the same way. "Thank you."

"Prego, Francesca," Tanya said, responding in Italian. "You're welcome."

"Tanya, do you really think this is the time to be matchmaking?" Mike asked. He shook his head as he climbed into the Jeep and fired it up listening to the quiet rumble. It represented power. Not too much, but just enough. The engine wasn't built for excessive speed or climbing up mountains, but it could more than hold its own.

"Mike, if I've learned nothing else over the years, it's there is always time for matchmaking, especially when you love the people involved. You mean so much to me and Kelly that you may never understand. We both want you to be happy," Tanya said moving in close and kissing him on the cheek. "Now get out of here and help us get our island back."

Mike pushed in on the clutch and moved the gear shift into first gear. "That I can do."

CHAPTER 25

Their other plans interrupted by the communications blockade, it was easy to recruit some additional divers for the search effort. Kurt Williams, Thomas "Shrop" Shropshire, and Eric Hexdall had all been friends with Kelly and Tanya for more than a decade. They had been there through the good times and the bad, even though they had all moved on to other parts of their lives. Shrop was the only one who was still even working in the dive industry on Cayman, but that didn't stop all three of them from volunteering to go out on the boat and help out. Everyone was inconvenienced by the communications breakdown they were experiencing, and they were all a bit nervous about the threats that were made, too.

Along with the three *cowboys* they recruited, Tanya, Kelly, and Rich had boarded the Sunset House dive boat *Manta*. They wanted to make sure they had enough people to handle the boat, dive and watch the metal detector system continually. At the same time, they didn't want too many people on board, getting bored, restless, or anxious. It promised to be a slow and tedious job. They brought Captain Biko along as well, to operate the dive boat and keep them out of trouble. Bill and his team were back at Sunset House working their computers and trying to determine likely locations. Everyone else felt they couldn't waste time sitting around until Bill figured something out. They were hoping they would get lucky, or at least be in the area, when Bill radioed that he had a site for them to check out. They were making educated guesses about the placement of the sensor units. To minimize communication issues caused by the water, they were working under the assumption that they could not be deep underwater and could not be spaced too far apart. To control them and have them function as a

115

network, there were limits. Before they took off on their treasure hunt, Rich and Kelly had reviewed Tanya's maps to plot out the most likely locations for the sensor units.

To perform the search, Rich hung his metal detector sensor off the bow of the boat. The metal detector itself wasn't new technology. He had simply disassembled a high-end land-use detector and spliced in additional wires between the sensor head and the control unit. That way, he could hang it 30 feet in the water below him and listen for "hits" while the boat moved forward slowly. Rich had fashioned a cradle for the metal detector head using white plastic PVC pipe that he filled with lead shot from the dive shop. He played with the balance for a few minutes to make sure the device was neutrally buoyant in the water. He didn't want it to float up or sink, putting additional pressure on the wires and lines he used to control it. He was able to control the sensor unit's depth while he watched the depth gauge on the boat that showed the distance between the boat's keel and the coral below them. To give them the widest sensor field, Rich had to keep the metal detector within three feet of the reef. He was wearing headphones so he could hear the metal detector squeal whenever they got close to anything metallic. Rich was in the shade of the boat's cabin, but he was sweating from the tension and strain of listening and watching for rapid changes in the depth that would either make his detector less effective or worse. If they ran into a coral head, slamming the sensor unit into the reef, it would damage the coral, but it would also destroy the sensor itself. And they only had one.

Compounding the problem was the debris buried inside the coral itself. Over the years, Grand Cayman had been hit by numerous hurricanes. Boats had sunk around the island in storms, by accident and on purpose. That meant there was a fair amount of metallic clutter underwater. Most of it had long-since been covered over by the living reef, but that didn't mean it couldn't set off the metal detector.

"And it's not like this sensor thing is the size of a car bumper," Rich said in frustration. "I mean, this's just about an impossible task to begin with."

"Rich, no one expects you to work miracles here. Unfortunately, we got the short end of the stick. But, it's a lot better than sitting back at the hotel doing nothing," Kelly said, playing the manager and keeping the crew on task.

"That's your opinion," Kurt said with a laugh. He was stretched out on one of the bench seats lined with scuba cylinders. Under normal operations, the benches would be filled with happy passengers looking forward to making a dive in the warm, clear water. Not today. "We could be sitting in the shade having a cold one."

"I could use a cold one right now, too," Shrop said, smiling from his spot near the stern. "Water isn't really cutting it."

"It's not helping that we are poking along either," Kurt said. "Can we push this thing a little faster and get some air movement?"

"You guys could have stayed home if all you're going to do is complain," Tanya snapped, glaring at the men, daring them to keep up their complaints. "Have you forgotten why we're out here? Do you think this is a fun trip? Want me to call some girls to come along, too? Maybe you can dance for a while."

"Can you all be quiet?" Rich asked, raising his voice.

"Tanya, settle down. They're just kidding around," Kelly said. "You know they don't mean any harm by it."

Tanya turned on Kelly and started to argue with him, and then deflated. "I'm sorry," she said to her husband and then she faced the guys who were sitting up a bit straighter on the back of the boat. "Sorry, guys. I'm just a bit irritable right now. And all this tension isn't helping anything. But please remember, we do need everyone to be quiet so Rich can monitor the metal detector."

"Yes, please remember that," Rich said catching everyone, including Tanya and Kelly, in his gaze. "Captain, can you come back around and go over that spot again. I think I heard something, but I can't be sure."

Everyone quieted down and gathered around Rich's equipment while Captain Biko maneuvered the dive boat in a slow arc. He was moving faster than he had been when they were actively searching, but he still couldn't move too quickly for fear of damaging the overboard equipment. It took them a couple of minutes to get back to a starting point that Rich identified on their GPS unit. When Kurt started to say something just as they began the search, Rich silenced him with a glare.

Just an hour into the search, they had already passed over three potential sites, but when divers went over the side, there was nothing. Still, the next one could always be the right one, so they kept taking it seriously.

The loudspeaker connected to the metal detector popped and cracked, but didn't give any indication they were close to anything metallic when Captain Biko began his second pass along the path they had just covered. Everyone gathered around close, barely breathing, hoping this time it would be *the one* they were all waiting for. No one knew exactly what they would do when they found one of the sensor units. And *when* was the way they chose to think. None of them thought of it as *if*.

Captain Biko kept a steady hand on the throttle and wheel, plodding through the water at barely two knots. They were almost back to where Rich had asked the captain to come about when they finally heard the tell-tale squeal of the metal detector. There was something below them. Just as quickly as the unit sounded, the noise went away. That was actually a relief to Rich as he knew what they were looking for was small. If the meter and the audible alarm had spiked and stayed that way for any distance, he knew it would be something that was too large. This time, though, it was an obvious hit, but a small one. Rich grinned. Time to get in the water.

"Captain, shut it down. Time to dive," Rich said, grinning with his normal enthusiasm. "This is so awesome!"

"We'll do it!" Kurt and Shrop said, grabbing their gear and running for the boat's swim step. They were almost in the water before anyone had a chance to say anything.

"Hold on guys," Rich started to protest.

"Let them go, Rich," Kelly said. "Those guys are the best you'll find, and I can't think of anyone I would want backing me up when things get dicey, but they need to blow off some steam."

They heard two splashes as the divers performed their giant strides, stepping out into the water from the boat.

"All right," Rich relented. "These are your people. You know them best. And they probably weren't going to listen to me brief them about what to look for anyway."

"No, twice is probably enough."

And then it was time to wait. Eric, Rich, Tanya, and Kelly moved to the bow to look over the side, trying to follow the divers' progress and see if they found anything. The water was clear and the sun was almost directly overhead, making it easy for the bubble watchers on the surface to track the divers. The bottom was less than 25 feet below them and conditions were perfect.

Shrop and Kurt took their time doing their search. They didn't want to overlook anything. And while this dive wasn't the most exciting thing they had ever done, it beat being bored on the boat. After entering the water, the two men allowed themselves to drift away from the boat, back along the line they had just come. When they reached the bottom, they began to swim forward, kicking slowly and hovering as close to the bottom as they could. They knew the sensor head on the metal detector would only react to metals within a small field, no more than three or four feet across if everything was perfect. They didn't have to perform a search pattern. They just had to follow the boat's path and make sure they didn't miss anything.

Both men were so intent on their search, they nearly didn't notice the high-pitched whining sound in the water. Propellers. Moving quickly from the sound of it. Shrop heard the sound first and glanced around, but from his position, face down just above the coral reef, he couldn't see anything. He reached out and tapped Kurt on the shoulder. When his buddy looked over at him, Shrop pointed to his ear and then gave another signal, cupping his hands together like he was holding water. The signal for boat.

Kurt signaled back with his hand in the shape of a hook, signaling a question mark.

Shrop replied with a simple shrug of his shoulders. Kurt shook his head and then pointed to his eyes behind his mask and then back at the bottom below them. They would figure it out when they were done. Both men knew the density of the water carried sound for long distances. The boat was probably hundreds of yards away. Being underwater made it hard to distinguish direction as well. The human brain determines direction based on the minor delay between when each ear detects sound. Sounds waves in water travel four times faster than in air so the brain can't decide which ear heard the sound first.

They returned to their search.

Topside, the four remaining searchers and the boat captain were startled when a large dive boat came right at them, only pulling back on its throttles and slowing the boat when they were within 20 feet of the *Manta*. The movement pushed a bow wave directly at the *Manta*, sloshing water over the stern.

Kelly ran for the stern of the boat, ready to give the other boat a piece of his mind. "Don't you know we have divers in the water? Can't you see the flag? Are you crazy or just stupid?" he shouted.

"We see your flag, but that's the problem. This is a private reef. No trespassing. You need to leave now," one man shouted back. Three others on board were carrying assault rifles. The guns were pointed at the deck, not at Kelly and the *Manta*, but the message was obvious. "And don't argue with me. You're not going to change my mind."

CHAPTER 26

Police Commissioner March felt good. He was away from his desk, doing *real* work, not just being an administrator. He knew he was good at his job, but it felt good to pound the pavement again. He rode the elevator to the top floor of the luxury building and knocked on the door to Jaylend Taylor's condo. The island was full of similar buildings and most of them left March cold. He wasn't impressed with money or the things it bought. Or the people who flaunted it.

It took a minute for someone to answer the door to the condo, but when it opened, March was surprised it was Taylor himself.

"Mr. Taylor, I'm Police Commissioner Alex March."

"It's a pleasure to meet you, Commissioner," Jay replied. "To what do I owe the pleasure of this visit?"

"I assume you've heard about the information blockade and how terrorists are holding our island hostage," March began.

"I saw that on the news. Pretty incredible stuff, really. It's amazing what crazies will do any more," Jay replied with a smile.

"You're right about that, Mr. Taylor. With your background, I was wondering if you might have some insight into how someone could pull something like this off," March asked, trying to angle himself to look inside Jay's condo. Jay moved to keep himself between March and a clear view of the room behind him.

"Don't believe everything you read in the magazines, Commissioner," Jay said with a laugh. "I'm pretty good, but this sort of thing isn't exactly my forte. I had lots of really smart people working for me at my company before I sold it. And I'm semiretired now. I'm just enjoying my money and my leisure. Not even keeping up with advancements in technology and if you are out of it for six months, well, you're pretty much left in the dust."

"I'm sorry to hear that, Mr. Taylor. I was hoping someone with your expertise would be able to help us figure out a way to break it down and restore communications to the world."

"Yeah, I'm sorry, but I don't think I'd be much use," Jay said. "I'm here offering my help to the Department of the Environment, but even with that I had other people do all the work. I gave them my vision and they put it all together for me. I'm just the money and idea guy anymore."

"All right, Mr. Taylor. I was really hoping you might be able to help us out, but I think I've taken up enough of your time. Thank you," March said, offering the younger man his hand.

Jay had already started to turn and shut the door when he realized March had his hand out. He stumbled and shook it quickly.

"I hope you catch the people who are doing this."

"I'm sure we will, Mr. Taylor. You have a good day."

When the door shut behind him, March headed back toward the elevator. He realized his energy from earlier was gone. This was the frustrating part of an investigation. What Taylor told him sounded sincere, but something about it didn't sit right with him. It was too polished, too practiced. And his hand shake was cold and soft.

Never trust a man with a limp handshake, he thought.

*****

Jay walked back into his condo, a laugh on his face.

"So the police commissioner came to see you? You don't seem worried," Matt asked, looking up from his computer. He had been able to hear the entire conversation.

"I handled him. That's what I do. He bought it hook, line and sinker. These island cops are no match for me, for us, I mean. They're bumpkins."

"I'm not so sure about that. I think we still need to be careful."

"Don't worry about that. You just hold up your end and I'll take care of the police. That's the way we've always done it. I'm the one with people skills, remember?"

Matt didn't answer Jay, opting instead to return to his work. He knew this argument was going nowhere quickly.

Realizing Matt was letting the conversation drop, Jay grabbed his keys.

"I'm going to get some coffee and some fresh air. You want some?"

"You're going to bring me some fresh air?"

"Haha, very funny."

"Yeah, I guess. I could definitely use some coffee. I've got to stay alert. Who knows when the real attacks are going to hit."

"I'll be right back."

CHAPTER 27

Mike and Frankie were sitting in the jeep on a side street near downtown George Town. Through their contacts, Kelly and Tanya had been able to track down where Jay was staying. Now, it was a waiting game. They couldn't just walk up and ask Jay what he was up to. And that meant they waited. Mike was used to this sort of thing. He had spent many cold, hard nights in the field waiting for a story to happen. This was different, though. Mike hadn't gone in search of a story. He wasn't on assignment. More importantly, friends of his were in danger. That bothered him.

And of course, to his right sat, well, the one that got away. He and Frankie had been close and he really cared for her. Their lives and careers had taken them in opposite directions. And suddenly she was here. Frankie reached out and put her hand on top of his where he was nervously resting it on the jeep's gear shift as if she knew exactly what he was thinking about.

"Are you happy to see me?" Frankie asked.

"Happy? Of course I am. I'm just a little confused about how you got here," Mike said. "I mean, it's been months since I've heard from you."

"Would you believe I missed you?"

"I should hope so!" Mike said. "Seriously, it is great to see you. I'm thrilled you're here. With everything that's happened since you landed, I haven't had a chance to say that. You look fantastic."

"Thank you, Michael," Frankie said, blushing. "It is great to see you, too. You look good. Healthy. I see a little more gray than the last time we got together, but it looks good on you."

"So, how did you end up in Rich's shop?"

"I got a call from a man named Theophillus Blackwell in the Anthropology Department at your university. He asked me to come lecture. When I realized it was where you were, I jumped at the opportunity," Frankie explained. "When I got there, they said Rich would know where you were. I hadn't been in his shop for 10 minutes when you called and now I'm here."

"I know Theophillus well. That old mountain man is always working some angle. And Rich is like a brother to me, but I'm not sure I would get on a plane with him after 15 minutes," Mike said as he scanned the streets around Jay's hotel.

"You have a way of making me make rash decisions," Frankie said with a wink. "And remember, I've got connections."

When Frankie and Mike found the Breastplate of Judgment, originally worn by the High Priest Aaron, brother of Moses, Frankie had put it on in an emergency. The breastplate was worn only by high priests and only when they entered the Holy of Holies, the inner chamber of the temple of Israel when coming before the Ark of the Covenant. She had never told Mike all that she saw when she did, but he knew that coming into contact with something so closely aligned with the presence of God had changed her.

"Hold on, I want to talk more about this, but there's one of the people we're looking for," Mike said changing the subject.

"Which one?"

"The one crossing the street. Good looking guy. Tan pants and the silk shirt."

"Do you know him?"

"No. Tanya showed me a picture of him. He was in the Caymanian Compass a couple days ago," Mike explained. He had the island newspaper in the back seat of the jeep.

"What's he doing?"

"Getting coffee from the looks of it."

Mike and Frankie watched while Jay casually unfolded a newspaper and ordered a cup of coffee at an open air coffee shop. The man smiled at the waitress who brought him his coffee and then returned to his paper. From where they sat, they could see that the headline on the paper trumpeted the communications blockade on the island.

"Doesn't seem like a terrorist holding the island hostage to me," Frankie said.

"He does seem awfully calm. Hmmmm."

"I know that sound. What are you going to do?"

"I think it is time I meet Jaylend Taylor."

*****

Before Frankie had a chance to protest, Mike hopped out of the jeep and headed across the street to the coffee shop. He was winging it and wasn't sure what he would say to Jay, so he didn't want Frankie to ask him questions he couldn't answer.

The coffee shop was island-typical, especially places that catered to tourists. Bob Marley was playing gently over the loudspeakers. It had a wide door to the inside, a small bar inside and a few tables. There were six small tables on the sidewalk in front, most with large shade umbrellas.

Mike crossed the street, approaching from behind Jay. When he walked up, a waiter told him to sit anywhere and pointed to the chalkboard by the street that had a list of their specialties and special offers. Mike took his seat, still unsure how he was going to break the ice.

Just before Mike got up to introduce himself, a pretty, slender blonde approached Jay. He missed his chance and he knew it, but Mike decided to listen for a few minutes and see what he might hear.

"Jay, I have called you many times and you have not answered," the woman scolded. Mike could detect an Eastern European accent. It wasn't Russian, but it was close. He had spent months in the region throughout his career. Looking more closely at the woman, Mike realized she had the high cheek bones and delicate structure of most women from the region. Mike made a mental note to ask Tanya about her. He didn't think his friend knew everyone from Eastern Europe on the island, but there was a good chance they had run across each other somewhere along the way.

"Sorry, Trina. We're a bit busy right now," Jay said, barely looking at the woman. Mike was surprised. The blonde, Trina, might not be a supermodel, but most men would notice her crossing the street. Jay looked as if he could care less.

"You don't look busy to me," Trina said, her voice developing an edge. "I'm part of this, too, you know."

"Trina, I'm just taking a break to relax. And you're making that hard to do," Jay said dismissively. "Matt needs his space when he's working. He practically told me to get out and stop looking over his shoulder. I'm going to go back to our suite and check on him in a minute. I'll take him a cup of coffee. I promise. If you'd like to help him relax a little bit, I'm sure he would appreciate it, but other than that, leave me alone."

"Why do you talk to me like that, Jay?" Trina pouted. "Matt is sweet, but he isn't my man. You are. I've done all of this for you. I've put my whole career on the line for you."

"Your whole career? You're a receptionist. That's not much of a career. And you'll get yours. Don't worry. I won't forget you."

"I know it's dangerous what you are doing, but it is also very exciting. We are really going to save the world, aren't we," Trina said, changing the subject.

Mike's ears perked up when he heard that. That was a good indication they were on the right track. Jay's reaction confirmed it. He sat forward, putting his head within inches of Trina's and hissed.

"What did I tell you about talking about that in public? Are you nuts? You have no idea who is listening!"

Realizing that what he just said sounded more suspicious than what Trina was saying, Jay got control of himself and leaned back in his chair.

"Is there something you need?" Jay's voice was cold. "Or did you just plan to irritate me today and remind me how insignificant you are?"

Mike watched out of the corner of his eye as Trina seemed to shrink inwardly. He could tell that any emotion in the relationship between the two people went only one way. She loved him, but he didn't feel the same way about her. If he felt anything.

"No, I don't guess so. I just wanted to check on you. I know you are under a lot of stress right now. I wanted to make sure everything was okay," Trina said, reaching out to put her hand on Jay's arm.

"We're fine," Jay said, twitching his wrist to push her away. Jay signaled for the waiter to order two coffees to go. "Now, I need to get back to work. And you should, too. This is an important time in the Department of the Environment. I would hate for someone to say something important and you not be there to hear it."

"You're right. Sorry, Jay," Trina said, her head hanging low at this point. "I need to get back to work. I'll let you know if I hear anything."

The pretty blonde slunk away from the coffee shop without another word, looking thoroughly defeated. Mike watched her go, feeling a mixture of sorrow for her and disgust for Jay. Mike had never understood why some men felt it necessary to make women feel smaller to make themselves feel bigger. Compensating for other inadequacies, he supposed. Jay paid the waiter for the coffees and stood to leave. Mike had confirmed his suspicions about Jay, but he couldn't resist the urge to look him in the eye and take the other man's measure. At 6'2" and 220 pounds, Mike cut an imposing figure. He was fit with broad shoulders and a trim waist line, although he wasn't anyone's idea of a fitness buff either. He stayed active, swimming, hiking and biking and that was enough. He rarely used his physical size to intimidate anyone intentionally. Rarely. In this situation, he thought it might be interesting. Jay clearly got a kick from making others feel small.

Mike stood quickly, rising into Jay's path and cutting off his exit. Mike intentionally looked down while he did so, pretending to look into his wallet so he had an excuse for blocking Jay's exit. Mike looked up when he saw Jay nearly run into him and then take a step backward, avoiding the collision by inches. Mike pretended to look surprised, and it took all of his acting ability to restrain a grin. Jay, for his part, took a step backward and looked up into Mike's face, confused and startled. Mike was only about two inches taller than Jay, but Mike was standing straight, gathering himself up, where Jay was slouching. It made the difference that much more pronounced.

"Oh, excuse me," Mike said.

"Ummm, yeah, excuse me. Do you mind?"

"Oh, hey, you're Jay, ummm, Taylor, right?" Mike stayed between Jay and the exit.

"Do I know you?"

"I work for *First Account* magazine. I think we did a feature on you a while back, didn't we?"

"Oh, umm, maybe. I'm not sure if I saw that story, but I've been traveling a lot since I sold my company. Maybe I missed it. Look, I really need to be going. My friend's coffee is going to get cold."

"Some strange goings on around, don't ya think? I mean taking a whole island hostage? That's crazy, huh?"

"Pretty crazy. Are you here covering it?"

"Nah, I'm on vacation, man. Just here to have a little fun and all this stuff happens. Who knows when we're going to get out of here." Mike gave

Jay his best "aw shucks" routine. He wanted Jay to underestimate him. "You're a tech guy, right? Any idea how all this could happen? I mean, I know you're not involved, but you would know how to do it, right?"

"I'm in technology, but not telecomm, so this is really outside of my realm, I'm afraid. I'm as much in the dark as you are. But, like I said, I've got to take off," Jay said, finally stepping around Mike. "I'm sure we'll get out of here soon. You take care."

"Thanks. You, too. Nice meeting you." Mike smiled a smile that ended at his eyes. He watched Jay walk away. When Jay went inside his hotel, Mike trotted back across the street to the jeep and a waiting Frankie.

"What did you learn?" Frankie asked when he got back.

"I think I learned a lot."

CHAPTER 28

Kelly stood stunned, staring at the men on the boat that had approached the *Manta*. They were clearly sending the message that Kelly and his people were unwanted in the area. It hadn't occurred to Kelly until that moment that Jay had an entire team. He had been so focused on everything else that had happened in the last few days and then the entire island being taken hostage, that he hadn't stopped to consider exactly what they were facing. Before he had a chance to respond, Captain Biko interrupted.

"Firs' mate Kelly, recall da divers in da water," Biko said, patting Kelly on the shoulder, but facing the man on the other boat. "Apologies, friend. I'm new to 'dis island."

Biko suddenly sounded different than he did most days. Kelly knew in the back of his mind that Biko wasn't from Cayman, but the dark-skinned boat captain sounded and looked Caribbean enough that Kelly forgot about it. Cayman was such a melting pot of people from all over the world; most of the time he dismissed accents anyway.

Kelly started to protest Biko's instructions. His own authority was rising in his mind, along with his refusal to back down to the men with the guns. There were no restricted areas around the island for boating. And this group of private boaters couldn't chase them off. *Who do these guys think they are?* Kelly thought.

"Kelly, do what the captain told you to do." It was Tanya, speaking evenly. She was almost quiet. The sound of his wife's voice broke Kelly's glare at the newly arrived boaters. He slumped and looked back at Tanya. She gave him a look that begged him to understand and to follow Captain Biko's lead.

"Sure, Captain. I'll get that started."

Kelly made his way to the pilot chair to activate the diver recall system. Kelly flipped it on and off several times. He knew Kurt and Shrop would hear the noise and understand exactly what they were supposed to do. Once he was done, he glanced over and realized Rich and Eric hadn't moved. They were still staring intently at the metal detector's speaker, straining to hear any sound.

*****

Kurt and Shrop heard the sound of the recall alarm underwater and turned to look at each other. *What's going on now?* both men thought. They looked behind them at the dive boat and were startled to see the second boat, uncomfortably close to their own. They had no idea what was going on topside, but it couldn't be good. The two divers turned and began heading back for their boat. They had moved 30 feet in front of the dive boat so it was going to take them a minute to get back. They chose to swim along the bottom on their way back.

*****

On the surface, Rich was surprised to hear the metal detector begin screeching. He quickly reached over and turned the volume down. Quieter, the detector kept signaling it had found something. But that didn't make sense. The boat wasn't moving. How did something metal suddenly move in front of the underwater sensor? And then it dawned on him.

*****

"Friends, I am sorry for 'dis intrusion," Biko said, smiling with his hands open and at his sides. "We didn't know 'dis was a protected area. These men jus' hired me to help them dive here. We will leave as soon as we get our divers back on board."

And then the captain moved a step closer to the other boat and turned sideways to keep an eye on his own people, while continuing to talk to the man on the new boat. He took on a conspiratorial tone. "You know 'dese rich tourists. Dey've no clue what they is doin', but 'dey t'ink they's gonna find da' treasure. Dey spend their money like that is all dey need do."

"I don't know who you are and I don't really care," the man on the gun boat ordered. "Get your divers out of the water now, or I'll take care of them myself." He wasn't going to get chummy with Biko.

"Calm down, mon, calm down. We's getting them back out now. Dey be here any minute," Biko continued. "See? Here dey come now."

Shrop and Kurt surfaced immediately behind the *Manta*, and Eric and Rich immediately moved to the swim step on the boat's stern to take their gear from them. With a quick look, Rich told the two divers all they needed to know. Stay quiet and get back on board.

"Hey Kurt, why don't you go ahead and pull your dive gear off in the water. You don't want to strain your knee," Rich said looking down at the diver in the water.

"What are you talking about? I don't need…"

"Kurt, you don't have to act like it's not bothering you. Take your gear off in the water and hand it up to Rich," Tanya said. She wasn't sure what Rich had in mind, but she was going to follow his lead. Rich took the scuba unit from Kurt, along with his mask and fins and carried them toward the front of the boat while Kurt and Shrop climbed on board. No one offered to take Shrop's dive gear from him.

"Let me see your men," the gunman said. "I want to make sure they didn't bring anything up or touch anything they weren't supposed to touch."

"Oh come on, man. This ain't right," Kelly said. "Who do you think you are? You can't order us around."

In answer to Kelly's protest, the armed men raised the barrels of their rifles and pointed them directly at the *Manta* and the crew on board.

"I've had about enough of you. I think you need to do what you're told," the leader on the gun boat said. "You two. Stand up and show me your stuff. I want to make sure you didn't bring anything back on board."

Kurt and Shrop stood up in front of two sets of dive gear and raised their hands.

"See, no collection bags. We didn't even have cameras with us underwater. We were just looking around," Shrop said. "We didn't bring anything up. Just be cool, man."

*****

As soon as Captain Biko had the men from the other boat distracted, Rich took Kurt's gear and slid it along the side of the boat, out of sight from the men. He never raised it out of the water where it would splash around and be noticed. Rich asked for Kurt's gear because the two men were about the same size. He had an idea, but it was going to have to go perfectly or he might not make it out of the water alive. Rich was glad when he saw light in Tanya's eyes and when she stepped in to convince Kurt to take his gear off in the water. She figured out what he was planning to do almost as quickly as he did.

Kelly was a step behind his wife, but only a step. He gave Rich the next distraction he was looking for when he protested the gun boat's leader's request to show them what they returned to the surface with.

"Oh come on, man. This ain't right. Who do you think you are? You can't order us around," was the last thing Rich heard before he slipped quietly over the side of the boat. He hoped Kelly's distraction didn't get the man shot. He liked the man, but Rich also knew he wouldn't survive long in the water once the shooting started.

Rich quickly deflated Kurt's dive gear, pulling his arms through the BCD jacket and strapping everything in place. He settled the mask onto his face and the fins on his feet with the practiced ease of a man who spent nearly every day in the water. A commercial diver, Rich was used to making dives in freezing cold water, wearing heavy equipment with a job to do. If anything, the recreational dive gear worn by the local dive guides was lightweight. Rich didn't notice the warmth of the Caribbean water as he quickly made his way to the bottom. His only thought was how to prevent the men above him from seeing his bubbles rise to the surface. All it would take was for one of them to look down into the water and see him swimming along.

Rich descended to the bottom as quickly as he could. He wanted his rising bubbles to have a chance to break up as much as possible. He was in good shape, and he tried to control his breathing, but he had to exhale. The most dangerous time would be when he was between the two boats. He just had to swim there, do what he set out to do, and get back to the *Manta* in time. Everything else would just have to take care of itself.

*****

"Give us jus' one more minute to get the anchor up, mon and we be out o' your way. Sorry about getting in a bad area, mon. We clear out. I'll teach dese guys for bringing me out to a restricted area like dis," Biko continued. "Can you tell me how big it is? I mean, I don't wanna come back out to where we aren't supposed to be?"

Eric and Kelly moved to the *Manta*'s bow and began pretending to raise the anchor. It had never been lowered. Biko had been following the divers in the water so they could continue to use the metal detector. They pulled the lower unit out of the water and rested it on the bow, securing it beside the anchor. They left a single line over the side, on the opposite side of the *Manta* from the gun boat.

"I count six of you. Where did the other one go?" the gun boat leader demanded. "I thought there were seven when we got here."

"No mon, just us. Dis everybody, mon. Dey was four of us on board when you got here. Den da two divers came back on board. You see everyone," Biko said. "Come on, mon. You t'ink I'm gonna mess wit' you? You got da' guns mon. We jus' get outta here."

The leader on the gun boat glared for a minute, but he couldn't see how anyone would have gotten off the boat. Or what good it would have done.

*****

"All right, Captain. Get your boat started and get out of here," the man said finally. This whole area is off limits. I don't want to see you back here or we won't be quite as friendly."

"Understood mon. I get you. We won' be back," Biko said, moving toward the pilot chair. He started the *Manta*'s engines and glanced at the others. Tanya gave him a quick nod. Captain Biko moved the *Manta* out slowly and then began picking up speed, moving away from the confrontation area. He was heading back toward Sunset House. No one spoke until Biko maneuvered the Manta around a rocky outcropping in the island and out of sight from the gun boat.

"That was impressive, Biko. You handled that really well," Kelly said, patting the captain on the shoulder. "I've never heard you talk like that, though. You really surprised me."

"Kelly, it's not the first time I've dealt with men with guns. They think they are in a position of power and those guns make them brave. There's no point in standing up to them. Showing them anger will just make them angrier, and things only get hotter and hotter until someone gets shot," Biko said. He returned to his normal speech pattern, but flashed a toothy grin. "And if I can disarm them and get us out of there by giving them what they expect, that's fine. If they look at me and think they see some uneducated islander just trying to get one over on some tourists, that's fine. It won't be the first time I've let someone underestimate me."

"I liked you before, Cap', but I've just gotten a new found respect for you," Kelly said, turning to look at the others. "Where's Rich anyway?"

"Captain, pull into that cove over there and you can slow it down a bit now. I think Rich has had enough of a ride," Tanya said grinning.

Kurt and Shrop moved to the bow and helped Rich climb back on board the moving boat. He had been hanging over the side from the line Eric and Kelly left for him.

"You took a big risk doing that," Kelly said when they got Rich on board. "You want to tell us what you did?"

"I thought it would be helpful if they couldn't follow us. They now have a piece of rope woven through both of their propellers. When they start their engines to move out, it's going to tear some things up," Rich said. "I figured in the confusion with Kurt and Shrop getting on board no one would notice if Kurt's gear didn't get back where it was supposed to be."

"What if they had started their engines to move out before we did?" Tanya asked.

"That was a risk, but I thought they would watch us leave to make sure we didn't hang around. And I had a good reason to want to slow them down."

"What was that?"

"I can probably answer that," Kurt said with a grin. "We found what we were looking for."

"And when I heard the metal detector go nuts like it was sitting right on top of something metal, I knew what these guys had done. They hid the control unit on the metal detector instead of bringing it to the surface."

"There are too many weird things going on around here," Shrop said. "When we found the control unit we were looking for, there was no question we weren't going to carry it with us."

"When did you get the idea to put all of this together," Kelly said, looking at his friends in amazement.

"The really cool thing is, no one had to talk to each other. We all just sort of knew what was going on," Kurt said, punching Rich on the arm. "Even the new guy."

"Does that mean I get to be a Cayman cowboy, too?" Rich asked with a laugh.

CHAPTER 29

Bill Gardner was focused on his computer, ignoring the beautiful surroundings of Sunset House. It was times like this, when he was faced with a challenge, that he could block out everything around him and gnaw on it like a dog on a bone until he reached a solution. He was easily distracted, but he could just as easily get so absorbed in a problem that he forgot everything around him.

"Bill, I don't understand what you're doing," Sherri asked him. The young blonde was there to support Bill and help him out, but she was also on the island for her Spring Break and was bored. "Bill!"

"What? I'm sorry. What did you say?" Bill looked up from his computer on the patio table, mildly confused for a moment. He had been lost in his thoughts.

"What're you doing?" Sherri asked again, a little louder.

"You were here for the discussion earlier. I'm trying to find the control units that have knocked out communications to the island," Bill said. Thinking that was explanation enough, Bill turned back to his computer. It wasn't.

"I know that much, but how're you doing it with the Internet down?" Sherri asked. "That's what I don't understand."

"Oh, sorry," Bill said, rubbing his eyes and realizing he probably needed to take a break for a moment anyway. "The control units this guy placed in the water around the island are scrambling the signals to the outside world. If I can find them and we can remove a couple of them, we can probably break through his barrier and maybe even take it down all together."

"Are you even sure it is Jay?" Miranda asked.

"Well, no, he hasn't been proven guilty, I guess, but a lot of evidence is pointing his direction. For now, my goal is to stop 'the terrorist'," Bill said, making air quotes around 'the terrorist' "and get communications back up. I'll let other people worry about who is to blame later."

"I'm not sure why you're trying to stop this guy, anyway," Miranda said sulkily. "I mean, we were just protesting the people hurting the environment a few days ago. Isn't that what he's doing? I mean, shouldn't we try to help him? I'm sure he could use someone like you."

"Are you kidding? This guy is holding an entire island hostage. That's like 50,000 hostages. I want no part of something like that," Bill glanced longingly at his computer. He liked the company of the two pretty young women, but he really wanted to get back to work. A problem like this wasn't going to solve itself. And reasoning with people wasn't his strong suit. "And frankly, I think he has someone like me already. Someone has set up this network and it's pretty impressive. I got a glimpse of it before he took everything down. Whoever is doing this has the island locked down tight."

"Well, okay, I'm not sure how I feel about what he's doing, but I agree with what he's trying to accomplish. He sees wrong with the world and is trying to fix it," Miranda said. "I think we should help someone like that."

"Tell me what you're doing, Bill," Sherri said, changing the subject. "I don't understand how you're going to track anyone down without the Internet."

Bill turned to the older sister, thankful for the reprieve. He wasn't in the mood to discuss the ethics of taking the entire island off-line.

"We know the locations of the undersea cables coming into the island. They bring most of the communications here. Phone, Internet, whatever. But he hasn't just cut communications at those locations. He has surrounded the entire island with these control units. None of them is all that significant, but they overlap and work together to form a network that is cutting the island off. It's actually a really slick way of doing things. If everything was in one unit, that would be easy to stop, but these things are small and hard to find," Bill explained. "So, I'm comparing the locations of the undersea cables with the underwater topography from Tanya's maps to find the most likely locations for the control units. When I find a likely spot, I call that into Kelly, Tanya, and the others out on the dive boat and they know where to look. Once they find one, they'll be able to track down several more. The units have to be close together and fairly close to the surface. That lets them work together and keeps them in contact with whoever is controlling them from the surface. There is a central control unit sending out the signals and blocking attempts to override the cone of silence. I'm sure by now the world outside is trying some pretty sophisticated methods to break the blockade."

"Why aren't you trying to find the central control unit?" Sherri asked.

"That's what Mike and Frankie are working on. They are following Jay to find out what he's doing and see how he is controlling the *cone*. If they're successful, great. But in case they can't figure it out, or can't get there fast enough, I'm trying to open the door for outside help. If we can take two or three of the control units offline, it might crash the entire cone or it might weaken it enough to get a signal out," Bill said. "Now, I really need to get back to work."

"I still don't understand why we aren't trying to help this guy," Miranda said, turning from Bill to stare out at the blue-green Caribbean water in front of her. She was in paradise, but she wasn't happy.

CHAPTER 30

"Guess what we found?" Tanya said into the VHF radio from the *Manta*. It was an open radio frequency, but they had agreed to monitor Channel 2 on the radio, trusting no one would be listening on that frequency. Still, they were being cautious about what they said.

"Something important, I hope," Bill answered.

"You could definitely say that. The fish that arrived to talk to us when we did aren't going to be very happy about it, either," Tanya continued.

"Can you tell me where you were?"

Tanya quickly read the coordinates from the GPS unit on the boat, and Bill entered the numbers into his computer.

"Okay, I'll know more when you find the next one, but my best guess is that they are within 100 feet of each other. Carefully move to the next location, 100 feet to the west and begin searching again," Bill said, staring at the mapping program on his computer. "I'll shoot you the coordinates for where I think it'll be."

"No. Don't bother. We had to leave the area. As I said, the fish that arrived when our divers found it were less than happy about our presence. We had to leave quickly. I have a good reason to believe they're still in the area."

"Oh, well, umm," Bill stumbled for a minute. "So, we're back to square one?" He dropped his head into his hands.

"Hold on a second, Bill. Just plot us out a bit further. We went west when we left that location. Just take us around the next bend and plot out the next several locations. We'll find another one. And a couple more after that," Kelly said, taking the microphone from his wife. "You said you wanted to take up several units, right? We'll find them. The boys know how to find the units. Just work your magic and get us some coordinates. We're not beaten yet."

"Okay, Kelly. Give me a few minutes. I'll get you some numbers."

"Thanks, Bill. We'll be waiting. We've slid into a little cove for the moment to stay away from prying eyes."

"What do we do now?" Shrop asked from where he lay on one of the diver benches on *Manta*.

"Thanks to Rich," Kelly said "I think we've got a little space away from the bad guys. So, we get some more locations from Bill and we go hunting. Unless someone tells me something different, we pick up as many of these control units as we can and we tear down the cone of silence." They had all begun calling the communications blockade that. It seemed less intimidating.

"I've got another idea," Kurt said.

"In place of mine?" Kelly asked, raising an eyebrow. The two men had long since buried any differences, but years before Kurt and Tanya had dated for a while. At this point, it was a friendly rivalry, but the implied challenge still got Kelly's attention.

"No, actually in concert with it. Come here and look at this," Kurt said. "I've found a port on this control unit. It's got a rubber plug covering it up to keep water out, but there is a mini-USB connection underneath. We can connect to this thing and see what makes it tick."

"You mean Bill can connect to this thing and see what makes it tick, right? Last I checked we don't have any computers on board. Or any computer geniuses," Kelly said, teasing his friend.

"Okay, that's probably true. I'm pretty good with computers, but Bill seems to know more than I do. I wonder if there's any way he can jack into it from there. I'd hate to waste time taking this thing in and then coming back out to search for more of them," Kurt agreed.

The radio crackled and Bill was back on the air. Before he got a chance to give them coordinates, they presented him with a completely different challenge. After a few minutes of discussing possibilities, Bill asked a question.

"Does anyone have their phone with them? And I mean a smart phone. Not some flip phone like the one I saw Kelly carrying."

"Oh come on," Kelly started to answer, but Kurt cut him off. "I have mine. It's an Android. Latest model."

"Okay, that's great. Do you have your charger cord?" "I do, but how is a phone going to help? I thought they had cut off all communications," Kurt asked.

"Not all communications. Just contact with the outside world. Cell towers on the island are still working. Even some of the on-island computer systems are still functioning. We can't talk to the outside world, but other than that, things are working normally," Bill explained. "Plug your phone into the data port on the control unit and let me see what I can do to jack into it. You'll need to leave your phone on and just let me do my thing."

"That's fine, but it only has about 50 percent battery left," Kurt said. He connected the phone to the control unit they recovered.

Bill found the cell phone, hacking into the cell phone tower network and connecting to the phone itself. He could *see* the control unit, but was not able to do much with it. Yet. He would work on that.

"Okay, I've got it. I'll see what I can do to connect to the control unit and run back up into their network. Maybe I can find a way to shut this thing down from the inside," Bill said. "In the meantime, I've got some coordinates for you. I'll give them to you as we discussed."

Bill prepared to read off the GPS coordinates, but since it was an open channel he planned to read them backward. They agreed to that precaution before the boat left the dock.

Suddenly a strange voice broke into their conversation. "Who is this? What are you people talking about? You keep popping up on my scanner."

Knowing they might also need to change channels in case someone was listening in, they also agreed to make a switch using a simple code word. Tanya wrote down three other choices before they left.

"Rum punch," Bill began. "I said, Rum punch."

"Your Rum Punch is on the way," Tanya agreed and switched the radio to Channel 79.

"Okay, I'm here," Bill said.

"So am I," Tanya agreed. "Anyone else on this channel? Hello? Anyone?"

Her query got no response. Bill began reading off the locations he thought they might be able to find another control unit.

"I've extrapolated my best guess of where they will be from what I know about the units. I'll know more once I break into the control unit you found. When you find a second, I'll be able to give you a better idea on where to find a third and a fourth one, too. For now, we are still shooting in the dark," Bill explained. "When you do find another one, let me know as soon as you can and I'll work my magic. In the meantime, stay at the same depth and follow the reef contours around the island. That should help."

"You got it, Bill and thanks for your help. *Manta* out."

CHAPTER 31

Jay was seething by the time he got back to his penthouse apartment. A geek most of his life, he had been bullied in school. He didn't have it as bad as some. He had the good fortune of being good looking even for a geek so the girls paid attention to him. The bigger, stronger boys weren't as accepting, of course. And probably even less so because the girls paid attention to him. When he got to MIT, everyone was a geek so Jay went from being picked on to being esteemed by his peers. He had better social skills and experience than many of his outcast contemporaries. At the same time, he went from being the smartest kid in his high school to one of the pack in college. Even geeks had their own form of bullying.

Never feeling like he could measure up, even after he sold his company and became a billionaire, left Jay with a chip on his shoulder. And it was easily jostled.

Jay slammed the front door to the apartment open, startling Matt where he sat at his computer. Matt was hard at work defending their blockade. It had been in place long enough: the governments were beginning to get their act together and launch attacks against the information blockade. They expected this would happen and both men knew it would be up to Matt to respond and repel those attacks. If they were going to be successful, they had to keep the island locked down.

"What's your problem?" Matt asked, irritated at the interruption.

"These are the times I envy you," Jay said, sulkily. "You sit up here and handle the network issues, but I have to go out and deal with people."

"You've been gone a half hour and you only went for coffee. How hard can that be?" Matt asked. "And where's mine?"

"You'd be surprised who you run into in a place like this," Jay said. He handed Matt his cup. "Trina started annoying me. She must have seen me on the street so she came running."

"You really need to treat her better. She has helped us out quite a bit. And you're the one sleeping with her. I know that's her mistake, but you weren't complaining," Matt said. He dared Jay to argue.

Jay stared at Matt for a minute, having a raging argument with the computer wizard in his mind before he answered. "You're right. I never should have mixed business with pleasure. That was a mistake on my part, but I thought it would get her to do what we needed. Now that it's almost finished, I don't need her anymore and she doesn't get it."

"It's pretty sad the way you think you can just use people and then throw them away," Matt said. He shook his head in disgust. It made him even angrier because he loved Trina, but she only thought of him as a sweet friend. Something he had dealt with all of his life. Jay would have been surprised to learn that Matt saw him as a bully, too.

"Is that what got you upset? Trina? I have no pity for you," Matt said, returning to his work.

"First that visit from the cop and then, when I was leaving the coffee shop, this thick-necked journalist got in my face. I'm betting he was a high school quarterback, the attitude he had. Kind of a dumb jock, too. You could just smell it on him," Jay said.

"He was a journalist? What did he say? Did he connect you to what's going on?"

"No, just here on vacation. Probably saved up his entire life for it. He asked me if I had any idea how this could happen, but I told him I didn't know telecommunications. He seemed to buy that. Idiot."

"If you say so, but it makes me nervous that guy is here. If he's any good, he might get bored and start digging around looking for a scoop. I mean, he has a front row seat for the end of the world. He's going to want to do a story on it and write off his trip. Who knows, he may already have dreams of a book tour. We need to be careful for the next couple days".

"Well, don't worry about him. I intimidated him some. He might have been bigger, but I'm smarter. I left him no doubt that we aren't in high school anymore and I can't be picked on like in 10th grade gym class," Jay

145

said as he poured a shot of rum into his coffee. He needed to steady his nerves and calm down from the confrontation. The extra coffee wasn't helping.

"You intimidated the big, thick-necked jock, did you?" Matt asked, with a sneer, knowing reality was likely much different.

Jay took a deep drink from his spiked coffee and let the rum seep into his blood stream for a minute before he answered. If he didn't need Matt so much, he would get rid of the twit, he thought to himself. *When this is all over, I'm leaving him far behind. I don't care if I ever look at another computer again.*

"How's your blockade defense holding up?" Jay asked to change the subject.

"Pretty much what I expected. There've been several attempts from outside the island trying to break through our firewalls. I've counteracted those without a lot of trouble. There's one from on the island that's giving me fits, though," Matt said, focusing back on the two computer monitors on the table.

"You said there wasn't anyone here who had the skills to give you any trouble."

"There isn't anyone who lives here that I know about. Of course, you never know when some kid savant is going to have the skills to put both of us to shame. And I told you there was that one guy I recognized before. I've seen him at a couple of the hacker conferences. I've heard he's pretty good."

"But he isn't an MIT guy, so how good can he be, really?"

"Like I said, you never know when someone is going to come up with a skill set out of nowhere."

"But you can handle him, right?"

"Yeah, I got him. But we need to keep an eye on him."

"Can you get a location on him? In case we need to take him off line or something," Jay asked. "We can shut down his connection if we need to."

"I'll get a location on the IP address he's using. That should get us pretty close. But like I said, he won't be a problem. I can handle him." Now it was Matt's turn to be defensive. His role was the head geek, and no one was going to push him off the mountain. He decided to change the subject. "That was a pretty slick change to the manifesto. The one about not interfering because we can fry all of the financial computers. You didn't mention that to me."

"Yeah, I wanted to keep the outside interference down to a minimum. I tweaked the system a little bit to make it look like we are messing around in the financial sectors, too. Just to give us a cover."

"It's a good bluff, but even better that we really aren't messing around in that area. That would be a great way to make some very powerful people very angry if we were."

Just then, Jay's phone chirped with an incoming text message. He turned and left Matt without further comment to read it in private. It read: *Thinks he is making progress. May be able to stop your efforts.* Just as quickly, another text message came through. *He doesn't want to protect the environment. Must stop him.*

This was a part of the operation that Matt didn't know about. Jay was in charge for a reason. He knew to keep things compartmentalized so people could focus on their jobs without worrying about what others were doing. And there were things he didn't want others to know about. Even Matt. He might think he could handle this hacker, but Jay's sources were telling him something different. While he was still staring at the message on his phone, debating how to handle this latest piece of information, his phone rang. Seeing who it was, he answered it immediately.

"Report," was all Jay said. And then he stood still, listening. It was Jay's dive team. Now that they had all of the control units in place, they were patrolling the waters around the island keeping people away from the sensors. Of course, they weren't going to intercede if a US Coast Guard cutter approached the island. Keeping small boats of divers away was their priority. Jay had given a 72-hour deadline, but he really didn't need that long to have everything in place. His team leader told him they scared away a small boat of divers, but then they had some engine trouble with the boat. They were limping back to the dock on one engine. The leader wasn't very forthcoming about the nature of the trouble. It made Jay nervous, though. And he decided he needed to act. He was tired of sitting on the sidelines doing nothing. He would show them who was really in charge and who could be bullied and who wouldn't. Jay gave the divers instructions and told him he would give them a location as soon as they reached the dock. It was time to get back to work.

Walking back into the apartment from the patio, Jay said, "Matt, did you happen to get the location of that IP address? I think I'm going to check it out myself. I know you're busy and I don't want you to have to worry about it."

CHAPTER 32

"Well, to begin with, Jay is a bit of an ass. He treats woman pretty badly if the way he was just talking to that girl is any indication," Mike explained, telling Frankie about the conversation he had just overheard.

"But you're sure he's the one behind this?"

"He didn't come right out and say 'now that I have kidnapped the entire island' but he hinted around it enough, along with being pretty paranoid. I'm confident he's our man."

"What do we do now? Do we go to the guardia?" Frankie used the name for the Italian National Police.

"Here it's the Royal Cayman Islands Police Service, but I know what you mean. I think we have enough to go on, but I don't know if I want to waste my time trying to explain it all to them and get them to believe me."

"And like before, we don't know who else is in on it," Frankie said. When Mike had helped her out in Italy, one of their biggest hurdles came from a man who worked for the city of Roseto, Italy, and should have been on Frankie's side.

"I don't have any reason to suspect the police, but since that girl works for the Department of the Environment and seems to be his spy, who knows who else he has on the inside. It's possible," Mike said, starting the jeep and shifting it into gear.

"What are we going to do now?"

"I want to talk to Kelly and Tanya and I want to catch up with Bill, too. I want to see if he's had any luck stopping this stuff. That might drive Jay out into the open and let us catch him doing something we can take to the police. If we can force him to react to something he didn't expect, we can swoop in. Why don't you use the VHF radio and call Bill or the dive boat and see what's going on."

Frankie picked up the radio microphone and tuned the dial to the channel they agreed to before she and Mike took off. Channel 2. It was a mostly unused frequency and shouldn't have anyone listening in. They had agreed to a couple other channels as well, but Channel 2 was going to be their primary.

"Gandalf the Grey, Gandalf the Grey. This is Blessed. Are you there?" Frankie began.

"Who in the world came up with these call signs?" Mike asked while he drove. He fell back into the routine of driving on the *other* side of the road, but he had to concentrate when he turned from one road to another.

"Mostly Bill. He said he was a gray hat hacker and Gandalf was the first thing that came to mind," Frankie laughed. "I came up with my own, but I'm not sure if anyone knows how literal I mean it."

"That's Gandalf, before he went through the transformation, of course," Mike said with a wink. "And you after yours."

"Of course," Frankie smiled. "Gandalf, this is Blessed. Are you out there? How about you, Archie and Edith? Are you on the radio?"

"That's for Kelly and Tanya? Now that's funny."

"Nothing. No one is answering," Frankie said.

"I don't like it, but maybe they changed frequencies for some reason. We'll be back at Sunset House in just a minute," Mike said, giving the jeep a little more gas.

*****

Bill Gardner was surrounded by beauty, but he really didn't see any of it. He was still sitting on the patio between My Bar and the Caribbean Sea where he had stationed himself since everyone left with their own particular missions. A gentle breeze pushed the air around, keeping things comfortable. His two friends, Sherri and Miranda, were still there. They had long since given up on talking to him and had stripped down to their swim suits and were intent on catching sun by the pool.

Sunset House was nearly deserted. It was the middle of the afternoon, and under normal circumstances there would still be people around. Since Kelly and Tanya had reserved the entire hotel for their friends to celebrate their 10th anniversary things were a little quieter. Add to that the communications blockade, and the party atmosphere had left the place. A bartender sat sleepily behind the bar, but other than that, nothing moved. His guards had wandered off for the moment.

The slow cell tower connection to the control unit Kelly and Tanya's group had found wasn't helping matters, either, but Bill was making progress. Just slowly. He could see the framework of the network set up by the control units. Since the unit they found was still out on the water, it was connecting to the network and communicating normally. For now, Bill didn't think anyone knew he was inside the network. He couldn't count on that lasting forever though.

Bill wasn't sure how much time had passed since he spoke to Sherri. It could have been a few minutes. Or an hour. He glanced up and rubbed his eyes. He had heard something that distracted him from his focus. He wasn't sure what he had found, but he was positive it had nothing to do with environmental issues. Why were the control units connecting to the international banking networks? He saw the encrypted data streams and what appeared to be a virus trying to hack into the network. This had to convince Sherri that their hostage taker, Jay, wasn't just doing everything to protect mother earth.

He had to talk to someone.

Where did the girls go? Bill blinked as he looked around. The girls were gone from the pool. He turned to look at the bar and the bartender was asleep, leaning back in his chair behind the bar. *Obviously, the girls haven't been talking to him.*

Shooting pain lanced through Bill's back. He lost control of his muscles. His arms locked straight out and his vision flared with light. The last thing he saw was a stranger's face checking his eyes. And then everything went dark.

*****

Mike rounded the final turn on South Church Street that ran directly in front of the hotel, but he didn't slow down. He was getting nervous. Pulling up to the hotel, Mike barely braked, just gearing down and hitting the entrance to the parking lot with a jolt. They slid to a stop near the bottom of the hill, just yards from the roped-off perimeter of My Bar. Mike quickly shut the jeep down and they both climbed out.

"Is that what you call being a cowboy?" Frankie asked with a twisted grin.

"Among other things," Mike said as he trotted around the side of the bar to the patio area where Bill had been set up when he left. The wires were there. The monitors were there. But Bill's computer was gone. And so was Bill.

"Do you think he went up to his room?" Frankie asked.

"Doubtful. He wasn't actually staying here at the hotel. He just came to help out," Mike said, growing angry. "And now it looks like we got him in trouble."

"Michael, you don't know what happened," Frankie said. "What about the two young ladies who were with him?"

"Last I saw them, they were hanging out by the pool," Mike said, walking 25 feet to the edge of the raised pool. There was no one there, either. "I would have thought the way we came down the hill would have attracted some attention."

"You'd think…"

"Let me see if I can raise the boat," Mike said. He returned to Bill's work station. The computer was missing, but the portable VHF radio was still there.

"I see why we couldn't reach them earlier. It's tuned to channel 79. They must have decided to switch for some reason."

Mike immediately called the *Manta* on that same frequency. Kelly came back almost immediately.

"Have you guys talked to Gandalf in a while? I'm at the hotel and he's not here."

"We spoke to him just a little bit ago. He didn't say anything about leaving. He gave us some new search coordinates."

"There's no sign of him anywhere. His laptop is gone, too. Monitors and other stuff are here, but no one else. Place is pretty deserted."

"We told everyone to take off for a while and check on their families. Most of the staff was a little freaked out about the terror threat. You don't think he took off, do you?"

"I'm worried someone might have taken him. If he was connected to the network and trying to lift the blockade, they might have figured it out and come after him."

"That's a definite possibility. He said he was making some progress. He was also trying to get inside of a control unit we found, using a remote connection. That would definitely raise his profile."

Kelly quickly explained how they had connected the control unit to the cell phone.

"Break that connection. I don't want them coming after you, too," Mike said.

"Too late for that. Your buddy Dirk Pitt disabled their boat, though. I don't think they're going to be chasing us down any time soon," Kelly said. Dirk Pitt was the code name for Rich. It was also Rich's favorite book and film character from the stories by Clive Cussler. Mike heard him tell Kurt to unplug the control unit and turn off his phone.

"Do you need us to come back in?" Kelly asked.

"No, you guys stay out there and keep looking for those control units. We need to break the cone of silence and get word out," Mike said. "Blessed and I will find the bad guy and see if he has Gandalf and his friends. Oh, one more thing. Is Edith around?"

"Hi, Clark. I'm here." They all decided to call Mike Clark Kent. Mike said he preferred Jimmy Olsen, the young photographer for the *Daily Planet* from the Superman series of DC comics, but no one else bought it.

"Do you know a pretty girl, blonde, Eastern European from the sounds of her? Name is Trina."

"I know her. Her full name is Ekaterina. She's the receptionist at the Department of Environment. Why?"

"She is in the middle of all this up to her neck. Seems to be the bad guy's girlfriend, although I'm guessing he's just using her."

"Oh no. I can't believe it, but that explains a lot. She would know about everything going on in that office. And really everything going on in the entire Ministry."

"Refresh my memory. What else is under that Ministry?"

"Sure. It's the Ministry of Financial Services, Commerce and the Environment."

"So, she has her ear to a lot more than just reef restoration," Mike said. "That makes me nervous."

CHAPTER 33

Bill woke up flat on his back on cold concrete. Every inch of his body hurt from the tips of his toes to the tips of his ears. His lower back was on fire. Swimming through the syrup that filled his mind, Bill remembered hearing a *zzzt* sound before he checked out. He realized he had been tazed. On one level, he thought that was funny. Someone was worried enough about him to take away any chance of him putting up a fight. He liked that. The more realistic reason for the tazer, though, was to put him down fast and stop him from running or warning anyone else. He didn't like that nearly as much.

The girls! Were they okay?

Bill struggled to sit up. His hands were bound with flex cuffs in front of him. He had to roll to his side and then struggle himself upright. His head swam with the exertion and the residual electrical shock. After a couple minutes, he stopped seeing spots and his eyes adjusted to the dim light. He was in some sort of warehouse. The stale smell of the ocean trapped inside the metal building told him it was on the waterfront somewhere. The only light in the room came through three windows high above the warehouse floor, but he could make out some old machinery boxes haphazardly positioned around the cavernous room. It was still daylight outside, but the sun was going down judging from the angle of the light streaming inside.

"It's about time you woke up," a man's voice said. Bill startled and tried to look over his shoulder to see who it was. The sudden movement made his head hurt again. Once his eyes cleared, the man was in front of him. It was Jaylend Taylor, the tech-sector golden boy. They had suspected Jay, of course, but Bill hadn't seen him yet. Regardless, Bill knew him immediately.

Jay had been on all the technology magazines and was the toast of the town for a while. Until the next big tech company sale and the next golden boy stepped forward.

"Why're you doing this? Let me go now," Bill began, keeping his voice tight. "And where are the girls? Sherri and Miranda? Did you hurt them? So help me, if you hurt them, I'll…"

"You'll what? You're tied up on the floor. You're a hacker. What do you think you're going to do? All those moves you pulled off in *Call of Duty*? Let me explain something to you. That's a video game. You can't really jump 50 feet through the air, and guns do run out of ammunition," Jay sneered. He had encountered these young punks too many times. They all played video games in their mamma's basement and dreamed of making it big without ever getting off the couch to do anything about it.

"It's Bill, right?" Jay said, changing tactics. He dragged a chair over to position himself right in front of Bill. "I don't plan on hurting you, or the girls. They're fine by the way. Very noble of you to be worried about them and ask how they're doing. You'll see them shortly. But here's the thing. I can't let you interfere with my plans. In just a couple days, it will be all over, but until then I have to keep you in here and out of the way. I can't let you stop me from what I'm trying to accomplish."

"So, this is all to make a statement about the environment? This is all to save the world and get world leaders to wake up?"

"Of course it is. Don't you believe me?"

"I guess I have to wonder why your communications blackout isn't just keeping electrical signals from going back and forth. You've accomplished that already, obviously. You could be spending the rest of your time fighting off breaches from outside and waiting, making your demands and speeches and prodding the world leaders to do what you've asked. But that's not what you're doing. Is it?"

"And that's why you're in here, Bill. I can't let you interfere with what else I'm doing."

"You're going after the banks. I knew it," Bill said. "Some environmental idealist."

"Did you know there are nearly 600 banks on this tiny island? Nearly every one of the 50 largest banks in the world has an office right here. There are only about 50,000 people. That's one bank for every 83 people, but of course that's not where most of the clients for these banks come from. There are major corporations and billionaires all over the world that have accounts here. I even have an account here," Jay said with a laugh.

Exploring Jay's network, trying to find a weakness in the system to exploit and shut the whole thing down, Bill noticed that the network *bots* were spending a considerable amount of time working on the network trunk lines dedicated to the international banking system. Those banks have their own firewalls and security systems, so Jay was having to find weaknesses and look for ways inside, just as Bill had been trying to do to Jay's technological curtain. None of those computerized attacks had anything to do with keeping the island on lockdown and Bill knew it.

"What does that have to do with saving the reefs? Or the island? Or me for that matter?" Bill asked.

"It has nothing to do with saving the environment," Jay agreed. "But saving the environment does give me a perfect cover to set up my network and get inside those banks."

"You're just a bank robber. A high-tech bank robber."

"When you've experienced the highs and lows of building your own company and selling it for billions, there aren't a lot of thrills left in the world. It's not like I could walk into a bank with a gun, of course. I had to do it this way."

"You're never going to let me leave here, are you?"

Jay stood up and turned his back on Bill for a moment. He actually saw Jay sigh.

"No, probably not. You know too much. I'm sure the authorities will figure out what I've done and come after me. But I want a good head start so I can get somewhere there's no extradition back to the United States or Europe. And you would be surprised how far a few billion dollars will go in some of those places. I can own an entire country if I want and have my own army to keep me safe." Jay's grin bordered on the maniacal.

"I want to see the girls. I want to make sure they're all right. They don't know any of this. They don't know what you're up to."

"There you go, playing the gallant gentlemen again. I'll let you see those pretty girls if you want. But here's the thing. You're right, they don't know what's going on. I've been talking to them," Jay said. "If they were to find out my other plan, well, then they wouldn't be able to make it out of here either, now would they?"

"So you want me to keep your secret?"

"This is definitely my little secret. My partner doesn't even know what this is really about," Jay said. He gestured with his arms wide, like the inside of the warehouse was his kingdom.

"I wondered about that. I heard Matthias Brun speak at a conference. He seems like a pretty stand up guy. I was having trouble seeing him turn bank robber. How did you fool him into setting it up for you? I mean, he was always the technical brains in your operation."

Jay bristled at the slight. "I set this all up myself. I'm the only one who knows how it works," he said. "I'm just as good as Matt."

"Eh, maybe. You could be. But I doubt it. He's the real genius in your little club. I have no idea why he let you hang around."

"He's so foolish. So idealistic. He really does think we're here to save the reefs or the whales or whatever. Like I care."

"You know he'll figure out what you're up to. Just the same as I did. He isn't a fool and he's deeper inside your network than I was. When he notices your resources are going after one sector, something he didn't set up, he'll wonder why and he'll investigate. When he sees where I was digging around, he'll know. He'll see what I saw and shut you down."

"Then I'll deal with him. The same way I'm going to deal with you," Jay said finally.

"Let me see the girls. I promise I won't tell them anything about your plans. But you have to promise to let them go."

"I will keep my promise as long as you keep yours. Not that I feel any need to worry about you. You have no leverage over me, but I really hate to waste good talent. They are both pretty girls. I haven't had the chance yet, but every guy imagines what it would be like to have sisters. I'm sure I can convince them. I can convince women to do a lot of things for me."

Jay raised his hand and waved to someone off in the dark. Bill heard a door open and three men came forward, escorting the two girls. When they saw Bill, the girls ran forward and hugged him. They were not bound in any way. Jay let them talk for a few minutes.

"Bill, keep your promise and you can all be comfortable. Girls, help Bill up off the floor. There's an old couch over there. You can go over there and sit."

"Thank you, Jay," Miranda said. "Can we take the cuffs off of him?"

"Maybe later, Miranda," Jay said with a smile. "Not right now, though. I can't let Bill interfere with my plans."

156

"Oh he won't, will you, Bill?" Sherri asked. "Bill wants to save the environment as much as you do. We're all on the same side."

"We'll see what side Bill is on shortly," Jay said. "Bill and I have had a good talk. I think we can see eye-to-eye on this, but I can't be sure just yet."

Sherri and Miranda helped Bill stand and walk to the couch. He was still moving slowly and gingerly from being tazed. While they walked, Bill looked at the men guarding them. A fourth man arrived. They were all carrying handguns in holsters and the man who walked up last was carrying an assault rifle.

"I see you have the beginnings of your private army," Bill said, looking at Jay, hoping the girls would notice what he was saying without him having to tip them off.

"These men are my dive team. I had to have someone who could place the control units in the water that would set up the information blockade around the island."

"Pretty heavily armed for a team of scientific divers," Bill said.

"They're mostly ex-military and commercial divers from several countries around the world." Jay smiled for the two young women. "Now that their dive duties are done, they're helping me keep things secure until I can force the world leaders to meet and do what they need to do. I don't expect they will need the guns, but I can't have anyone interfering before it's time. I'll do whatever I have to do to make sure that doesn't happen."

*****

Jay walked back into the apartment, wary about Matt, Bill's words echoing in his head.

"When he sees where I was digging around, he'll know. He'll see what I saw. He'll just shut you down."

Bill was probably right. Matt was no slouch. It wouldn't be difficult for him to figure out what was going on. Jay had probably left Matt in the network long enough. He made his decision to move on Matt now, but he was waffling seeing Matt sitting at the table, working away. They had been through so much together. They made it through their time at MIT leaning on each other and helping each other along. Jay knew he wouldn't be where he was today if it weren't for Matt. But that couldn't be helped. He needed a final score and he was going to get away. He knew Matt would never follow him on this one.

"What are you looking at?" Matt asked from across the room.

"What? Oh sorry, man, just thinking," Jay said. He had stopped just inside the door and was looking around the room. "I'm sorry I got you into this."

"What do you mean by that? We're not done yet. We've got two days before the deadline. I'm sure the world leaders will accept our conditions and do what we've asked. It is time they wake up and pay attention. How many times did we talk about this over the years?" Matt said, looking back down at his computer monitors. He knew Jay often got jittery at this point in any project. Jay might be the *leader* but he wasn't necessarily the strongest-willed part of their partnership. He had second thoughts and doubts that Matt never had to deal with. "You didn't get me into anything."

"Okay, well, I don't want you to resent me later."

Matt looked up at Jay and shook his head. "I know what we're doing is risky. That's fine. This is about principle. We have the skills and the resources to act on all those things we planned to do when we were poor and struggling, drinking cheap beer in the garage."

Before Jay got a chance to respond, they both heard a knock at the apartment door. Jay checked the peephole and groaned. This was all he needed right now. Trina. It was getting more and more complicated by the minute. Jay hesitated for a minute opening the door, then made his decision.

"Hi, Trina. So what do we owe the pleasure of this visit?" Jay said smiling.

"Ummm, I, ummm, hi, Jay," Trina said, brightly. She had expected to continue the argument she had with Jay at the coffee shop. His change of attitude had her off balance.

"Hi Trina!" Matt said from across the room.

"Oh, hi, Matt. How're things going?" the woman asked as she entered the apartment.

"Really good. We've had some outside groups testing the firewall we've set up, but no one has been able to find a way past our defenses. There was a challenge to the blockade from inside, but that suddenly went away."

"You're a genius," Jay said. "No one out there's better than you are. I'm sure the one inside just gave up. He couldn't figure out a way through your defenses and quit." For a moment, he thought he might be lucky enough to not have to do anything about Matt. At least not yet.

"I don't know. I'm actually beginning to think someone has hijacked what we're doing for their own purposes. Come and look at this," Matt said gesturing to his friend. "My firewall is pretty consistent, blocking out all incoming and outgoing signals. So, there really isn't a weak link to go after. But I see all this activity in this one area. It's a protected area where the banks route their business. I'm able to shut out the attacks on the blockade, but it almost seems like someone is inside the firewall, using our work as a cover to attack the banks."

"That's pretty incredible. It's someone on the island, you say? You think it is that hacker you mentioned before? Could he be the one doing this?"

"That's horrible! I can't believe someone would turn our efforts into something evil like stealing money," Trina said. "We have to find them and stop them."

"Trina, the hacker could be anywhere. I don't know how we can track him down in time, and we don't have the resources for something like that. If he's good enough to hijack our work and try to break into the banks, I'm sure he knows how to hide his location. Let's just hope he isn't good enough to get inside the banks before the world leaders come to their senses," Jay said, moving close to Trina and putting his arm around her shoulder. "It's almost like someone is taking advantage of the threat in the manifesto to undermine the banks."

"You have got to be kidding me!" Matt shouted at his computer. "I can't believe it!" Matt stood and glared at Jay and Trina.

"What is it, Matt?" Trina asked. "Did you find the hacker?"

"Yep. I found him." He continued glaring at Jay. "How could you?"

"How could I what?" Trina asked, confused.

Matt shifted his gaze slightly to look directly at Trina. "I'm not talking to you right now. It's Jay." And then he shifted back to Jay. "You might be smart enough to hide your location, but you aren't smart enough to avoid using signature pieces of code to get the job done. You're a pig."

"I was afraid you would figure it out quickly, but you got to it faster than even I expected," Jay replied calmly.

"Jay, what's he talking about? You aren't the one stealing money. Tell him," Trina said, the pitch of her voice rising.

"Gawd, that was always the worst part of being with you. The tone of your voice," Jay sneered. Trina tried to pull away from him, but Jay held her tight. Before Matt or Trina knew it, Jay was pointing a gun at Trina's ribs. "Like I said, you got there faster than I expected, but I was prepared for it anyway. Boys!"

When Jay shouted, two more men entered the apartment. Jay hadn't shut the door completely when Trina arrived. His men were waiting outside the whole time, just in case he needed help.

"The good news is it's too late to stop my plans now," Jay said with a smile as he pushed Trina into the waiting arms of one of the divers. "Without access to your terminal, you can't stop me."

Matt only hesitated a moment before he dived for his computer keyboard again. Jay lunged forward and hit Matt in the back of the head with his semi-automatic.

"Even you couldn't do anything that quickly to stop me. What were you thinking?" Jay asked, standing over his now ex-friend. "I really didn't want to hurt you."

"Give me a break. You don't care about anyone but yourself. That's the truth and it always has been."

"I'm not going to argue with you, Matt. I'm still in charge."

Jay gestured to his other man who came over and lifted Matt to his feet.

"We're leaving now. I'm sure your blockade will be fine without you. I can handle the rest, and I'll have accomplished what I want long before our deadline runs out, anyway," Jay said grimly.

"What are you trying to accomplish?"

"To steal money, of course. Now listen to me. I know you care for Trina. I have no idea why, but I know you do. I'm going to take you somewhere out of the way while I do what needs to be done. If you promise to behave, she'll be fine. But if you don't, well, she will pay the price."

CHAPTER 34

Mike and Frankie jumped back into Kelly's jeep and headed back into town. They weren't sure what they were going to do, but there was no way they were going to do nothing. Mike headed for the apartment building he saw Jay entering before. He hoped he would get lucky and Jay would make a mistake.

Throughout Mike's career, he took calculated risks to get the story. On a couple occasions, he had jumped into stories himself, moving from a reporter to an active participant. As much as Mike wanted to help people and solve problems, he didn't like to put his friends in danger. He liked having Frankie with him and her arrival had awoken thoughts in him that had been locked away. Having her in the jeep with him, chasing bad guys who threatened their friends on the boat with guns was an entirely different thing. These were the times Mike preferred to be alone.

Mike was about to suggest to Frankie that she check into a hotel and stay safe while he looked for Jay when they saw him coming out of the apartment building. He had two rough-looking men with him along with another, smaller man and the pretty girl Mike saw Jay arguing with at the coffee shop. He couldn't see any obvious weapons, but the two men *escorting* them were probably enough. Mike wasn't sure who the smaller man was, but he remembered Bill saying something about Jay having a partner who was really the technical brains of the operation. Matthias Brun was his name. Judging from the way they were walking, Mike guessed the partnership was at an end. There was nothing friendly about their little group and Matthias and Trina didn't look happy. They looked scared.

"Well, this just keeps getting better and better. Doesn't look like I'm going to get Frankie anywhere safe now," Mike mumbled to himself. He frequently talked to himself when he was troubled or trying to figure something out.

"No, it doesn't," Frankie said, cocking an eyebrow at him. "I think the last thing you need to be worrying about is protecting me. Let's get this island free and then we'll talk about my safety."

"What? Oh, sorry. Was that out loud?" Mike looked over at Frankie sheepishly. He had been watching Jay and his group intently and had forgotten Frankie was right beside him.

"Michael, I know how you are and what is on your mind. But let's concentrate on what is in front of us. Those people are in danger and we need to help them. Not to mention Bill and the two young ladies," Frankie said, putting a hand on his arm.

Mike liked the feel of her warm skin on his.

"Where do you think he's taking them?" Frankie asked, bringing Mike back to the present.

"No clue, but I'm guessing it's the same place he's holding Bill. I mean, how many secret hiding places could he really have on this island? The place just isn't that big."

"So, we follow them?"

"We follow them and see what's going on. Once we determine if those people are in trouble and if Bill and his friends are there, we go to the police and tell them everything. How does that sound to you?"

"It sounds like a perfect plan to me," Frankie agreed. "And no more silly thoughts about getting me somewhere safe."

Before Mike could argue, they watched Jay's group load into a small Toyota van and pull out of their parking place. And then it dawned on Mike that the van was coming right at them. Jay was in the front seat and he would surely recognize Mike from their meeting earlier that day at the coffee shop. Mike twisted around and pulled Frankie in close for a kiss. It was the first time he'd had a chance to hold Frankie, much less give her a kiss, since she arrived. It felt good and lasted much longer than actually necessary for Jay and his people to pass them.

"I like it. Thank you," Frankie said with a smile. "Don't wait so long next time."

"Yes, ma'am," Mike replied, giving Frankie a look that told her it had fired his imagination as well. If they could just stop working in crisis mode. "Looks like it's time for us to go." Mike started the jeep and slid it into gear.

CHAPTER 35

Mike had to give Jay and his people credit. They were doing their best to make sure they weren't being followed. They took a series of turns and dodged in and out of traffic. Mike lay back as much as he could, doing his best to stay out of his quarry's line of site. It was a small island and that worked to his advantage and disadvantage. Evening was coming so traffic was light. Most of the tourists left the island when the cruise ships pulled up anchor to move to their next port. The tourists who were staying on the island were mostly at their hotels for the evening or in a restaurant somewhere. That made it harder for Mike to hide and follow Jay's van without being seen.

On the other hand, it was a small island that Mike knew well. There were only a few places Jay could go to hide his captives and only so many roads to get there. He was able to take alternate turns and race ahead a few blocks so the van never got too far away.

It didn't take long for the van to pull up to a gate near the waterfront. They were outside a gravel parking lot beside an old warehouse and fish cleaning facility. It appeared to have been out of use for quite some time, although there were a few lights on inside. Mike parked the jeep a block away where he could keep an eye on the structure. Before one of Jay's men closed the gate, he saw Matt and Trina being taken from the van and dragged inside. Trina was struggling and fighting, but Matt seemed subdued. He simply followed where the men pointed him.

For a few minutes after everyone was inside, Mike sat quietly staring at the warehouse.

"Michael," Frankie said, breaking the silence. "What are you thinking?"

"I'm trying to figure out the best way to get a look inside the building and see what's going on," Mike said. He tore his eyes away from the warehouse to face Frankie. "I need to figure out how many people are in there. How many bad guys and how many people are being held captive. We know about Matt and Trina. And we can assume Bill and the two girls he was with; Miranda and Sherri. That's a lot of people to watch. Unless Jay has a big team, it will be difficult to keep them all under control. I need to know how they're keeping them captive and what they're doing."

"I can help."

"Frankie, listen, I've done this sort of thing before. You haven't. I can't let you risk it."

"I don't recall giving you that choice. If you remember, we've been through this sort of thing together. We confronted a mad man with a gun. And then a couple more mad men. And a couple more after that." She ticked them off on her fingers. "I think I handled myself pretty well. I'm going to help."

Mike looked at Frankie and saw the steely determination in her eyes. He was about to argue, when she gave him a final look that told him he was going to lose.

"I know you want to protect everyone. You want to save everyone else, no matter what it does to you. I get it. It's in your DNA. But no one asked you to be the hero. At least not all the time. We're all here to help you."

Mike laughed.

"All right, Dr. DeMarco, what do you have in mind?"

"Well, there is no reason to be that way," she grinned. "And frankly, my idea has a lot less to do with me being Dr. DeMarco and a lot more to do with me being Frankie, the Italian tourist."

Frankie quickly sketched out her idea. The men working for Jay and guarding their friends were, after all, men. Although Frankie did very little to accentuate her own physical attractiveness, she wasn't completely oblivious to the effect she had on men, especially men who thought of women more as possessions than people. She was making an assumption, but the rough look of the men working for Jay told her that they weren't the kind who liked long walks and talking about their feelings.

"So, I'll go play the lost tourist looking for the party in the warehouse. Sort of a rave or something. That should give you time to look around and see what's going on."

"Can't say I'm thrilled about dangling you in front of wolves, but that should work. I shouldn't need a lot of time. Just be careful. Please."

"Michael, you would almost make a girl think you care."

Mike growled in mock frustration.

Frankie hopped out of the jeep to get ready. She was wearing shorts and a t-shirt already. There wasn't much she could do with her clothes. But this was a tropical island. And the more skin, the better. Frankie was wearing her hair in a pony tail, so she let her long black hair out and shook it out so it flowed down around her shoulders. She pulled her shorts up, folding the waist line down over itself, showing off more of her long, tanned legs. Then she took the pony tail holder and tied off her t-shirt at her hip. That had the double bonus of pulling the shirt down and showing off a bit more cleavage while exposing a hint of her flat, toned stomach. From her bag, she pulled out some lipstick and gave her lips some highlights.

"What do you think?" she asked Mike with a smile that said she knew exactly what his reaction would be.

"I, umm, wow. That's about all I got," Mike said. He looked her up and down. "I see how this plan might just work."

"Might? Really, Mike? Might?"

"Okay, I'm sure it will work. Getting you away from there might be the problem," Mike said with a laugh.

"Don't you worry about that. We women have our ways," Frankie said. "You spent all of your time watching me. Do you know how you are going to sneak in there and get a look around?"

"That much I got covered," Mike said. He turned his attention, regretfully, back to the warehouse and the matter at hand. "But we might just have to discuss you and this look again later."

"Why, Michael, I'm afraid I don't have a clue what is on your mind."

"Yeah, right."

Mike crossed the road and began working his way toward the warehouse while Frankie made her way down the street, heading straight for the building's front door. He paused for a moment to watch her walk. She was already in character, playing the tipsy tourist out looking for a party. He smiled to think about the difference between the brilliant woman and the one she was playing. But she hadn't hesitated for a second to do what needed to be done. And he thought she was sort of enjoying it, too.

"I will never understand women," Mike said out loud. And then he got back to work, focusing on the job in front of him. He guessed the men were armed. What he didn't know was if they were professionals or just thugs with guns. Professionals would be likely to have lookouts posted around the warehouse and would be focused on their job. Thugs would be looking inward, bored and only worried about their pay day. He hoped for the latter.

About 30 yards away, Mike noticed that the fence around the parking area beside the warehouse didn't extend all the way to the water. It was simply there to discourage casual visitors. Not real security. Mike made his way along the fence line and down to the water where delivery boats would access the warehouse. He picked his way along the rough exposed coral and around the fence line. The fence stopped about five feet from the water, although a few feet of it hung out in the air as if the ground had slipped in beneath it.

Dusk was falling and the light was failing. There were street lights at the main road, but nothing deeper in. Another check in his favor. Before coming around the fence and into the gravel parking lot, Mike paused to look for security cameras, but he didn't see any. He was able to stay close to the water and in the shadow of the drop off until he got within 15 feet of the building. From there, he saw no cover until he got to the outer walls of the building. Mike paused for a moment, wondering how he was going to cross the open ground, when he heard Frankie shout.

"Hey in there! Open up! Is this where the party is?"

Mike smiled to himself. She was definitely putting on a show. Her distraction gave him exactly the break he needed. Keeping low, Mike ran across the open field, nearly crashing into the warehouse wall. Mike stayed still for a moment. If anyone saw him, the response would be, should be, immediate. He didn't hear anything.

Mike could hear Frankie talking at the front entrance, but couldn't make out what she was saying. Or what the man was saying to her. He felt a twinge of jealousy, too. Hearing Frankie giggle. Mike shook his head and filed that reaction away. There would be time to sort that out later. He scanned the building, looking for a way inside. He had to know what was going on inside before he talked to the police. He knew he couldn't just point the finger at someone like Jay without a good reason. If they tipped Jay off, and didn't really know what was going on, Jay could escape. There wouldn't be a second chance to stop him.

Toward the back of the building, Mike saw a fire escape from the second floor. The ladder was halfway down and appeared rusted. Any metal close to the ocean salt air would only last a few years, or weeks, before it began to rust. Mike worked quickly, stacking the few crates he found by the warehouse dock to climb up. He got within four feet, but couldn't find another box to raise him any closer.

Looking around, Mike saw a small run-about boat. It looked like it was from one of the luxury yachts that frequented Grand Cayman. Mike wasn't sure if it had anything to do with Jay and his group or just happened to be there. He decided to file the presence of the boat away for later. With no other boxes he could pile up, he knew he was going to have to leap for the bottom rung of the ladder. He hoped the fire escape would hold his weight. No time like the present and no way to test it without taking a leap. Mike gathered himself up and jumped. With his arms outstretched, he had to jump two feet straight up to reach the bottom rung of the rusted fire escape ladder. Missing the leap was not an option. He knew he wouldn't get a second chance. Crashing back down into the boxes he had stacked up would surely make a racket, if not causing them to collapse beneath him, taking him all the way back to the ground.

As he jumped, one of the boxes fell from the pile. It didn't make much noise, but Mike knew it would complicate getting back down. But he didn't have time to worry about that right then. Mike's right hand hit the ladder at the third knuckle. His left hand missed. He grabbed hold as tightly as he could with one hand and swung in place. He controlled his swing and then took another swing with his left to connect both hands. The ladder rungs felt rough under his hands, but the ladder itself felt solid. There was no movement from the apparatus, so Mike judged it was rusted in place. Good for him, but bad for anyone inside in case of a fire. Not his problem at the moment, though. Fire was the least of his worries.

As quietly as he could, Mike pulled himself up the rusted ladder. He held on with his left hand while he threw his right a notch higher. With each rung on the ladder, he paused to listen for sounds that would tell him he had been discovered. He knew he had to work quickly, Frankie wouldn't be able to keep the men inside distracted for too long, but he also knew tipping his hand wouldn't help the captives, either. Mike was beginning to sweat in the heat and humidity of the day, but he kept going, pulling himself upward. After a few more lurches, his body was resting against the metal. One more swing and he got a foot on the lowest rung. He was able to pull himself up the rest of the way quickly.

On the fire escape platform, Mike knelt and pulled himself together. He focused on his breathing and tried to still his trembling arms. Panting like a dog wouldn't help him go undetected. As soon as he had himself mostly under control, Mike edged toward one of the high windows that would let him look inside the warehouse and see where Bill and the others were.

*****

"Hey in there! Open up! Is this where the party is?" Frankie shouted at the front of the warehouse, knocking on the door. She was doing her best to channel a girl she knew from college in America. She saw the girl talk her way into parties and events, simply by flirting and showing a little skin. Silently, she thanked God she enjoyed a theater class in school.

Frankie was just about to knock again when the door in front of her opened swiftly, pulling her off-balance. She actually stumbled forward as her arm came down to knock harder on the non-existent door and fell into the arms of the man who opened it. Frankie's hand hit the man in the chest and her knuckles rapped against a solid wall of flesh, not unlike the metal door she had knocked on moments before.

"Oh, excuse me. Oooh, you're a big one," she purred, while she stood up and smoothed out her clothes, repositioning everything for the maximum effect. "Are you in charge here? Is this where the party is tonight? My friends really want to come, but we weren't sure exactly where it was so I told them I would come down and see. I was sure someone would be here setting things up. I know how much effort it takes to set up a good party and make it look like you didn't do any work at all. There was this one time last year, my boyfriend was throwing a party, we're not together any more, by the way, but anyway, he was throwing this big party, but he wanted it to look like he hadn't done anything at all. And so we--"

"Stop!" the man barked, towering over her. "I don't know who you are but you have the wrong place. There's no party here and there won't be. This is a private business. We don't host parties."

"Ooooh, where are you from? I like your accent. That sounds sexy," Frankie said, ignoring the man's comments entirely. She purred again, touching the man's chest with her hand open this time, "Are you German? Dutch? I'm Italian…"

"I'm from South Africa," he said. "Now it's time for you to leave. There's no party here."

"Are you sure? The guys at the bar last night said there was a big rave tonight at the warehouse on the water front. I'm sure this is the place. Is there someone else I can talk to? Maybe someone else knows what I'm talking about." Frankie tried to push past the man and into the warehouse. She was determined to cause as much of a distraction as possible. And if she got a chance to go inside and see for herself, even better. Too much information was never a bad thing. The large South African diver put his bear paw hands on each of her shoulders and held her in place. She felt like she was in a vise and knew he could crush her without working up a sweat. She immediately began reconsidering her attempt to get inside.

"I said, it is time for you to go. There is no one else for you to talk to."

Before she got a chance to answer, another voice interrupted.

"I don't know about that, Frans. You're always so serious. Maybe we could have a little fun with the lady. I think a party would do us all some good right now."

"Albert, I think you better mind your own business. The lady is just about to leave. She's not your kind," Frans growled.

"Come on, Frans. We're on this island with beautiful women all over the place and we haven't gotten a chance to touch any of them. The boss has kept us cooped up in here the whole time," Albert said. And then he looked at Frankie. "And none of the women I've seen even come close to this beauty right here."

"Oh, Albert, you're so fun," Frankie giggled. "I'm sure you know where the party is. Let's go and I'll introduce you to my friends. Frans, we might even take you along, too. You look like you need to loosen up some."

*****

Only a few minutes had passed since Jay arrived with two more captives, but it only took a second for Bill to recognize one of them and realize there was definitely something out of whack. He knew Matthias Brun immediately. What he didn't understand was what Matt was doing there. He knew the whole story, like everyone else in the high-tech/hacker community. But now Matt was dragged into the room by Jay's men and dumped unceremoniously on the floor, just a few feet away from Bill. He had never thought much of Jay, but seeing Matt treated like an outcast had renewed his faith in the man. And left him confused, too.

"I've got to find out what's going on," Bill mumbled as he looked around the room, taking stock of where their captors were. Once Jay had come in, all the guards had followed him, leaving the captives alone on the warehouse floor.

Bill's hands were still cuffed in front of him, but he did his best to shuffle across the floor to Matt, staying low and as quiet as possible. He was surprised that Matt didn't look up as he made his way over. Matt simply sat on the floor, his hands bound with flex cuffs and his head hanging low. Bill couldn't tell if Matt's eyes were open or closed, but he was afraid Matt had been drugged.

"Hey, man, are you okay?" Bill said, whispering when he got close. Matt didn't stir.

"Are you okay?" Bill asked louder. With his shoulder, he shoved Matt and knocked him off balance.

"Leave me alone," was all Matt said before returning to staring at the floor.

"Man, I was just checking on you."

"Leave me alone. It's all over. I just can't..."

"Are you kidding me? You got us into this trouble. You're going to help us get out of it," Bill said, his voice rising. "Time to suck it up, buttercup. I don't know what you think's going on here, but this is real life. You don't just get to take your ball and go home." Realizing he probably got too loud, Bill looked around to see if he had attracted the attention of any of the guards. No one came to see what was going on, so he relaxed. "Did you hear me?"

"Yeah, I heard you. Now, leave me alone. I don't care anymore. Jay has destroyed everything. He has ruined everything we built. For greed," Matt said, his Belgian accent peaking through.

"Okay, so what're you going to do about it? Are you just going to let the bullies win? Again?"

For the first time, Matt looked up at Bill, a blaze in his eyes. "What would you know about it?"

"Look at me. I'm a geek just like you. But I didn't have the money to go to MIT. At least there, everyone is a geek so they at least sort of understand. In my world, in the real world, there are plenty of bullies. I know exactly what they look like. Jay might be a geek, but he's still a bully. I can smell it on him."

"He protected me from the worst of it at school, and I helped him when he didn't quite measure up with the academics. He didn't bully me."

"If that's the story you want to keep telling yourself, go ahead," Bill said with a snort. "If you're so upset at what he destroyed, let's take it back from him. I'll help you."

Matt looked up at Bill for a minute. "What's in it for you?"

"Me?" Bill asked, genuinely confused by the question. "Good karma, I guess, but that's about it."

Before Matt had a chance to respond, they all heard a female voice and someone knocking at the front door. One of the guards walked through the warehouse floor to see what was going on and all of the captives got quiet. The man didn't seem to notice that Bill had moved over or that Bill and Matt were talking.

"Look man, I was trying to stop you guys, but I saw some things that confused me. I thought this was all about the environment, but I saw an awful lot of activity in the financial sectors. It looked like your bots were going after that infrastructure hard. I find it hard to believe Jay did all of that. Did you guys have a falling out? He didn't want to split the money with you?"

"That was you? You were the one trying to break through my firewalls from the inside? You have some mojo. You just about had it, and then you went offline."

"A tazer will do that to you," Bill said and then he realized what Matt said. "You think I've got some mojo?"

"Dude, you were taking all of my energy and I wasn't going to be able to get ahead of you. That's probably what brought you to Jay's attention. Sorry about the tazer," Matt said, looking genuinely sorry. "But believe me or not, I don't really care. I had nothing to do with the banking system stuff. Jay's not a complete idiot. He knows how to piggy back off my work and get what he wants. I didn't realize what he was doing until it was too late."

"Then I think we need to work together and stop him," Bill said.

"Have you seen the guys watching us? There are a lot of things I can do, but I don't know about fighting them. Jay hired them as divers to place the control units around the island, but most of them had prior military experience, too. He said it would come in handy. I just let him do it."

"I'm not big on fighting our way out of here either, but I don't think we'll have to. I was working with some people on the outside. Something tells me, they won't be lying down and taking it."

*****

Looking through the high window into the warehouse, it took Mike a moment to get his bearings and let his eyes adjust. He had been in the gloom of the evening and then found himself looking into the warehouse. He counted five captives? hostages? prisoners? He wasn't sure what to call them. Bill, Sherri, Miranda, Trina, and Matt. He had met or encountered each of them except for Matt, but Bill's description of him affirmed who he was. The big question of the day was what had happened between Jay and Matt that would change Matt from partner to prisoner.

Mike scanned the room. He knew Frankie couldn't keep them busy for long so he didn't have time to waste. The five prisoners were in the middle of the warehouse floor and they all appeared to have their hands cuffed in front of them. It didn't look like their feet were bound, though. That was a good thing. Mike was a little surprised to see Bill talking to Matt. The three women mostly looked miserable, but they didn't appear to know each other or be interested in talking. He could tell there was one guard at the door talking to Frankie. He saw another in the room, watching over the prisoners, but he didn't really seem to care what they were doing as long as they didn't try to go anywhere. He could see two, no, three more in a room off to the side with Jay. There were a total of five men, other than Jay, they would have to deal with. They all had a rough look about them that told Mike they were used to doing whatever they were told. Legalities and ethics were not their biggest problems in life. The guard he could see clearly was carrying an assault rifle. He could only assume that the rest of them were similarly armed. They didn't appear to taking the job seriously, though. They weren't posting multiple guards to keep watch outside and that sort of thing. The man watching their prisoners was only halfway paying attention.

Mike laughed to himself when he saw the one guard who was supposed to be watching the prisoners leave his post and head for the front door. "I guess he couldn't stand for his buddy to have all the fun with Frankie," Mike said. "Lots of luck there, fellas."

He was about to leave and head back down when Mike saw Jay come out of the side room with the other three men. He immediately started yelling about the prisoners being left alone. Mike couldn't make out what he was saying, but by the hand gestures and body position, he could tell Jay was angry. Then Jay saw Frankie at the door talking to two more of his men and decided to take over.

*****

"Just what do you two think you're doing? You're supposed to be inside guarding, umm, doing your job!" Jay said, shouting at his men when he saw them at the door to the warehouse. When he realized they were talking to someone he shifted his language. Admitting to having prisoners under guard was probably a mistake. "Now get back to work!"

Frans and Albert both grinned at Frankie and Frans tipped an imaginary hat to her before they turned and headed back inside the warehouse. Neither *jumped* when their boss commanded.

Frankie turned to leave, but Jay stopped her.

"And just who are you?" Jay said, the anger gone from his voice, replaced by a different tone that told Frankie she could keep him distracted, too. And if Jay wasn't paying attention, she guessed his men weren't exactly going to be working hard, judging from their reaction to him.

"My name is Billie," Frankie said, using her college friend's name. It was the first one that came to her. She added a lilt and a giggle and took a deep breath to keep Jay focused. "I just love this island, don't you?"

"I sure do, Billie. What can I do for you?" Jay asked, looking her up and down. "And I hope there's something."

"I'm looking for a party. Some guys at the bar last night told me it was here, but I can't seem to find it. Those guys didn't know where it was."

"I might know about a party. I'd be happy to take you there," Jay said. He looked her up and down before he continued. "But you'll have to come back in a little while. Maybe in an hour? I have a couple things to do first."

Frankie knew exactly what sort of party Jay was talking about. She really hated that there were women who might be tempted to fall for his line. He wasn't bad looking and she knew he had money, but she also could tell he was a slime ball just by listening to him speak for two minutes. Before she responded, Frankie looked up and saw exactly what she hoped she wouldn't. Mike was in sight and in trouble. She knew she was going to have to act fast and make sure no one turned around.

*****

Mike could tell Frankie had things well in hand. Jay was talking to her and he could tell the man was drooling from where he stood. On the far side of the warehouse. Mike didn't blame the man for his reaction. He even felt a little sorry for Jay knowing how things were going to turn out. Even with Frankie's distraction, Mike decided it was a good time to make his exit. He wasn't going to be able to break Bill out by himself and he didn't think there was much more he could learn. His mind went back to the stack of boxes he had used to jump onto the fire escape and he remembered the box on the top that fell when he jumped. If he left the same way, he would have to drop an extra four feet.

"That's not going to work out too well," Mike said. He was sure the remaining boxes would never hold him and the potential noise from his crash landing couldn't help but attract attention.

To Mike's right there was another walkway that lead to an access ladder for maintenance workers to climb to the warehouse roof. There were only two problems. It was closer to the street and in sight of the front entrance. The sun had set and it was dark outside the warehouse, but it would still be a touch-and-go thing to get away without being seen. Still, Mike didn't see that he had much choice. It was time to move.

To get to the walkway and down the ladder, Mike would have to pass by another of the high windows and then he would be in sight of the entrance. He began moving as quickly as he could while hunched over, touching the metal walkway with his finger tips for balance. He got past the window quickly and then slowed down to think about the best path to the ground. He needed Frankie to leave and send Jay back inside, but there was no way he could communicate that to her.

And then another problem dawned on Mike. The walkway was slowly pulling away from the walls of the warehouse. The bolts had rusted through and were beginning to give way. He couldn't stay there, but if he moved too quickly, there was no way he could do it without being seen. He kept moving cautiously and willed Frankie to look up and see him. Finally, she did and he saw the recognition in her eyes.

*****

Two options presented themselves to Frankie. Either one would probably work to distract Jay, but she needed to make sure everyone inside was in an uproar. After watching Jay's men with him for 30 seconds she knew they weren't exactly loyal to him. And that told her which option to choose. She exploded.

"You slimeball!" she screamed at the top of her lungs as she caught Jay full in the face with her open hand. The smack was audible to everyone inside. "How dare you say something like that to me!"

Out of the corner of her eye, she saw Mike start moving again, a little faster. Jay for his part was completely shell-shocked by the slap. Two of his men came to help and he stumbled backward past them shouting, "She's nuts. I didn't say a thing to her! Get that crazy woman out of here!"

Frankie started to lunge forward to go after Jay again, certain the men would stop her. The last thing she wanted to do was go inside the building, but she had to make it look convincing. Frans was there and held her back.

"Miss, I think it's time you took off. I don't know where your party is, but it's not here," Frans said to her.

"I can't believe him. Uuugh," she said, gathering herself up.

"I'm sorry about that, Miss. You take care of yourself, okay? And stay away from guys like that. You're too pretty to mess with men like him."

Frankie stood tall and looked Frans in the eyes. She saw more there than she had realized at first. He was a big, strong man, but she could see a depth behind those eyes that surprised her.

"Thank you, Frans. I can see you're a gentleman, at least." She patted the man on the shoulder and then turned to leave. Frans simply smiled and closed the door behind her.

*****

Mike took advantage of Frankie's explosion to move quickly. With each step, he felt the metal walkway begin to sag, but he didn't slow down. There was no going back from this one. He tried to stay as close to the building as he could, hoping the metal would be stronger there. As Frankie's hand connected with Jay's head, Mike jumped from the walkway to the access ladder. In the air he prayed it was stronger than the walkway and would hold his weight.

Mike landed with both hands and both feet connecting to rungs on the ladder. It held. He did his best to hold on and hold still. He hoped Frankie's instincts were correct. He heard her speak softly to the man who came to the door and then saw her walk away. He watched her for a second thinking just how remarkable she really was and then made his way down. Frankie's outburst had ensured that no one inside would be looking out the front door for a few minutes. They would be inside having fun with Jay for getting slapped.

Mike actually felt relaxed by the time his feet made it to the ground. He was still cautious when he left, but no longer concerned about getting caught and shot while hanging on the side of the building.

He didn't see the infra red video camera hanging from the fence post that caught him creeping away. Or know that Jay was inside the warehouse watching him go.

CHAPTER 36

Mike met Frankie back at the jeep, relieved it went as well as it did. They both climbed quietly inside and Frankie adjusted her clothes to restore her personal comfort level.

"Awww, I kind of liked that look," Mike said teasing as he started the jeep and put it in gear.

"Keep it up and that will be the last time you see anything like that," Frankie shot back.

And then they both started laughing. The stress of the last few minutes bleeding off while Mike headed back toward Sunset House. He wanted to compare notes with his friends before going to the police. Now that darkness had fallen, he guessed Rich, Kelly, and Tanya would be back at the hotel. He chose not to call in, by phone or radio, though, in case someone was listening. He knew they would be back home in a few minutes. His instincts were rewarded when he saw his friends seated around a table, with a few local cowboys hanging around, too. Mike was relieved to see the others, knowing they were going to need additional back up. He wasn't sure how or why yet, but he had a gut feeling they would come in handy. Everyone regarded Bill's kidnapping like he was one of their own. They had only known him a few hours, but recognized his contribution. And they were angry that one of theirs had been taken right under their noses.

Kelly quickly caught Mike and Frankie up on their success for the day while Frankie and Mike. The team from the *Manta* found three of the control units in the water, but decided to leave them in place until they talked to Bill or someone else who could tell them what to do with them. They knew they didn't want to tip Jay off too soon.

"But you can trust that we marked them and know how to find them again in just a couple minutes," Kelly finished up.

"That sounds good," Mike agreed. "I think your instincts were spot on. Frankie and I did well, too. We found out quite a bit, but before I tell you about it, I think it's time we involved the island police. We have enough of an idea of what is going on that they will believe us. And judging from the men and weapons we saw in the warehouse, we can't do this alone."

"It's a good thing I'm here then." Mike was startled by the voice approaching out of the semi-darkness behind him. It took him a moment to recognize Detective Alex March from the Royal Cayman Islands Police Force. Detective March had been instrumental in their take down of Gray Walker 10 years before.

"Detective! It's good to see you," Mike said, rising to shake the man's hand. March had been frustrated with Mike and Kelly during the investigation before, but they had ended on good terms, especially considering the way it all worked out. Mike could see the passage of time on March's face.

"Ummm, Mike, he's the Commissioner now, in charge of all the police on the island," Kelly said, coming forward to greet March as well. "I called him when we got back to the dock."

"It's okay, Kelly. There are times I wish I was Detective March again. I spend too much time shuffling papers and not near enough time in the field stopping criminals," March said.

Mike and Kelly quickly caught the police commissioner up what they had discovered since the blockade was put in place. March listened, asking a few questions, but mostly sitting still and taking it all in.

"I see you people have been doing my job again. I really wish you would come to me first with these things," March said.

"Honestly, we didn't think you would believe us without more to go on. Especially since it is someone like Jay Taylor. He's powerful and influential," Mike said.

"Understood, but you should know that I've never been afraid to take on the powerful and influential before. And now it might have put your friend in danger."

"You're right, sir," Kelly replied.

"Of course, I never thought someone would try to take the whole island hostage. I don't know how you negotiate with people like that. It seems to me that our first task is to get the people who are in danger safe and then let the rest of it fall where it will," March said, finally. I talked to Taylor a little while ago and something didn't seem right about him. I just couldn't put my finger on it. I guess my instincts were right, if a little rusty."

"There's a good chance that once we get Bill free he can help us break out of the cone of silence, too," Mike said.

"Cone of silence?"

"It's something we've been calling it. We had to call it something," Mike said.

"I like it. And that's even more reason to get your friend free," March agreed. "I'm guessing I can't tell you all to stay out of the way and let the professionals handle this?"

"Sir, I saw some pretty heavy weapons in that warehouse when I was sneaking around, so I will defer to you, however you want to handle this. I'm not nearly as young as I once was and far less dumb, too. But I think I can speak for everyone when I say we'd like to help out," Mike said.

March looked around at the faces gathered around their table. March knew most of them in one capacity or another. It was a small island after all. A few he had arrested for one reason or another. Most he knew as stand-up members of the community.

"I agree. I want you there to help out, but you have to follow my instructions," March agreed.

"We understand completely, Commissioner, but I have a suggestion on how this might work. If you're willing to listen," Mike said.

CHAPTER 37

Commissioner March rallied the police quickly, but it still took them a few hours to get everything together. It was just after midnight when the SWAT team from the Royal Cayman Islands Police Force was in position to raid the warehouse. The island didn't see much crime in the way of police stand-offs and raids, so the group wasn't especially large. They were well-trained, however, each taking rotations to work and train in the United States, and they worked well together. To cover the perimeter of the building, they used regular duty officers to fill in the gaps.

The plan was to take as many of the hostage takers prisoner as possible, but the police unit expected resistance and they were prepared for a fire fight. They took Mike's reports of the number and types of weapons seriously. Frankie had gotten the distinct impression that the two men she met, before Jay, had military training as well.

Everything outside seemed dark and quiet. They were confident that a guard or two inside was still awake, but there were no signs on the outside that anyone was aware of the police presence ready to come through the doors.

When everyone was in place, Commissioner March signaled Mike and Frankie to start moving.

*****

Inside the warehouse, the prisoners were all still awake. Bill and Matt had continued talking about Jay's plans to steal from the Cayman banks, plotting how to stop him if they got the chance. That left the three women

181

to talk amongst themselves on the old couch. The few guards that were still awake had long since stopped caring if they talked quietly. They decided it would keep them calm. They all hoped the situation would be over soon. One by one, as the guards led them to the bathroom, the men had removed the women's flex cuffs and had not bothered to put them back on. They didn't see much threat from them.

"We're going to be okay," Sherri said. "I'm sure of it. Jay just has us in here to cover up what he is doing. We're not in any danger."

"What do you mean?" Trina asked, wondering how the young American woman even knew Jay.

"I met him earlier this week in a bar. We've been out a couple times and I slept with him. It has been an absolutely amazing romance. I've never felt like this in my life. He's not like the boys at school. He has money and class and taste," Sherri gushed. "He trusted me so much, he asked for my help. He asked us to keep an eye on Bill and let him know what Bill was up to. He told me that he respected what Bill was doing, setting up the protests and all that, but he had something bigger planned and he didn't want Bill to mess that up. Now I guess we see what that was. Can you imagine taking an entire island hostage for your ideals?"

Trina sat shocked by what the college girl was telling her. Not at Sherri's betrayal of Bill, but of Jay's betrayal of her. She began to suspect that they were in more trouble than any of them imagined. Until just a few minutes before, Trina had been thinking almost exactly the same thoughts. She imagined they were just there so Matt and the other one, Bill, didn't suspect them. Now, she wasn't so sure. She wasn't sure which upset her more.

"So, you've been dating Jay?" Trina asked, trying to sound innocent and unconcerned.

"Just this week, but he told me he thought he loved me. It's been amazing. I've never dated a rich guy before. He hasn't had a lot of time for me, but when we got together, it was amazing," Sherri continued. "Now I know why he was so busy."

"Has your boyfriend told you what's going to happen next? I really don't want to spend all of my spring break being a hostage in a warehouse," Miranda sneered at her sister.

"You're just mad because he liked me best," Sherri said.

"He just liked you best because he knew you would sleep with him," Miranda taunted right back.

"Did he tell you what would happen?" Trina asked, interrupting the family argument. She had sisters and knew how things could go if left unchecked.

"No, not really. And he hasn't said anything to me since we've been here. I'm sure he just wants to keep his cover intact and keep us safe, too."

*****

Mike and Frankie crossed the parking lot, walking straight up to the front door of the warehouse. In case anyone was watching, they walked straight for the door like they were on a mission. Mike stepped to the steel door and banged with his fist. They could all hear the booming sound echoing through the nearly vacant building. He convinced March to let them act as a distraction and keep the guards inside the building off balance. The last thing they wanted was for one of the hostages inside to get shot. A full-scale building breach with stun grenades and a heavily armed SWAT team raised the stakes on the situation. Mike's plan was to keep the men inside from thinking there were police anywhere nearby, so the police could enter though the rear. March agreed to the plan because he wanted to avoid the possibility of bloodshed. He also understood that the man who was holding his island hostage was inside and so were two people who gave him the best chance of breaking down the communications blockade. The last thing he wanted was to lose a hostage in the raid and end up losing his chance to get his island free. March's team was set up around the back of the building.

Mike hammered on the door again with his fist. Albert answered the door.

"What do you want?" the man demanded. He was smaller than the first man Frankie met, standing 5'8", but he was still solid, with a shaven head and a scar on his cheek. He looked like he could handle himself. Mike noted Albert was carrying a rifle, but had it hanging at his side, tucked behind his leg.

"The lady tells me some guy here was rude to her, and I plan to make him pay for it," Mike snarled, adding a slight slur to his voice. They had both washed their mouths out with rum and Mike spilled some on his shirt. He wanted to make the guard believe he and Frankie met in a bar and when she told him the story his drunken chivalry had sprung up, ready to defend her honor. "Was it you? Were you rude to the lady?"

"I think you and the lady need to go home. Or go back to the bar or go to your hotel room. I don't care where you go, but you best get out of here," Albert said.

"You can't tell me what to do. If it was you, I'm gonna bust you up," Mike said, closing on the smaller man. Albert didn't budge. He was carrying a gun after all and he was the sort who didn't back down from a challenge.

"I'm giving you one last chance, old man." Albert noted the wrinkles around Mike's eyes and gray at his temples. He immediately dismissed Mike as an older guy chasing younger women. He was sure Mike wasn't a threat.

"Or what?" Mike growled.

"Honey, no, this isn't the weasel who was mean to me. It's not him," Frankie said. "He's prettier than this one."

Albert didn't anticipate Mike's next move. Mike reached forward and grabbed Albert by the shirt. Thinking Mike was going to try to enter the building to find Jay, Albert surged forward. Going inside was never on Mike's mind. Instead of pushing forward, he pulled backward, using Albert's momentum against him, pulling him out of the building and onto his face on the gravel.

"Out of my way cupcake," Mike shouted, saying the codeword that told the police to enter the building from the rear. The uniformed officers around the front of the building swarmed onto Albert and had him handcuffed before the man knew what was happening.

The noise of the confrontation had the men inside, the ones who were still awake, distracted and watching the front for some action. They were taken completely off-guard when the SWAT team entered the rear, blowing down the door and pouring into the building.

*****

The lights inside the warehouse were low, mainly so the guards could sleep. There was some disturbance at the front door, but no one other than Albert moved to take care of it. And then the back door exploded. The noise, light and smoke inside the warehouse was awful. Noise bounced off the metal walls and concrete floors like hundreds of ping pong balls dropped from the ceiling. Everything was chaos and confusion. Except for March's SWAT team. They entered the room with set objectives.

Through a small camera snaked through a hole in the wall, the team had noted the locations of the hostages and the guards. Men were assigned to each one. And they went directly after their assignments. Three SWAT team members moved directly toward Bill, Matt, Trina, Sherri, and Miranda, gathering them up and shielding them with their own bodies. The rest of the team went after guards, with two heading for the office near the front of the building where Mike described seeing Jay.

*****

Jay smiled as he slipped through the escape hatch in the floor of his office. *These idiots think they're going to outsmart me. I'll show them who's really in charge.*

He had set up closed circuit cameras outside the warehouse to watch for trespassers. When he saw Mike and Frankie leave just a few hours before, he knew the inevitable was about to happen. But he had planned for that. He knew the police were coming. From inside his office, Jay watched the police get set up and ready and watched Frankie and Mike approach the front door, playing their roles. He didn't bother to tell his men or try to move the hostages. This was exactly what he wanted to happen. The men served their purposes and now he didn't need them anymore. Just like the two young women sitting on the floor in the warehouse. They both thought they knew him and that he loved them. They couldn't have been more wrong.

Jay jumped when the police breached the door and he stayed put a few more seconds, listening for his men to react. Nothing. He would fix that.

Jay picked up his nickel-plated .45 and racked a round into the chamber, just like he saw in the movies. Then he stuck the gun out of the door of his office and fired. He didn't aim it. The last thing he cared about, or even wanted to do, was hit anything. *That's what I hire people to do.* The heavy report for the large caliber gun echoed in the silence that settled after the police blew the door open and tossed in their flash-bang grenades. Jay was rewarded with the sound that came next. More gun fire. That was all the cover he needed. *Everything is going just as I planned it.*

*****

Out of nowhere, a gun shot rang out. It seemed to come from the front of the warehouse, but it really didn't matter. That one shot caused every other itchy or nervous trigger finger to contract and start shooting. Bullets rang out and sprayed the room.

Firing continuously from the hip, a man stepped from the shadows. He was blinking from the effects of a flash-bang grenade. The police returned fire with controlled bursts, catching the man directly in the chest. His knees gave way and the man hit the floor face first without ever seeing who shot him. A second guard began firing from an overhead spot. He never came close to hitting anyone, but he attracted the attention of the SWAT shooters who quickly returned fire.

In just a few moments, it was over. The air was choked with smoke from the flash-bang grenades. There was a tang of fear, sweat, and blood in the room as well.

*****

"I'm so worried about Jay," Sherri whined while a paramedic checked her over. The young woman was unharmed, just scared and a little dehydrated. "They haven't said if he got hurt or anything, but I haven't seen him, either. I hope he's okay."

When Sherri looked up, she saw Trina standing over her and was startled by the look on her face.

"You said you're in love with Jay, right?" Trina said, her Slavic accent coming through. Trina looked as if she was in a daze. "He took you on dates this week and you slept with him, right?

"Umm, yeah, that's what I said. What's wrong with you?"

"Until this week, he told me he was in love with me. And when he met you, everything changed," Trina said, her voice still neutral, flat.

"Look, Trina, I'm sorry about that. But you can't stand in the way of love," Sherri said, backing away. "We met and fell in love. That's the end of the story."

"I don't think so, Sherri. I think he's just using you to get what he wants. He asked you to spy on your friend over there, didn't he? He told me he had someone on the inside watching him," Trina said.

"You're lying. He loves me!" Sherri said, growing agitated.

"Honestly, I don't think he loves anyone but himself."

"You can't say that! He loves me! You're just jealous," Sherri said.

"No, Sherri. He was using me, too. But now I see that was all it was. And right in front of me, there was a man who loved me, but I ignored him, blinded by Jay." Trina was looking at Matt when she said the last. "I doubt he will ever want me now."

*****

Mike stood outside talking to March, staying out of the way until given the all-clear.

"Commissioner, I have to hand it to you," Mike said. "That went about as well as any take down I've seen. And I hate to admit it, but I've been around several."

"Thanks, Mike. The SWAT team trains very hard. Fortunately, they haven't really been tested until now, but I think they passed this exam with flying colors," March agreed. Both men were quiet and grim. Two men lost their lives tonight and while neither was a police officer, it still wasn't anything to laugh about. The fact that the situation got this far was troubling. "Of course, it will take a while to sort it all out. I'd like to know who started the shooting. I was really hoping to get out of this without a shot."

"You may never know exactly what happened inside," Mike said. "I've covered several battlefields as well. About the only thing that's consistent is the confusion."

"I think it's time I made it inside to start debriefing the hostages," March said. "I'm hoping we can get a couple of those guys to a computer and tear down this cone of silence as you call it." He started to walk toward the door, Mike following him when they both heard a single gunshot.

*****

Sherri stood looking at Trina's back, trembling.

Was it true? It couldn't be. It had all felt so right. Had Jay used her? No, there was no way. He loved her. That was real. She felt it. It had to be real. Trina was just trying to confuse her. That's it. She's trying to get rid of me so she can have Jay. She just wants me gone. I won't let that happen. I told Jay how to find Bill. I helped him because I love him. He isn't just using me!

When Sherri decided to act, she did so in the blink of an eye. Everyone around her was relaxed, the threat over. Jay's team was subdued and all the guns were locked away. They had already escorted the men out of the building away from the hostages and the police were beginning to let go of the adrenaline that had been coursing through their veins just a few minutes before.

The uniformed officer standing beside Sherri never thought for an instant to protect his gun from the young college girl. Before he knew what happened, Sherri hit from behind, knocking him off balance and pulling his sidearm from its holster. Sherri pointed the gun at Trina's back.

"You're lying!" she screamed.

Matt looked around and saw the gun pointed at Trina's back. He moved to protect Trina, the woman he loved, from danger. He wasn't fast enough.

The gun fired, Sherri's finger on the trigger. Matt could see the bullet flying through the air and his eyes met Trina's. He could see she finally saw him the way he wanted her to. The bullet struck Trina between the shoulder blades and knocked face down on the concrete floor. Matt was there a half second too late.

*****

Everyone stood still in shock after Sherri shot Trina in the back. People mumbled things like:

"The stress of being a hostage."

"Stockholm syndrome."

"Too much violence."

The medics immediately jumped on Trina and worked to stop the bleeding. She wasn't dead, but no one had much hope she would make it. The gun shot was too close and the bullet had passed near her heart. The internal damage had to be extensive. The only thing keeping her alive was the fact that paramedics stood within ten feet of her when it happened and were able to respond within seconds. Sherri was handcuffed and arrested, but she was taken to a hospital as well for psychiatric evaluation. Matt knelt beside Trina while the medics did their job, holding her hand and praying. He didn't let go of her hand until the medics loaded Trina in an ambulance and whisked her away. Then he went to find Bill.

Commissioner March got a final report from his men and stood talking to Mike.

"It looks like we can account for everyone except for Jay Taylor," March said. "You said you were confident he was here, right?"

"He was here when Frankie and I did our surveillance, but he could've left after that, I guess. We didn't keep a watch on the building."

"It's a small island and I have people on the lookout for him. We'll find him. He won't get away," March said. "He has a lot to answer for."

"Were any of your men hurt?"

"Fortunately, no," March said, shaking his head. "The odd thing is we discovered a closed-circuit television system in the office. If he had been there, he would have seen us coming and been prepared. I guess we got lucky that he wasn't around or it could have been a lot uglier."

"That's pretty scary," Mike agreed. "If they knew we were coming and had put up a fight, there could have been a lot more body bags. The hostages would have been in real trouble. It's funny, though. I didn't see the cameras when I was climbing around the building. But if they were there, it seems like he would have seen me climbing around or at least when I left."

"This doesn't seem like a real professional operation. I guess no one was watching the cameras when you were here. Whatever happened, we all got lucky and got the hostages out safe."

"Except for the one girl, of course."

"Jay will face the music for that, but I'm looking at that as a separate incident."

"Fair enough, Commissioner," Mike agreed. "Let me know if there's anything else you need from us."

When March left, Frankie came up behind Mike and put her arm around his waist.

"You sure know how to show a girl a good time," she smiled.

"This is not exactly how I envisioned seeing you again, that's for sure."

"But you had imagined it?" she asked, a sparkle in her eye.

"Do you really have to ask that?"

"So, is it all over now?"

"Honestly, I'm not sure. This all seems like it went too easy. It's like we're missing something. And Jay's still on the loose. Of course, the cone of silence is still up, too," Mike said. "But we've found the control units and got the hostages back. So, I'm guessing it will all wrap itself up pretty soon. Tomorrow would be my guess. It is just amazing to me that someone would go to these lengths to make a political statement about the environment. He's got to know it will just backfire."

"Mike, we need to talk to you." It was Bill and Matt.

"Sure, guys. What's up?"

"We were talking inside, before the police came in. And we've been comparing notes since then," Bill started out. "Jay has an agenda that no one could see. I was beginning to see it and Matt here has confirmed it. Matt is the architect of the cone of silence, but it was doing something he didn't expect it to do. He figured out that Jay was going after the Cayman banks and that's when he got kidnapped and put in there with the rest of us."

"Wait, what? What's going on?" Mike asked, suddenly confused. "I knew this seemed too easy."

Matt and Bill did their best to explain what Jay was doing. Mike had to ask them to stop and clarify several points as the computer genius hackers in front of him frequently drifted into technical speak.

"So, in essence, the cone of silence is just a cover to hack into the Cayman banks and steal money?" Mike asked. "How much money are we talking about?"

"Once he breaks through the firewalls of the banks, and he's probably really close now, he'll have access to billions of dollars," Matt confirmed. "He was getting close a few hours ago before he took me and Trina away and put us in there," Matt said. The young man winced when he said Trina's name.

"I saw the way you were with her after she was shot. She's special to you. I can tell. Are you okay?" Frankie asked.

"Jay uses people. I knew that, but I never let it bother me before. I don't know what it is about him, but he has that effect on people," Matt said, his eyes flat and his voice dull. "Trina thought he loved her and I couldn't convince her otherwise, or that I would be a better choice. But yes, I love her. It'll probably sound stupid, but the last thing I saw in her eyes was recognition that I was the one. Now, I'll never get a chance to find out."

"It's not over yet," Frankie said. "I can feel it." She put her hand on Matt's arm. He looked up at her and she could see the fire return.

"I… I can't do anything about that. It's up to God and the doctors, I guess. But what I can do is stop him. I can make Jay pay for what he's done. I should have done it months ago, but he swayed me, too. I thought we were going to do something radical and good."

"And that's what I want to talk to you about," Bill interrupted. "Matt and I can stop this and shut Jay down before he gets any further."

"That's going to be a problem," March said, coming back to join the conversation. "I didn't realize it until now, but this man is part of the plot to kidnap our island and shut down our communications. He's going to Her Majesty's Prison and he may never leave it."

"But he can help us!" Bill shouted.

"And who are you again? Oh, wait. You're the hacker who was protesting on my streets. We suspected you at the beginning of this," March said, his look turning grim. "And now you want me to trust you and this man, who was part of it. How can I know you aren't working together?"

"We want to help you!" Bill said. "I can't believe this."

"Commissioner March, can you trust me?" Mike asked. "I'll take personal responsibility for them both."

"Do you know these men, Mike? You have proved yourself to me more than once. But you're asking me to take a big risk," March said, doubtful.

"Honestly, no. I don't know them very well. I've only just met Matt and I only met Bill a couple days ago. But he has been a stand-up guy so far and I get the feeling Matt here has every reason in the world to make sure Jay pays for what he's done."

"I'll make you a deal," March said after thinking it through for a few moments. "I'll give you custody of Matt, but I want one of my officers on hand to keep an eye on them, too. I won't take him to jail immediately, but if he does anything that looks even vaguely suspicious, he goes there without argument. Can you accept that? How about you?"

March looked at Mike and then at Matt.

"Sir, I accept that I've broken many laws here and will face whatever punishment is coming to me. But thank you for giving me the chance to make this right. I will accept whatever limitations you put on me," Matt said formally, looking March in the eyes.

"Do you think you can find Jay and pull down the cone of silence," March asked.

"I know I can pull down the cone," Matt said, smiling. "I like that name for it. Never thought of calling it that. And I will do my best to find Jay. I want to see him pay."

"We've got computers set up at Sunset House. How about you bring Matt's equipment there and they can work together," Mike suggested. "Kelly and Tanya can go out on the water and lift the control units that they found from the water. That should take down the cone, too, or at least weaken it."

"Mike, I'm putting my faith in you. But you keep an eye on them and make sure this goes as planned."

*****

When Jay scouted the warehouse, his plan had begun to form. He told Matt he needed it for the dive crew to use as a base of operations. They had to have some place to work from and store the control units they would eventually use to encircle the island. It wasn't like he could just charter a dive boat. All of that was true, of course. He just didn't tell Matt his entire plan. When he saw the trapdoor to a tunnel underneath the warehouse floor and out to a small dock in the harbor, he knew exactly how it would go.

Jay slipped away from the action. The old smuggler's tunnel came out beyond the police lines. It wouldn't matter much anyway. Their attention was focused entirely inside the building. He slipped over the side of the small boat behind the warehouse and released the lines holding it in place. He started the boat's small motor and moved away from the harbor to his own personal retreat. The one only he knew about. That was where he would wait out the last phase of his plan. And then he would be gone. They would never find him where he was heading.

Jay noted that the shooting inside the warehouse had already stopped by the time he was pulling away. He thought he heard one more gun shot, but he couldn't be sure.

CHAPTER 38

The sky was beginning to lighten and dawn was close at hand when the group was finally reassembled. They stood around in the cool, damp morning air yawning and stretching. The Sunset House Sea View Restaurant made strong coffee and breakfast sandwiches at Kelly's request. They were up against a deadline and no one planned to sleep.

"All right, guys, settle down," Kelly started things out, gesturing to his friends and the people who had turned out to help. There were a dozen men and women, from their early 20s to early 50s, but they were all there to do whatever they had to do to stop Jay and get their island back to normal. Kelly had asked everyone to huddle up so they could make sure everyone was on the same page before they took off on their separate tasks. "Thank you all for coming out this morning. I know most of us are running on little or no sleep, but of course this isn't the first time any of us have been there, right?" That drew some laughs from the Cayman cowboys in attendance.

"This has been a pretty strange couple days and it definitely hasn't gone the way any of us imagined," Kelly continued, looking at Tanya. "Now it turns out some lunatic has shut us off from the rest of the world. He's basically taken the island hostage and is using the pretense of saving the environment to steal money. We now believe he set up the cruise ship grounding that almost killed Mike and me as part of this whole plot. We're not sure why, yet, but it was part of the plan. He attempted to kill Tanya, too, and I can't let that go. I know most of you couldn't care less about the banks on this island, but I'm asking you to step up and help because there is a bigger issue here as well. We can't let someone come in and steal from us, and from this island. Right?"

"Yeah!"

"You tell 'em, Kelly!"

"Let's get that bastard!"

We're going to break into three teams," Mike said, stepping forward. "Bill and Matt are going to stay here at the hotel and work their computer magic to try to tear down the cone of silence. We've got a police officer who is going to stay here to keep watch over them, but I'd like a couple of you to hang around, too, to help out however they can. And also to provide a little extra security. I don't like it that Jay and his goons were able to waltz in here and take Bill and the two girls, yesterday."

Two men and a woman raised their hands and stepped to the side to see what Bill and Matt were doing. The two computer wizards were still setting up the computers and getting things straightened out. Jay had taken Matt's primary computer from the apartment, but Matt had a backup they were setting up. Jay had also taken Bill's computer when they took him hostage, but he hadn't done anything with it, so Bill was able to plug it in and fire things right back up. With Matt's knowledge of the network and the blockade causing the cone of silence and the attack on the island banking system, they expected to be able to go right after the system, although both men knew that Jay had most likely set up defenses they didn't know about and would be prepared for their attack. The banks had confirmed they were under attack through their networks, but nothing had gotten through so far. The police officer Commissioner March had assigned to watch over Matt was the department's white collar crime expert and had at least a functional understanding of the problem.

"The second group will go out on the *Manta*. The dive team marked the location of three of the underwater control units that are the physical cause of the cone of silence. They will pull those things out of the water and shut them down," Mike explained. "That should break the stranglehold on the island. If not, they'll keep searching for the units and pull as many off the reef as it takes until the cone fails."

"Frankie, Rich and I are going to look for Jay. We took out the team that was backing him up, but it seems like he may have planned for that. We think he knew we were coming and didn't let his guys know, so that means he planned to leave them behind the whole time. This guy has set this all up, and we don't know his exact end game, other than to steal money. He has a plan that even his partner didn't know about, so we can be sure he has a place to hide and it will have defenses as well," Mike said.

"Can we help you look for this guy?"

"Absolutely, but I only want people out on the road who have older vehicles, like the jeep. Anything with electronic controls and on-board computers is grounded for now. We don't want a repeat of what happened to Tanya. And no one goes alone. I want teams out looking. We'll divide the island up into segments and you can search for him. Bill and Matt think they should be able to get a location on him when they begin trying to tear down his computer defenses. He'll fight back and that should give him away. From there, they should be able to guide us in."

The remaining cowboys quickly divided up into teams, based on the people they had left and who had the oldest cars and trucks. What had once been a sore spot for a couple of them, driving the roughest vehicles on the island, quickly became a source of pride when they realized they were needed. They had two more search teams ready, beyond Mike's group.

"This is going to be a coordinated effort. Everyone start on Channel 79 on the VHF radio. We'll call for switches if we need to. And remember, this is all going to work together. Every part is important. Bill and Matt will be attacking from here and that will help us get a location on him. The divers on the boat will be working to take down the cone of silence and slow down or stop his attack on the banks. And when we find him and get close enough to harass him, he won't be able to defend his network and the guys here can finish the job. Every part of this is important to stopping this guy. The police will be out looking, too, and they need our help, but they don't have a lot of vehicles that are up to the task. And frankly I don't think they know the island as well as we do," Mike finished.

"Thank you all for being here and helping out," Kelly said. "Get something to eat, get a fresh coffee and let's get to work people. Daylight will be here soon and there's no time to waste. But remember, be careful out there. No heroes. This guy is willing to hurt people to get what he wants. We aren't soldiers and we aren't cops. I want all of you back here this evening and we'll have the party we've been trying to have all week. You got that?"

"I heard that!"

"You got it, Kelly!"

"Where's that coffee?"

CHAPTER 39

As the sun came up over the Caribbean Sea around Grand Cayman, Kelly and Tanya as well as Kurt, Shrop, Eric, and Captain Biko, the same crew that found the control units in the first place, were back on the water to clean up *their* reef. As divers and dive professionals who made a living from diving on the island, they had a vested interest in the health of the reefs. They didn't like anyone to mess with it. Collectively, if they had a chance to lay their hands on Jay, he wouldn't enjoy the experience.

They all appreciated the opportunity to return to the reef and do what they did best. They got to clean junk from their reef and undo a wrong. That worked.

When they found the control units on their first trip out, they left them in place while they waited on someone to tell them what to do with them. There had been some concern about connecting to the units and leading Jay's people back to them. So, they just marked the boat's GPS unit with the coordinates and moved on to the next location. That made this return trip easy. Captain Biko was able to direct the boat directly to the closest location and when they arrived, two divers were able to go over the side in minutes. Kurt and Shrop did backroll entries into the water as soon as Captain Biko said they were on site and pulled the twin in-board engines into neutral. There was no need to drop anchor. They were the same two divers who found this unit the first time and discovered it right where they left it the day before. They were all stunned by that. It was just the day before, but an awful lot had happened since then. Just a few minutes later, both men surfaced right behind the boat and began climbing out of the water. Shrop held the control unit in his hand and tossed it on the deck.

"What should we do with it?" Kelly asked when everyone was back on board.

"I say drop a tank on it," Kurt said.

"Or a crate of lead dive weights," Shrop agreed. "Smash that puppy."

"I agree with you both, but I'm not sure that's the best idea," Tanya said, picking up the microphone to the VHF radio. "Wonder Twins, Wonder Twins, you there? This is Edith calling Wonder Twins."

There was silence for a moment until Bill came back. "Wonder Twins here. What can we do for you, Edith?"

"We've got the first package. Should we destroy it?"

There was a pause for a moment. Tanya could tell Bill and Matt conferring over the best way to handle the control units.

"My twin brother says it will be best to shut them down all at one time. They'll get a little fuzzy when you move them around, but it won't shut down the network. He thinks when you take out three of the units at one time, it will make the whole net stumble. You got that? But also, let us know when you have them. We want to be ready on our end."

"Understood, Wonder Twins. Will do as directed," Tanya said. They were trying to be obscure about what they were talking about, just in case Jay was paying attention, but the code names lightened the mood a bit, too.

The location for the next control unit was only 100 yards away and they were on the site quickly. This time it was Eric and Kelly's turn to go in the water. There was no reason Kurt and Shrop couldn't make the second dive, but they had alternated dive teams before when they expected their searches to take longer so it made sense for the same people who found the devices to recover them.

As quickly as the two divers hit the water, they were surfacing. Kelly tossed the second control unit onto the deck. When they cleared the water, he gave Captain Biko the signal to move out.

"You guys in a hurry or something?" Shrop asked.

"Well, no. We just wanted to show you how real divers do it," Kelly said.

"Oh, is that how it is, huh?" Kurt asked. "I think it's time for us to get back in the water and show these jokers up."

When the boat approached the third control unit they found, Kurt and Shrop slid into their BCDs and jumped off the sides of the boat before

Biko even had the engines stopped all the way, their competitive nature getting in the way of good sense.

"Kelly, if one of you idiots gets hurt doing this, I'm going to kill all of you," Tanya said sternly, ignoring the irony in her sentence. She cared about all of them and the last thing she wanted to see was someone in trouble. Even if it was self-inflicted. And definitely not if it was purely out of competition.

"It's been a tough couple days, Tanya. We all just need to have a little fun. And this is how we do it," Kelly said, sounding as reasonable as he could, while he backed away from his wife. She was even touchier than usual lately.

"You heard me," was her only response.

"Eric, what's taking those guys so long? This should have been an easy one," Kelly said, changing the subject. This control unit was the first one they found after they were confronted by the armed dive team on the boat. They found three units after their escape and they had already recovered the first two.

"You got me," Eric said, shrugging his shoulders. He looked over the side of the boat to see if he could tell if the divers were heading toward the surface. The water was clear and the sun was climbing into the sky, allowing the people on the boat to see the reef below them clearly.

*****

Kurt and Shrop hit the water and immediately dropped below the surface, clearing their ears and inverting to kick to the bottom. Kelly's challenge to get the control unit and get back on board the boat quickly was pushing him to get this job done.

Kurt swam for the bottom, scanning from side to side looking for the control unit. A lot had happened since they found this unit and he was struggling to remember where he last saw it. Shrop saw the control unit first and signaled to Kurt that he got it. Both men swam in the direction, wanting to get the unit and get back on board the boat.

Shrop was the first one there. He reached for the computerized octopus-looking device, already thinking about smashing the device with the bottom of a scuba tank. This whole turn of events frustrated him and he wanted to bring it to an end. Inches before his hand hit the control unit,

Kurt grabbed his wrist and pulled him back. Shrop wheeled around and looked at Kurt. *What are you doing? Let go of me!*

Kurt gestured to him to stop, holding his hand up like a traffic cop. Then he pointed to his eyes, signaling "look" and then pointed just below the control unit. There was something there that hadn't been there the day before and wasn't present underneath the other devices they picked up that morning. Finally, he waggled his finger back and forth to signal, "Don't touch."

The control unit rested on top of a coral outcropping that appeared to be mostly dead. Changes in water temperature or salinity had taken their toll. Kurt couldn't tell exactly what was below the control unit, but he was afraid of what it might be. He held his breath as he moved in close to get a better look. Kurt could see the playing card-sized case of the control unit with its tentacle sensor arms arrayed around it. Below it, he saw a smaller block and then saw a straw-like device with a wire from its end stuck into a separate block below everything. The final layer looked like putty. Kurt kept holding his breath and backed away. He signaled for Shrop to move away and gave him a thumbs-up signal to say they needed to surface.

They were only in 25 feet of water, so Kurt and Shrop were back at the boat in a moment.

"You guys took long enough," Kelly said. "Get on board and let's get out of here."

"Can't do it, Kelly. We have a problem," Kurt said. "It looks like this one is booby-trapped."

"You're kidding me."

"Nope. We found the device and it's resting on a couple other pieces. Looks like some sort of sensor along with a blasting cap and what looks like a package of C4. Those guys from the other boat must've figured out what we were doing and laid a trap for us. If we pick this thing up, it goes boom. Even a little C4 down there is going to mess up anyone in the water. The water will transmit the pressure wave," Kurt said, treading water behind the boat. "I can't really tell what sort of trigger it has. It may be a motion sensor, or it could be acoustic. Or even magnetic. It may blow when a diver exhales near it or when a tank gets close. No way of knowing, really."

"Then we leave it in place and go looking for another one," Kelly said.

"We don't have time for that, Kelly. We have to deal with this one."

"What do you have in mind?"

"We blow it in place. We were just going to destroy it anyway, so that doesn't hurt us any."

"I know you have to do what you have to do, but is there any way you can get it off the reef first? I'd hate to blow another hole in a living reef. They've already torn up so much around," Tanya said. She had been listening quietly up until that point. "I understand if you don't have any choice."

"It's resting on an old, dead coral head, but I agree with you," Kurt said. "I have an idea." He quickly told them the tools he would need to put his plan in place.

"Okay, while you work on that, I'll call Bill and let him know what's going on. It looks like we'll be taking out one control unit before the others. Shrop, get on back to the boat. I don't need two lunatics in the water," Kelly said.

Kurt was a champion freediver, often descending to 100 feet or more on a single breath to take photos or spearfish. He liked the freedom of diving without scuba gear and could easily hold his breath two minutes and often could go three minutes without a problem. In 25 feet of water, freediving wasn't even a challenge and ditching his scuba unit seemed the best way to avoid setting off the sensor and detonating the explosive. He wouldn't make a sound and wouldn't have anything metallic hanging off him. Tanya brought Kurt what he asked for and then knelt down on the stern swim platform to talk for a minute.

"Don't do anything stupid down there. If you can't get it off the reef, we'll blow it in place and come back to fix it later. It'll just be one more thing to blame those guys for," she said.

"I know, Tanya. Don't worry. My hero days have long since passed me. I'm just trying not to make a bigger mess than I have to."

"Remember that," Tanya said. "When this is all over, we're finally going to have that big party and I want you there."

"Roger that, Tanya."

"How are you going to get away from it?" Kelly asked, coming back to the stern. "The shock wave can still mess you up."

"That's a very good question. I'll figure something out. But you should move the boat a little farther away," Kurt said. "Now, let me get ready."

To prepare for the freedive, Kurt closed his eyes and relaxed. He needed to slow his breathing and his heart rate. He didn't want his body to use up the oxygen in his lungs too quickly or he would be forced to surface. Freedivers used to hyperventilate, taking multiple deep breaths to flush the carbon dioxide from their bodies and packing in as much fresh oxygen as possible, but that could also cause them to black out as they surfaced after a long dive. Kurt preferred to still himself and breathe normally before a dive. When he was ready, he piked his body, using his body weight to force him underwater and back toward the danger.

The plan was relatively simple. He was going to wrap a short piece of monofilament fishing line around the control unit and the explosive. He would then connect the fishing line to a lift bag. He was carrying a small air cylinder with him to fill the lift bag with air. He planned to fill the bag completely before releasing it. He expected the bag would jerk upward, pulling the explosive off the coral head quickly. He hoped it would raise a few feet anyway before exploding. That was about the best he could do on short notice. He thought about swimming upward with the monofilament line and jerking it upward from the surface, like setting the hook on a fish, but he was concerned he would jostle the explosive or the drag from the fishing line would set things off early. He couldn't take that risk. And it wasn't like they had a freediving bomb squad.

Kurt saved his energy, sacrificing a few seconds by allowing himself to sink passively rather than swimming down. He wasn't racing against a clock so there was no need to rush. He got to the coral head and moved closer to the control unit and the bomb. In spite of what he told Tanya and Kelly, he was guessing about the triggering device. It might go off simply because he touched it while sliding the monofilament beneath it. Nothing he could do about that. He got to work.

On the surface, Kurt had prepped the fishing line. One end was already tied to the lift bag. He sat the bag and the small air cylinder down to the side of the coral head and then unspooled the monofilament up to the top of the three-foot-tall brain coral to look at the bomb. *Just like he left it.* Above him, Kurt heard Captain Biko start the Manta's engines and move the boat out of the way. Regardless of how this ended up, there was going to be a blast underwater and he was relieved to know his friends were at a safe distance.

Everything was quiet as Kurt gently snaked the end of the fishing line under the explosive and out the other side. He would have preferred to wrap it underneath the device several times to make sure there was a solid connection, but he didn't dare take that risk. The more he messed with the bomb, the greater the risk of blowing it, and him, up. He cautiously pulled the end of the fishing line out the other side and tied a slip knot in the end of the line, allowing him to tighten the line down without disturbing the detonator.

Satisfied everything was as it should be, Kurt moved to the lift bag and the air cylinder. The lift bag was relatively small, but it still had more than 25 pounds of lift when fully inflated. His plan was to add as much air into the bag as he could and then release it suddenly. The bottom of the bag was open with straps hanging below it to connect to the fishing line. He could open the valve on the air cylinder and fill it quickly. The bag would shoot for the surface and he hoped it would protect the reef from the blast. Kurt took a quick breath from the air cylinder before he began filling the bag. He didn't need a breath yet, but he didn't want to hurry either. To offset the lift generated by the bag, he kept his scuba weight belt in place for this freedive. He hoped it would be enough weight, at least for a few minutes. That was all he would need.

Kurt began filling the lift bag, opening the valve wide open. After the silence, the air rushing into the bag sounded almost like a roar. But in the background, he heard a beeping noise. He turned the valve, stopping the air flow to listen. It was still there. He looked around, trying to figure out where the sound was coming from and then he felt a stone in the pit of his stomach. The bomb. He moved back to the top of the brain coral head and looked. A small light was blinking on the block immediately beneath the control unit, what he assumed was the detonator. He must have activated it, but not enough to set off an instant detonation. Kurt grabbed the air tank and immediately returned to filling the bag. He held it as deep underwater as he could, hoping the difference would allow the bag to pick up speed on ascent. He had no way of knowing when it would blow, but he had to hold onto the bag until it was full.

With a free hand, Kurt pulled his weight belt off his waist and held it across his lap. He needed the ballast right then, but if something happened to him underwater, knocking him unconscious, he wanted to float freely.

Beep.

Beep.

Beep.

Air began to flow out of the bottom of the lift bag. Now or never. He released the bag, almost throwing it straight up. In the same motion, he dived down into a crevice in the coral beneath him. It wasn't a swim through with a roof, but he hoped it would shield him from the blast.

*****

Without warning a water spout blew 15 feet straight into the air. Captain Biko had moved the *Manta* 50 feet away from the location of the control unit so they were safe, but they still received some of the spray from the blast.

"We need to get back over there now!" Tanya barked.

Captain Biko didn't hesitate. The boat's engines were still running and he immediately engaged the boat's propellers, moving back to where the water spout had been moments before. Everyone on board crowded the rails, staring into the water, desperately looking for any sign of Kurt. The explosion had turned the sea into a foamy mess, cutting visibility to nearly zero. They were all looking for any sign of their friend.

"I'm going in!" Kelly said, pulling his shirt off.

"Right behind you!" Shrop and Tom said together. "We'll find him."

"That won't be necessary," Kurt called out from behind the boat. "I'm over here."

Everyone on board the *Manta* stood still for a minute, having trouble comprehending that Kurt was there in front of them.

"But you could throw me a line. That would help," Kurt said.

Quickly, Kurt was back on board, drying off. He was having trouble hearing them, but other than that, he seemed fine. He told them about setting off the beeping and rushing to get away from the bomb blast in the crack in the coral below him. The concussion from the bomb blast had been severe, knocking the air from his lungs. As a last thought, he had kept the air tank he used to fill the lift bag with him and had been able to get a quick breath of air while still underwater. He waited a minute after the blast to let the water blown into the air come back down before he surfaced. It wouldn't have done much good to get to the surface and then be knocked unconscious by a few hundred pounds of falling water.

"Tanya, the reef looked fine. Some soft corals were knocked over, but I didn't see any major damage from the blast. It got far enough from the coral head before it went off," Kurt said. "No more damage than a good storm blowing through. It'll recover on its own."

"That's good to hear, Kurt. Thank you."

"Believe me, I wanted to do it. They've done enough damage around here. No more."

"That was a heck of an explosion," Eric said. "Those guys were really playing for keeps."

"I guess they were upset about having their boat sabotaged," Kelly said with a grin. "We'll have to let Rich know that his message was received. Now, one more thing."

Kelly went to the captain's area and picked up the microphone for the VHF radio.

"Wonder Twins, Wonder Twins. This is Archie. We've destroyed one of the cattle rustlers. No casualties. Are you ready for the last two to die?"

"That's a roger, Archie. Take the last two cattle rustlers out. We're ready on this end."

On the boat, they were ready for this order. The two remaining control units were on the deck and Eric and Shrop had scuba tanks ready. They picked the tanks up and slammed them down onto the computerized control units as hard as they could. They were concerned about the fiberglass deck, but too angry at everything that had happened to really care.

"How is that, Wonder Twins? Should be off-line, now."

"Hold on, Archie," Bill replied over the radio. "I see the hole you've made in the system. My twin here is going to use that opening to shut the whole cone of silence down."

There was silence for a moment as they let the men work their computer magic.

"Oh my God! I didn't expect that!"

CHAPTER 40

"What in the world is going on?" Bill asked, staring at his computer. He put down the radio microphone from where he was talking to the divers on the boat. "Are you seeing this?"

Matt was seated across the table from him and was equally confused.

"The whole thing is just shutting down," Matt mumbled. "That doesn't make sense. It's not the way I built it. I set up this network to withstand an attack like this. It should have given us an opening. We should have found a weak spot to make our attack and take it down ourselves, but not just collapse."

"That's a good thing, then, right?" one of the divers on guard duty asked. "I mean, you wanted the system to collapse and now it has. We're free!"

"It just doesn't make sense. And I'm not entirely comfortable with things that don't make sense," Matt said.

"You don't date much, do you?" the diver asked.

"What's that have to do with…Oh, never mind. Bill what do you think?"

"I'm pretty surprised, too, but I can't look a gift horse in the mouth. Maybe Jay changed something that made it less stable? Is that possible?"

"Wonder Twins, this is Archie. Care to tell us what's going on?" Kelly asked over the radio.

"I'm kind of curious myself," Mike asked over the radio as well. He, Rich, and Frankie had been listening in while searching their section of the island for any signs of Jay.

"Sorry guys, but we're still trying to figure it out. The whole cone of silence just collapsed. Archie removed units and the whole thing went out."

"That's great, guys. Good job!" Mike said. "That makes our lives a whole lot easier."

"It makes us nervous, Clark," Bill said.

"Explain."

"My twin brother here says he built the cone better than that. It had redundancies and back-ups. Taking out three units would have weakened it, but not crippled it. But it just fell down like a house of cards."

"I'm not sure I understand the problem," Kelly said. "Are you saying you want us to put the units back? They're pretty beaten up. And one, well…"

"No, Archie. Turning them back on wouldn't help anything. I guess we'll just have to wait for the other shoe to drop. And hope it never does," Bill said.

"Hey Bill. Look at this," Matt said, gesturing Bill to look at his screen.

"Hold on everyone. My wonder twin wants to show me something," Bill said into the radio before setting the microphone down and moving around the table. The white-collar police officer and the divers who stayed to watch them crowded around Matt's computer as well.

"What's that?" Bill asked, looking at the activity on the screen.

"It's a Trojan Horse. I recognize it. We built it in college for an assignment. It was particularly good."

"Where is it? What's it doing?"

"It's going after the financial sector," Matt said.

"I thought he was using the cone of silence to shut everything down and go after the banks," Bill said. "Now that the cone is broken, how's he still active?"

"That's just it. He's not going after the local banks anymore. The Trojan Horse is in the dedicated secure networks for the international banking system. Most of the largest banks in the world are on this island. They need secure communications for their operations and wire transfers. The Trojan Horse is in that."

"Okay, hold on. I need to let everyone know what's going on."

"Hey, guys, the other shoe just dropped," Bill said over the radio, before explaining the situation. It took a few minutes, trying to use his vague language and finally he just gave up and said it plainly.

"Are you telling me this was his plan all along?" Mike asked. He was faster than the rest at understanding computer and hacker logic. "He set all this up so he could plant his Trojan Horse in the international banking networks and get inside every major bank in the world? He'll be able to steal from anyone and everyone and no one will be able to stop him."

"It seems that way. I wondered why he was so focused on Grand Cayman when we started talking about this scheme," Matt said. "We looked at several places, but he kept coming back to Grand Cayman."

"I'm still confused," Kelly said.

"When we took down communications, Jay was able to attack the firewalls of the local banks and there wasn't much they could do. If he had the time, eventually he could have gotten into those banks, but it seems now that was never his plan. He just needed to get into the networks so he could insert his Trojan Horse. Now that the comms are back up, he can get into banks anywhere in the world. It's pretty ingenious," Matt explained.

"Well, let's not pat him on the head too much," Mike said. "He's got a long list of criminal offenses to answer for. Bill, is the officer still there with you?"

"I'm here, Mr. Scott," the officer said, taking the microphone.

"You need to let Commissioner March know what's going on. We'll keep looking for Jay and will try to stop him."

"Mike, I do have some good news. Now that the cone of silence is gone and we can see what he's doing, I can see where Jay is. I can lead you to him," Bill said.

"That's great!"

"Give me a few minutes and I'll let you know," Bill replied.

"And I have an idea how we might be able to set up a DoS attack to at least slow him down before he can get inside the banking systems," Matt said.

"A DoS attack?"

"It's a denial of service attack. You've heard about it on the news from time to time. Hackers will take over thousands of computers and direct them all to one website, basically overloading the web servers and shutting it down. It's really a nuisance attack, but keeps people from paying their credit cards and that sort of thing."

"Can you get that started?" Mike asked.

"Yeah, we can get it set up pretty quickly," Matt said, thinking through the steps to take. "The problem is, a DoS attack isn't exactly legal either. Even if we are using it for good."

"Officer, did you hear that? We need to get permission to use an illegal tool to stop something more illegal," Mike said over the radio. "I think you need to talk to your boss. And guys, get me those coordinates as soon as you can. I'm about done with this nuisance."

CHAPTER 41

When Jay fled from the warehouse in George Town, none of the divers believed he would stay close to town. There were too many people looking for him there. They left that area to the island police. The three teams of searchers divided the rest of the island between themselves. It was a small island, but there was still a lot of ground to cover. One team took the West Bay region of the island. A second took the far East End, from Frank Sound Road to the end of the island. Mike, Rich, and Frankie took the East End, from George Town to Frank Sound Road, including Rum Point. Frank Sound Road was a roughly north-south route that cut directly across the eastern end of the island, providing a short cut to get to Rum Point and several of the other more exclusive areas.

Grand Cayman covered 76 square miles, but most of the residents lived on the fringes of the island, facing the beaches and the water, or in George Town. The interior of the island was largely uninhabited and rough terrain. And that made it the perfect place to hide.

Mike hung up the radio microphone in the jeep and continued driving. He didn't have a destination in mind. He was just looking for anything out of the ordinary that would suggest where Jay was holed up while he waited for something more definite from Bill and Matt.

"So, Jay has been playing us from the beginning," Rich said from the back seat of the jeep CJ-5.

"It sure seems that way," Mike agreed. "He's planned this every step of the way. He knew we would take down his cone of silence. Actually, he wanted us to do it. That's what opened the door for his end game."

"That's important," Frankie said. "If he planned every step like this, it means he isn't on the run. He isn't reacting. He knew we would take down the warehouse, and he would make his escape. He knew we would shut down his network. He's hanging around long enough to make sure it works and then he's gone. But I'm sure he's in a place of his own choosing."

"In other words, we're not looking for someone whose plans are falling apart. We're looking for someone who is on schedule," Rich agreed. "Lovely. We need to get a step ahead of this guy."

"I'm not sure we aren't," Mike said. "Think about what we know about him. Matt and Bill both said Jay was the leader, but Matt was the better hacker. Jay probably didn't expect Matt to survive the warehouse or be in a position to help us."

"That makes sense," Frankie said.

"So, we have a tool that Jay didn't plan for. And he didn't plan for Bill to be here, either. That's why he took him hostage. He wanted Bill out of the way. He probably hoped Bill would die in the shooting at the warehouse. Next, what we've seen of him, he's a bit of a pretty boy who likes his luxury, right?"

"And his women," Frankie said with a smile.

"Good point," Mike agreed. "Do we really think Jay's going to be hiding in a tent on the beach somewhere?"

"Not likely," Frankie agreed.

"We know he's staying in a decent house somewhere with some luxury," Mike finished.

"The downside to that is there are plenty of luxury homes on this island with absentee owners. He could be in any one of them," Rich offered. "How do we narrow that down?"

"I think he'll do it for us. He'll still have his computer and his toys. He isn't finished yet and he'll have to respond to the DoS attack the guys are setting up. He'll be preoccupied," Mike said. "With a little luck he won't even see us coming."

"With a little luck, he won't have a second security team guarding the house," Rich said grimly, looking around him at the houses they were passing.

Without warning a drone passed the jeep. It was flying directly over the road and its four propeller fans making a sound like an angry bee's nest.

"Wow! What was that?" Rich said from the back seat. Mike and Frankie were in the jeep's front seats and were protected from the elements by the jeep bikini top. The cover provided sun protection between the windshield and the jeep's roll bar, but didn't cover the back seat. Rich was the only one who had gotten a good look at the drone, at least until it passed them.

"Did I forget to mention he has a drone?" Mike asked, tongue in cheek. Rich and Frankie had arrived after Tanya's accident in the harbor, and they hadn't seen one since then, so it was possible with everything else going on that it had slipped his mind, Mike conceded as he caught them up.

"So, that's why you insisted on everyone taking older vehicles. I get it now," Rich agreed.

"Does that mean he saw us?" Frankie asked, scanning the skies for the aerial spy.

"Won't know until it comes back, but there's a good chance he didn't recognize us. Rich hasn't been around Jay and we were out of sight," Mike said, thinking things through. "If we see it come back and check us out more, we'll deal with it. The biggest question I have now is was the drone headed out or heading home? If it was heading home, we can follow it and find Jay."

"I've used drones some to inspect dive sites from the air before I get in the water," Rich said. As a commercial diver, he was often asked to dive in places with zero visibility and plenty of obstructions. He took any edge he could come up with to get the job done as quickly and as safely as possible. "They don't have much battery life. I mean like 15 or 20 minutes, tops. And that's the bigger ones, not the kind you get at the department store."

"The drone Jay used in both the cruise ship grounding and sending Tanya's car into the harbor was clearly a higher-end machine," Mike agreed. "But it's good to know those things can't stay up indefinitely. And that means whoever is flying it is pretty close."

The radio crackled to life. It was Bill confirming what Mike had just realized. Jay was close to where he was, based on the IP address location he was using to break into the banking system. He gave Mike GPS coordinates to where Jay was hiding.

"Has he been able to plant his Trojan Horse?" Mike asked.

"No, not yet," Bill replied. "We were able to get the DoS attack going before he got all the way in. But he's close. If it weren't for Matt, he would be in already. This guy is great."

"Tell him I said thanks. And keep me updated," Mike said. "Out."

Rich pulled out a portable GPS unit and pinpointed Jay's location.

"We can be there in about five minutes," Rich said, pointing in front of the jeep. "And the drone was heading home."

CHAPTER 42

"I understand from my officer you two are breaking the law," Commissioner March said as he approached the table where Matt and Bill were hard at work.

"Umm, what? No, sir. I mean, yes, sir, but…" Bill stumbled, trying to decide whether to own up to what they were doing or to deny it. Breaking the law for a good cause was still breaking the law and he wasn't sure how much March knew or how he was going to handle it.

"It's all my fault. I'm the one to blame. Bill hasn't done anything illegal," Matt said, standing up and facing March. He knew he was already in trouble, so one more strike wasn't going to make that much difference.

"Both of you sit down and tell me what you're doing. We'll discuss who's to blame for what later," March said, sternly, but with a hint of a smile to show that he understood the situation.

"As you know, Jay is trying to insert a Trojan Horse into the secure connections maintained by the international banks on the island. If he's successful, it'll give him a back door to any bank in the world. At least the ones who do business here on the island," Matt explained. "He could siphon off money from any bank he wanted. Or worse, he could shut down that bank and hold it hostage. That could trigger worldwide financial chaos."

"And that is pretty much all of them," March said. "Continue."

"We've enlisted the aid of just about every computer on the island to stop him," Bill offered.

213

"Is that the illegal part? Those computers you have enlisted into your fight didn't give their permission to do it, right?"

Both of the hackers just stared at March for a moment, unsure how to react.

"Boys, I understand the big picture. Just answer my questions, please."

"Yes sir. That's correct. We were able to insert a bot into the local networks as they came back on line and took control. The owners don't even know we're there. They probably think their computers are running a little slow, but that's it," Matt explained. "It just so happens that taking the entire island down and then letting everyone get back on at one time was a perfect time to insert our bot into the system."

"I'll remember that. You do plan on removing it when you're done, right?"

"Yes, sir. Of course, sir."

"Are you being successful with your attempts?"

"Mostly, sir. But it's hard to anticipate Jay's moves. We're constantly playing catch up," Matt explained. "Frankly, you don't have a lot of computers here, compared to a city in the US for example. So, we don't have a lot of horsepower behind us."

"What would you say if I could get you more horsepower. A lot more?"

"That would be great!" both hackers replied.

"I've been on the phone with the NSA now that we're back on the grid. They have some concerns about what happened and want to make sure it doesn't happen again. I told them about you two and it seems that they know who you are. Both of you," March said, raising an eyebrow.

"Well, yeah, umm, about that. I can explain," Bill began.

March held up his hand. "I really don't want to hear about it. Anything that's a concern of theirs is out of my jurisdiction. They told me to support your efforts. They said you two were on the ground and could do the job. But they did offer to hook you up with some reinforcements." He handed over a slip of paper with contact information. "They probably expect you to burn that once you use it. Or maybe it just self-destructs. I don't know."

"I have a couple old classmates who work at the NSA," Matt said, grinning. "They couldn't get real jobs…"

"Me, too, now that I think about it. Not the sharpest tools in the shed, but nice folks," Bill laughed.

March stood and began to walk away, and then turned back. "Boys, my officer will stay here and keep an eye on you. If you need anything, let me know. But please don't be tempted to do anything foolish, either."

"We understand, sir."

March began walking back up the hill to the main road in front of Sunset House where he left his car when Matt ran after him.

"You need something already?" March asked when he heard Matt coming and turned.

"No sir, not about this. We'll take care of it. I just wanted to ask about Trina. I haven't heard anything about her. Is she going to make it?"

"Son, all we know now is that she's still with us. She's in deep trouble. That gunshot tore her up inside pretty badly, but our doctors are working on her. They say it is mostly just a waiting game at this point," March said, his eyes softening as he put a hand on Matt's shoulder. "They told me one of you cared about her. If I hear of anything else, I'll let my officers know to tell you."

"Thank you, sir," Matt said. "Please let me know either way. Both will give me motivation."

"That I understand."

CHAPTER 43

The house had a perfect view of the Caribbean Sea north of Grand Cayman. Only about 180 miles separated the house from the southern beaches of mainland Cuba. The sun was bright and the air was warm. It should have been a perfect day to nap in the hammock, listening to the sounds of the ocean and thinking about his recent successes. That wasn't in the cards for the day, though. Not yet anyway. Soon, though. Very soon.

Until recently, Jay might have headed to Cuba when he was done with this project in Grand Cayman, but things were loosening up between the United States and Cuba, so that was his best option. He had decided to head to Venezuela. He had made some initial contacts with the government and they had confirmed for him that a healthy donation to the national treasury would go a long way toward ensuring his protection. They wouldn't ask too many questions and the money he was planning to siphon off would still allow him the best of everything, including a private army. Jay was an American citizen, but Grand Cayman was a British Protectorate so he was fairly confident he was going to have the governments of both nations out looking for him. He laughed. That was fine. There was no way they were going to catch him, though. Both of them were too dependent on electronic footprints and he was a master at corrupting and changing those. They couldn't catch him, because there was no one better at erasing a digital trail. That was what he told himself anyway.

If he could just get the Trojan Horse loaded and working. But that was the problem. He knew Matt was on the other end of the computer fighting him. He could feel it. He had an advantage over Matt, since he knew how everything was set up, but Matt was foiling his efforts at every turn. They were playing cat and mouse. The DoS attack was a good idea and would certainly slow him down, but it wouldn't stop him. Just in the last few minutes, though, they hit him with something even stronger and it was taking all of his attention to fight it off. Once the Trojan Horse was seeded in the system, it was done. There was nothing they could do about it. He might even offer to remove it for them in a few years, for a price, of course. But he still had to get it out there.

Jay was glad he had brought his drone home and landed it just a little while ago. On the drone's last flight, he had performed a sweep for digital signatures, but saw absolutely nothing. There were a few cars on the road, but nothing indicated they were searching for him. They were all pretty basic. He didn't even pick up any cell phone signals radiating from them. Jay liked the drone, he thought of it as his toy, and if it had been in the air when Matt started this latest attack he might have had to ditch it. There would have been no way he could have flown it and concentrated on his computer screen. Jay wasn't sure what Matt was using to get the additional computing power he was throwing at Jay's system, but it was definitely a handful. It was too late, but it was a handful.

Everything on this project had turned out even better than he had planned it. Jay was sure that meant he was a genius. In his mind, taking over the communications system was just another project, another challenge and another soon-to-be success. He even expected they would write magazine articles about him. He doubted they would be as flattering as some in his past, though. He smiled at that. Everything had worked perfectly. Even setting up the cruise ship to drop its anchor and tear up the reef in the harbor had been perfect. It had galvanized Matt to do his job and forget his ethics. The island government had been eager to accept his help in the restoration process. They knew it was going to be expensive and time-consuming, but when a rich benefactor had shown up throwing money around, they had greedily accepted it. He hadn't planned on people being there, in the water right where the anchor chain dropped, but that just made it that much more dramatic and got that much more international news attention. The whole thing served his purposes and let him bribe his way in without actually having to bribe anyone. It proved his good intentions and he didn't actually have to spend any money. The wire transfer hadn't gone through yet. He laughed. "I truly am a genius," he said out loud.

No one could catch him now. His escape route was planned. Everything was in place. His runabout boat was resting at the dock behind the house. He just had to run it out to the yacht just off-shore and he would be gone. His crew was already waiting on him, ready to go wherever he told them. And they were going in style.

CHAPTER 44

Mike, Frankie, and Rich sat outside the front entrance to Jay's house. They weren't sure what to do next. They told Commissioner March where they were and what they saw using the VHF radio. March told them what was going on back in town, with the NSA helping out the hackers. He laughed when they called them the Wonder Twins, but said it would be at least 20 minutes before he could get an officer to that side of the island. He asked them to stay put and keep an eye on the place.

The coordinates Bill gave them earlier were 19°20'48.54"N and 81°10'42.68"W. It led them to a house just east of Old Man Bay on the island's north side. Frank Sound Road came to a Y. From there, they turned left onto North Side Road and parked 20 yards away from the house's entrance. It was situated on the right side of the road, facing the ocean. Before they parked, Mike drove the jeep past the gated entrance a couple times. He hoped Jay wasn't looking out the front and watching the road, but there wasn't much he could do about it if he was.

The house had a gate just off the main road, but the house itself set back 60 feet from the gate. Either side of the long driveway was bounded by wind-swept scrub bushes and iron shore; exposed ancient coral reef that was jagged and impossible to walk across. It ate shoes, tires, and just about anything else not constructed of steel. Approaching on foot was out of the question. Mike had to give it to the guy. He had picked well, from a security perspective, when he selected this remote house. It was difficult to approach and Mother Nature kept all but the most determined visitors away.

But Mike was pretty determined when he needed to be.

"How do you want to play this, Mike?" Rich asked.

"For the moment, we hang tight and see what happens," Mike said. "You're looking at the same thing I am. No way to approach quietly."

"If we had the time, we could swim up from the ocean side," Frankie offered.

"Not a bad idea, but I don't think we have the time. It sounds like everything is just about to come to a head," Mike said. "You guys heard March. He said he had delivered some pretty serious back-up to the wonder twins. The question is, will it be enough?"

"And if it's not?"

"You have both been through some adventures with me. We'll figure it out," Mike said with a smile.

"And I've read about some of your others," Rich laughed, too. "Just think of the story you'll get out of this."

"That's funny. I'd almost forgotten about that. The last couple days have had me thinking more like a cop, or a private detective, than a journalist. I'm sure my editor is going to want full-blown coverage on this. Someday, I'm going to have a real vacation."

"You wouldn't know what to do with yourself," Rich said.

"I have a couple ideas what we could do on a vacation," Frankie said, with a look that told Mike she wasn't thinking about playing shuffleboard.

"I like the way you think," Mike agreed. "Sorry we haven't had any time to be together since you got here."

"Michael, there's no place I would rather be right now."

"Something tells me I'm not old enough to hear this conversation," Rich joked. He was about to lean back in his seat when the radio crackled to life. It was Bill.

"Clark Kent, this is the Wonder Twins, are you out there Clark?"

"What's up, Wonder Twins? Have you shut this thing down?"

"Unfortunately, no. Even with help from Big Daddy, it looks like we're still going to lose. He's too agile and able to react to our attacks," Bill said.

"Okay. What should we do on this end? March is still 15 minutes out," Mike replied.

"Mike, he said it wasn't over yet, right?" Frankie asked.

"Yeah, I guess. He said Jay is reacting to everything they try. Why?"

"What if we distract him?"

Mike thought for a second and then keyed the microphone.

"We aren't done yet, Wonder Twins. Give us a couple minutes and then throw everything you have at the problem."

"Do I want to know?" Bill asked.

"When I figure it out, you'll be the second to know. Out."

Mike stared at the locked gate at the front of Jay's compound. That was the only way in.

"What's the plan, boss?" Rich asked.

"I think Kelly's going to be really mad at me," Mike said. "Everyone get ready. We're going to knock on the front door."

Mike started the jeep's engine while the other two prepared themselves. Kelly had done a great job restoring the jeep to its original condition, with the addition of some over-sized tires and a winch on the front. When they were ready, Mike explained his plan.

The wrought-iron gate looked solid and well-made. Whoever built the house wasn't interested in visitors. Mike revved the jeep's engine and shifted into first gear. He slipped his left foot off the clutch and slammed his right one down on the gas pedal. The jeep lurched forward, its tires barking on the sand-covered pavement before they took hold and the jeep took off. Mike didn't let off the gas until he slammed headfirst into the gate, twisting it and knocking it off its hinges. The threesome in the jeep had braced for the collision, but it still knocked them forward and bounced them around quite a bit. Rich was the first to look at the gate.

"Still up!" he barked.

"Get to it!" Mike agreed. He restarted the engine and shifted into reverse while Rich unbuckled and jumped from the back of the jeep. Rich quickly unspooled the hook and steel cable from the winch on the front of the jeep and snaked it through the bars on the bent and twisted gate. He gave Mike a thumbs-up. Mike eased the jeep backward until the cable was taut and then he hit the gas, digging in hard against the iron. At first nothing moved, the jeep matching its will with the gate. After a breathless moment, the gate began to give way. Mike poured more juice to the jeep, causing the rear tires to break loose and howl. With a sudden jerk, the gate snapped and the jeep was free. Mike backed up far enough to get the broken gate out of the way and then slipped it back into first gear while Rich unhooked the cable. He wound it up out of the way as quickly as he could and then jumped back into the back of the jeep. Rich stood in the backseat, leaning on the roll bar and gave his best war whoop.

"Company is coming!"

"Time to say hello to the guy who is causing all these problems," Mike agreed and he took off down the 60 foot-long drive way and skidded to a stop in front of the house. "Knock, knock!"

*****

Jay was feeling good about himself. He was even whistling as he packed up the few things he had with him. He had planned to leave most of his stuff behind. He had sacrificed his dive team in the warehouse, because he didn't want their baggage either. He was wealthy anyway, but he was about to become so wealthy he would never need to ever wear any article of clothing more than once if he needed to. He could buy anything and anyone he wanted. Just a few more minutes. He threw the last few items in a bag and turned back to check the computer. Yep, he had the people on the other end, it had to be Matt, beaten. He had answered every feint and outright attack and blocked them. Even when they found renewed strength, Jay had deflected their attacks. He was the king. And really, that was what was most important. Money was just a way to keep score. But being the king of the metaphorical mountain was what it was all about.

Just another minute and he would be in. The Trojan Horse would be released and the international banking system would be at his mercy. Jay laughed. *They all said Matt was the brains of the outfit. I'll show them.* And so much for his "partners" overseas as well. He had needed to join forces with them, to put a few things together, but the crime syndicate couldn't touch him now. He had no plans to follow through with that agreement, either.

Jay's head whipped around toward the front of the house when he heard the crash. It was the front gate. *They've found me. How did that happen? I didn't read anyone nearby…*

The next noise Jay heard was the iron fence screaming as it was twisted backward. A moment after that, Jay heard a vehicle accelerate down the driveway. He froze in place. *I can't fight the police. Too many guns, too many men.* He crept to the front of the house so he could see who was there. His gut told him to run for his boat and make his getaway. The police would be cautious and wouldn't be able to do anything to his computer in time. If they even understood what to do. But something didn't seem right. Jay looked out a window, hiding behind the curtains as best as he could. He saw a jeep sitting diagonally in the driveway, blocking his car in. Three people got out, slowly.

It was that woman from the warehouse. And the guy with her. And another guy. *How did they find me? Are they working with the police? That big one looks like the guy climbing on the side of the warehouse. He was in the coffee shop, too. What's going on here?*

Jay went back to his desk and grabbed his nickel-plated .45. *They do not know who they are messing with. I'm going to show them once and for all!*

Jay whipped the front door of the house open and stepped outside, pointing the gun at Mike, Frankie, and Rich.

"You people need to leave. You're in way over your heads," Jay shouted, waving the gun around.

"Oh, I think we do, Jay," Mike said calmly facing the man while gesturing to Rich and Frankie to spread out. The last thing he wanted was for them to group together and give Jay an easy target.

"You think you're on to some big story, but if you don't leave now, you're never going to get a chance to tell it. Now go and maybe you can still collect your Pulitzer."

"I already have one of those, Jay. And that's not what we're here for. You're a geek who sold his tech company and made a mint. But you couldn't leave that alone. You couldn't try to do something altruistic or save the world. You needed to prove yourself on an even bigger stage. Isn't that right?" Mike asked, trying to goad Jay into arguing with him. All Mike needed was for Jay to argue with him while Bill and Matt worked their magic back at Sunset House and the police raced across the island to where they were. He wasn't thinking about playing hero.

"How do you know…"

"But what you don't get is you're just a bank robber. A common thief. You broke into a few banks and stole some money. So what? Any idiot with a handgun can do that," Mike sneered. "You think you're making a statement, but the only statement you're making is how pathetic you really are."

Jay grew angry at Mike's challenge. He had always hated men like Mike. Good looking with broad shoulders. Mike was the proverbial bully on the beach in Jay's eyes.

"So you think you know my plans," Jay shouted back, growing agitated. This was exactly the point he was trying to make. "You don't care what I've accomplished. You still think you're better than me. But you just don't get it. Your kind will always work for me. You call me a geek, but I wear that label proudly. The jocks and the popular kids in school don't understand that they will work for the geeks one day. And then who has the last laugh? Huh? The geeks, that's who. You call me a bank robber, but you think too small. I'm not robbing one bank. I'm robbing all of them. I'm in control of the world banking system. I can take money from any account in any bank in the world. When this is done, I'm going to come after yours. I'll clean you out and you won't be able to do anything about it."

"Oh no, Rich. He's going to take the $258 dollars from my bank account and wipe me out," Mike quipped. "How will I ever recover?"

"You got that much? Can I borrow some money? This trip has just about cleaned me out. I'm not sure I have enough to pay my bar tab," Rich laughed.

"Your threats aren't worrying me or my friend over there," Mike said. "Just like a geek. Making threats he can't back up."

"I'll show you," Jay said, becoming enraged at Mike's taunts. "I'll show you how I back up my threats."

Jay raised his gun back up and extended his arm, pointing it at each one of them in turn. "You think you're tough, but you're not tougher than a bullet."

"Is that thing chrome-plated?" Mike laughed and shook his head. "You can't even get a gun right. Blued steel is for professionals. Shiny guns are for amateurs. You probably don't even know how to turn the safety off. Have you ever fired that monster? Did you load it? Amateur…"

Mike knew he was playing a dangerous game. Jay seemed like he was about to crack, but Mike needed to keep him preoccupied for another couple minutes. The police had to be close now.

"It's nickel-plated, not chrome," Jay said, stealing a quick look at the left side of the gun to make sure the safety was off. "I know what I'm doing. Maybe I'll just shoot the woman to prove it to you."

"Why would you shoot her?" Mike asked, edging toward Frankie.

"Come on, Jay. Don't listen to him," Frankie said, speaking for the first time. "I kinda liked what you said at the warehouse. I thought maybe you and I could get together later. And you'll have so much money. Are you sure you don't want to get to know me better?"

"Aaagh. Just shut up. Get out of here! I'm tired of all of you. It's time for me to leave!" Jay remembered his computer in the house and his escape plans. He needed to go. And he knew a way to make sure the three of them were distracted long enough for his escape.

"You slapped me. No woman gets away with that. No one," Jay screamed as he extended the gun straight at Frankie and squeezed the trigger.

*****

Mike saw the muscles in Jay's shoulder tighten first and watched the tendons in his forearm contract as he squeezed the heavy pull on the trigger. He began moving immediately.

The gun bucked in Jay's hand. Mike was nearly right. It was the second time Jay had fired the gun. The first time he had fired it was at the warehouse where he was just shooting into the air to cover his exit. In the calm of the morning beside his house, and without the benefit of the police-raid-induced adrenaline shot, he was surprised by the kick as the powder in the .45 ACP cartridge exploded, sending the heavy lead bullet out of the barrel. The gun automatically ejected the spent shell and loaded another bullet into the chamber, leaving the hammer back and ready to shoot again.

Mike leapt toward Frankie, hoping to knock her out of the bullet's path. He reached Frankie before the bullet got there, but not fast enough to get out of its path himself. The .45 caliber hunk of lead hit Mike in the back, tearing through his lung and knocking him the rest of the way to the ground.

Pain. Mike's mind seared with pain. Everything in his mind went red as he fell to the ground. Mike was having trouble breathing. He realized the damage the bullet had done to his left lung. Mike could smell his own blood. It was bubbling up into his throat with each breath. He heard Frankie scream and felt Rich and Frankie at his side.

Then he lost consciousness. And began dreaming.

The pain receded somewhat, although it was still hard to breathe. Mike wondered if he was dying. Is this what it feels like? He had seen death many times, but he didn't know, no one really knew, what death was like. Mike thought about his friends. Kelly and Tanya were so happy together and he was proud of them. He knew a relationship like theirs took a lot of work, and he knew it wasn't easy, but they were making it. That was all that mattered. They knew what it was like to be loved. That was all that mattered.

He had never slowed down, never taken the chance on love. There had been moments, he knew, but opening himself up to that risk hadn't been possible. He had always told himself that he was being brave, facing dangers, and that he couldn't do that to someone else. He couldn't let someone care about him and then worry while he was out doing his job. But now he was going to die alone, and no one was going to even miss him. He was going to die. Might as well surrender to it.

The pain lessened even further.

Those were the thoughts rattling around in his subconscious. Until he felt another presence and another voice.

"Michael, you're not alone. I am here and you are loved." It was Frankie. He knew it immediately. She was there in his mind. "You can't give up. You have to fight the despair. You are a fighter. Don't give up on me now."

The pain in Mike's chest returned.

"It hurts so much, Frankie. I just want to rest for a while."

"Michael, listen to me. It hurts, but that tells you that you're still alive. That you have a chance. I need you to fight and come back to me. Help is on the way, but you can't give up."

The pain grew more intense.

"How are you here, Frankie? Or are you really here?"

"It's me, Mike. It's me. You forget, I truly am blessed. Putting the Breastplate of Judgment on opened up parts of my mind and exposed me to things I never knew about and I didn't know how to handle. I was close to God. I touched God and he touched me. He is giving me the ability to talk to you right now. God wants you to fight. He wants you to live. He has plans for you. I know that."

Mike's chest was on fire again. He was having trouble breathing, but he could feel the struggle now. He wasn't going to give up.

"Frankie, don't leave me. I love you."

"I love you, too, Michael. I'm not going anywhere. They would have to drag me away from you."

CHAPTER 45

Jay stood stock still for a moment. The blast from the pistol in his hand and the sight of the bullet striking the man, his friends called him Mike, shocked him deeply. When the other two rushed to Mike's aid, he ran. Jay knew exactly what he had to do. He still had one card up his sleeve.

Reaching his desk, Jay turned to a different computer than the one he was using to attack the financial sector. He punched in a few commands and reactivated the remaining underwater control units ringing the island. There was still one task they could do. He turned them on and sent out the final message. He saw every light turn green and then go out. They were done.

Without glancing at his primary computer, Jay closed the cover, grabbed the bag of things he was planning to take with him and headed for the small runabout boat tied to the dock in the back of the house. It was time to get to his yacht and get out of here. He liked this tropical paradise, but he knew he had worn out his welcome. He smiled. He got everything he could out of it while he was there.

Jay quickly untied the lines holding the small boat in place, started the engine and pulled away, heading north away from the island. He heard sirens arriving at the house, just before he pushed the throttles forward and left Grand Cayman. Forever.

*****

Rich and Frankie were dimly aware of Commissioner March's arrival, but they were focused on controlling Mike's bleeding. Rich looked up and

227

told the officers with March that the shooter had just run back in the house. They immediately began preparing to enter the house when they heard a small boat engine start. Two officers rushed in the front door while two more ran around the outside of the house heading for the dock.

March grabbed his phone to call for an ambulance, but he couldn't connect.

"What happened?" March asked, quieter than you might expect while he continued trying to call. "I told you to wait."

"Jay screamed. I think he was losing it. And then he tried to shoot Frankie, but Mike stepped in the way," Rich said. "They told us that Jay's program was about to break in, so we decided to distract him and give the guys one more chance to stop it."

"We'll talk about it all later, but my phone isn't going through. That jeep has a VHF radio, right?"

"Yeah, it does. The radio still works. The rest of it is iffy," Rich said then he looked at Frankie. She looked like she was praying. She was kneeling beside Mike, applying pressure to the wound on his back and concentrating. Rich reached out his hand and touched Frankie. "Stay with him sweetheart. Don't let him die. He's too important. To all of us."

"We've got problems," March said as he ran back to Rich, Frankie and Mike. "Everything in George Town is a mess. All of the street lights and cell towers just went off. They are trying to get everything restarted, but it is going to take time. Traffic in town got snarled immediately and there are a bunch of wrecks. About the only communications that are working is radio."

"What caused it?"

"I'm guessing we have our friend Jaylend Taylor to thank for this one, too," March said. "But I don't know when we can get an ambulance out here. They are either tied up in traffic or already responding to other calls. The whole island is a mess."

"We'll have to load him in one of the police cruisers and drive him to town. I'm just afraid of the roads right now," March said.

"I've got a better idea," Rich said with a smile. "Look."

The *Manta* with Kelly, Tanya, Shrop, Eric, and Kurt pulled up to the dock that Jay had just vacated. Rich ran to let them know what was going on and get the backboard they kept onboard to get injured divers out of the water. Within minutes, the group had Mike on the backboard and were heading back to the boat.

"How did you know we needed your help?" Frankie asked as they pulled the boat away from the dock. She was still holding pressure on Mike's wound. They were pulling first aid supplies from the boat's kit and had set up a pressure bandage, along with putting Mike on supplemental oxygen to offset shock from the blood loss and the damaged lung.

"Something told us we needed to be here. We weren't about to go back to Sunset House and sip rum punch while you guys had all the fun, of course, but as soon as we got rid of the last control unit, we headed this way. We heard Bill send out the coordinates and knew right where to come," Tanya said gently. "And we thought we could help. That's what we do for each other. Cayman cowboys look out for each other. Mike has saved every one of us at one time or another. There's nothing we wouldn't do for him."

"I understand. And it's possible, there might be someone else guiding us all as well," Frankie smiled and then she closed her eyes again and concentrated on Mike.

"What's she doing?" Kelly asked, looking at Frankie.

"I think she's talking to Mike and keeping him with us."

Frankie could feel Mike's pain, but she also felt his strength and knew he was going to fight. He wasn't about to quit now.

"You've got some amazing friends, Michael," Frankie said to Mike. "These cowboys definitely have your back."

She could feel Mike relax, understanding where he was and surrounded by friends. Everything was going to be all right.

CHAPTER 46

Mike hurt. Everywhere. His throat was raw. His body was stiff and he couldn't move, or even feel, his left arm. He opened his eyes and saw white all around him. The lights were blazing. He could hear voices, but not make out anything other than a few shapes. Maybe he was dead.

Mike blinked a few times and things began to clear up. All his friends were there. Frankie, Rich, Kelly, Tanya and a few others as well. He was surprised the hospital hadn't thrown them all out.

"How…" Mike croaked.

"Hold on, Mike. They just took the tubes out of your throat a few minutes ago," Frankie said as she elevated the head of his bed and gave him some ice chips to suck on. "You got shot."

"I remember an angel talking to me, telling me to stay here. The angel said my friends needed me and loved me," Mike said with a smile for Frankie. His memories were fuzzy, and he didn't know how she did it, but he was certain she was inside his head talking to him.

"I'm sure the angel was right, Michael," Frankie said patting him on the shoulder.

"What happened after that?"

"That's when things got messy," Kelly said, taking over the story. "Somehow, Jay shut down the cell towers and streetlights. He really messed up traffic and they couldn't get an ambulance to you. Fortunately for your lazy hide, we showed up and started running you back to George Town on the boat. A Coast Guard helicopter met us halfway here and picked you up and then got you to the hospital. That was two days ago, by the way. You've been out and worrying us all half to death."

"What? Do I still owe you money?"

"Have you seen what you did to my jeep? You're going to have to pay for that," Kelly grinned.

"Stop it, Kelly. You know the answer to that, Mike." Tanya interrupted, punching Kelly on the shoulder.

"Did you get Jay?"

"The Wonder Twins were able to stop his Trojan Horse before it got into the banking system. They keep saying they give you guys full credit for distracting Jay while they worked. If he had been fighting them, they say they couldn't have done it," Kelly said. "But somehow Jay escaped. He took off from the house in a boat. He was headed to a yacht offshore, but the Coasties were there already. They had ringed the whole island, making sure no one left. We think he's still here, somewhere, but no one has found him yet."

"Oh, I almost forgot. Your magazine editor called on your cell phone. I answered it. Since you're laid up, they're sending down a writer and a photographer to interview all of us. She expects an exclusive, of course," Rich said.

"Of course," Mike said. "She can't pass up a really good story."

"Not when her golden boy was on the front row."

Mike looked around the room and realized there was someone else there. Except this person was in a hospital bed. It was Trina.

"She made it?" Mike asked, surprised and pleased.

"She was in worse shape than you, but she's going to pull through. It was touch and go for a while, but she's doing much better now."

"How much trouble is she in?"

"Some, but I don't think they're going to send her to jail. She'll probably be deported, though. The girl who shot her is going to stand trial for attempted murder. Trina will have to stay around at least until that's over."

"Sorry to hear that, but being sent home is better than spending the rest of your life in jail."

"What about Matt? He was a big help. Are they taking that into consideration?"

"He's in more trouble, but they're being fairly lenient," Kelly agreed. "Commissioner March vouched for him. Matt didn't know Jay's real plan and then he worked hard to stop him once he found everything out. I think they're looking at some sort of work release. He's agreed to help the international banks protect their systems better. And he and Trina will get to be together while the courts do their thing."

"The great thing is he's figured out a way to reprogram the control units all around the island to do what they were supposed to do in the first place. We're already gathering all sorts of data on the reefs around the island," Tanya chimed in.

"That sounds great," Mike said, already growing tired. "Seems like you don't need me around here after all. You've got it all figured it out."

"What we need is for you to get out of this hospital so we can finally have our party and renew our vows," Tanya said, patting Mike on his good arm.

"I'll get right to work on that…" And then he was back asleep.

*****

It took a few more days for Mike to get out of the hospital, but that gave Kelly and Tanya a chance to get everything ready at Sunset House. When Mike arrived at the hotel, driven by Rich and Frankie, everyone was waiting on him. The party for Kelly and Tanya's renewal of their vows had grown to encompass much more. They were celebrating Mike and Trina's recovery, getting the island back and new friends on top of the beautiful ceremony.

As things were winding down, and many of the party-goers were gone, the core group was seated around a table on the patio at My Bar. Kelly and Tanya were there, along with Rich, Frankie, and Mike.

"Michael, we have one more surprise for you," Tanya said. "Have you noticed that I haven't been diving and haven't been drinking either?"

"I hadn't, I guess, but now that you mention it…wait, you're pregnant?"

"It's a boy, Mike. We'd like you to be the godfather to Michael Kelly Anderson."

"You're naming him after me?" Mike was stunned. "Really?"

"Of course. How many other friends have saved both of our lives and are responsible for us being here together in the first place," Tanya beamed and patted her belly.

"And all of those awards you've won have to be worth something," Kelly joked. "Raising kids is expensive these days."

"That's wonderful guys, and I'll be honored to be his godfather," Mike agreed, tearing up. "I'm sure he's going to grow up to be another little cowboy, too."

*****

Tanya had experience restoring coral reefs from her work 10 years before, following the damage wreaked on the reef around Cayman by developer Gray Walker. Still, to help organize the efforts to repair the damage caused by the cruise ship anchor in the George Town Harbor, she called in the Coral Restoration Foundation for their advice. Since she couldn't dive, she was relying on her divers to give her reports and handle all the work, while she stayed on the boat and directed traffic. It wasn't where she wanted to be, but it was a small sacrifice for the safety of her baby, her unborn son. And there would still be plenty of work to do after he was born.

To restore the reef and repair the damage, the divers had to remove the rubble and debris to help the corals that were still attached to the reef live. They sorted through the damaged and broken pieces and found viable pieces of elkhorn and staghorn coral and were taking them to a protected bay not far away to set them up as a nursery. Once the reef was cleaned and prepared, they would reintroduce the broken pieces to the damaged reef, along with some corals brought in from other nurseries, to help the area regrow. Corals grow extremely slowly and this was a long-term project.

They had decided to rename the reef after Bubba, the ancient Goliath Grouper that hung out in the coral swim-throughs, but had died when the anchor chain came crashing down. Mike had the last photos of the enormous fish taken immediately before the accident.

Mike was on board the boat, photographing divers coming in and out of the water. He wasn't allowed to return to diving, either, so he was taking the time to work on stories about the entire affair for his magazine. Mike's editors at *First Account* magazine were salivating for another of his man-in-the-middle of the action stories. He had won them several awards for his past adventures. Mike was taking some leave to work as a Fellow at his alma mater, helping groom up-and-coming journalists, but he was still contributing from time to time.

Bill was still around, too. He stood on the shore flying drones over the research area. He had come with his own drone, but he had been able to commandeer Jay's drone, too. It was larger and stronger and was able to carry more equipment. They fitted the quadcopters with downward looking radar that was designed to penetrate the water. He was working to build a comprehensive map of the damage zone. The drones had limited flight times, but he would fly one until it ran low on battery life and then recharge that one while he flew the second one. He was making really good time with the mapmaking.

Mike was growing bored and frustrated at not being able to dive. He understood why he couldn't, the damage to his lungs from Jay's gunshot had not healed completely. But that didn't keep him from getting irritated. When all the divers were in the water and he wasn't needed at the moment, he picked up a pair of binoculars to look around. It was almost time to go home and while he had many memories of the island, he wanted to lock everything in. He scanned the pastel-colored buildings and the aquamarine water in the shallows above the white sand. There were no cruise ships in today so the streets were relatively quiet. *It really is paradise*, he thought.

As Mike scanned the docks with his binoculars, something caught his eye. It was a person, but someone who looked familiar. It was Jay, still on the run, but not looking like the Jay they had seen up until now. He was torn up, dirty and a mess. He looked exactly like you would expect someone to look who was on the run. He needed a bath and a shave. And clean clothes. When Jay had escaped, both from the island and then from the Coast Guard when he tried to board his yacht, the Grand Cayman and US government froze his assets. He was unable to access any of his money so he had to live off the land. It didn't look like it was going so well for him.

"Couldn't happen to a nicer guy," Mike said to himself. Jay had shot him, of course and Mike wasn't about to let that go.

"What was that, Mike? What are you looking at?" Tanya asked.

"I see the one loose end left from our little adventure," Mike said with a grin. He pointed where he was looking and handed the binoculars to Tanya.

"You've got to be kidding me. He looks like crap," she said, equally pleased by the turn of events. Jay had tried to kill her, too. "What's he doing?"

They both watched Jay for a few minutes. The man prowled along the docks, checking out boats. He did his best, but it was the middle of the day and Jay wasn't really cut out for burglary so it was fairly easy to keep an eye on him.

"Probably trying to find a boat he can steal to get off the island. If he can get to Cuba, maybe they'll give him asylum," Mike said. "Of course, our situation with Cuba is changing so they may not be as receptive to that as he might think. I doubt he's thinking too clearly at this point."

"You keep an eye on him. I'll call the police and let them know where to pick him up," Tanya said, grabbing her cell phone. Communications had finally returned to normal on the island. With divers in the water, they couldn't move the dive boat to try to intercept Jay, no matter how much both Tanya and Mike would love the experience.

"Tanya, we might have a problem," Mike said, never taking his eyes from the binoculars.

"Hold on," Tanya said, speaking into the phone. "What is it, Mike?"

"It looks like he's found a boat he can steal. He has climbed aboard that cruiser over there and I think he has started the engines. Owner must've left the keys on board." Mike quickly read off the Hull Identification Number and the boat's name and Tanya reported it to the police.

"They are sending someone out to get him, but it's going to take them a minute to get here," Tanya said after conferring with the police.

Mike looked around, trying to think of anything they could do. The boat was tied to a mooring ball and they had divers all over the dive site beneath them. It would be too dangerous to start the engines and take off in pursuit now. And then Mike got an idea.

"Hey, Bill!" Mike called out over the VHF radio. They didn't have to use their code names any longer, but Mike still wanted to call the computer hacker Wonder Twin.

"What's up, Mike?"

"Does Jay's old drone have any battery left in it?"

"Yep, I was just about to launch it. His drone is pretty amazing. It's got great battery life and we can get all sorts of information from it. It is still connected to the island network."

"Bill, that's all great, but I need you to do one thing for me right now."

"What's that?"

"Shut down a boat. Can you still do that?"

"Watch me!"

Bill launched the drone almost immediately and flew it out over the water, going away from the island and then angling back toward the harbor and the boat Jay was stealing. He didn't want to try to chase the boat down over open water.

Jay paused to grab some food out of the boat's refrigerator. The man tore into the packages like he hadn't eaten in days. Mike smirked at that. They all heard the police sirens as the authorities raced to the harbor and Mike watched as Jay realized they were coming for him. He saw Jay scramble around the boat to release the lines holding it to the dock.

The police came racing across the dock, but Jay was able to move faster. He was far from an expert at handling boats, but he really wasn't concerned about the niceties. He slid the boat he was stealing down the side of another boat tied off at the dock as he made his way out of the slip and then slammed the throttles forward, digging the propellers deep in the water before the cruiser began to move away and out to sea. The Cayman police officers ran for the police boat docked 100 yards away and got ready to give chase. If Jay made it too far away from the harbor, it would be difficult to track him. Larger boats had active radar systems that could keep an eye on him, but it would take time to get them involved.

Mike watched as Jay believed he was getting away. He saw the man stand behind the boat's wheel and shout and pump his fist into the air. Jay was convinced he was going to make it. He never saw the drone hovering directly in his path. When the boat got within 25 feet, the boat's engine began to sputter and lurch. The boat immediately lost headway and Jay was thrown forward against the wheel. He looked around in a panic, trying to restart the engines and flipping switches. In the silence of the moment, Jay finally heard the drone overheard. He looked up and recognized his own quad copter, the machine he used to cause an environmental disaster with the cruise ship and attempted murder sending Tanya to the bottom of the harbor. His own toy was going to be his undoing.

Jay slumped back into the captain's chair on the stolen boat and began to cry. The police boat caught up with him two minutes later. By then, Jay was inconsolable, in the midst of a complete breakdown.

*****

Everything was finally settling down. Kelly and Tanya were getting back to business, running their hotel and working to restore the coral reefs around the island, preserving diving for many years to come. Rich had flown home a few days earlier. He had to get back to work. Mike and Frankie were leaving Grand Cayman for home the next morning, but for the moment they were sitting on the patio at My Bar, staring out at the warm Caribbean water as the sun slipped into the ocean. Mike was smoking a Partagas Serie D Cuban cigar, sipping a CayBrew Ironshore Bock and relaxing. In spite of the gunshot wound and the stress of the last week, he felt great.

"Did I ever tell you about the time I met the Castros?" Mike asked, looking at the cigar.

"No, I don't think you did," Frankie smiled. "But you'll have plenty of time."

"How is that?"Mike asked looking at the beautiful woman beside him.

"I've been in touch with Dr. Blackwell at Marshall University. I had to explain to him why I came to town to give a guest lecture, and see you, and then disappeared for two weeks," Frankie said. "He told me a visiting fellow position has just opened up. He said it is similar to the one you are filling at the moment and asked if I would be interested. I told him I would take it. It's only a year, but I thought it would give us a chance to spend some time together and see if this could all work out."

"That's fantastic!" Mike said truly pleased. He slipped his hand into Frankie's and then turned to look out across the water at the sunset as the sun slipped below the horizon.

They saw the green flash.

"That has to be a sign," Mike said, happily.

EPILOGUE

This story is obviously a work of fiction. But the underlying story line is all too real.

On August 27, 2014, the cruise ship Carnival Magic dropped its anchor in a restricted area near Don Foster's dive shop. The grounding tore up more than 12,000 square feet of coral reef.

Criminal charges are unlikely for the captain and cruise line, but there may be fines. Volunteer divers from dive operations all over the island are coming together to clean up the reef and reattach surviving coral. Divers have worked to clear off the torn up coral, salvaging the still-living pieces and moving them to an underwater nursery to keep it growing until the site can be cleaned and repaired. Once everything is ready, the volunteer divers will reattach the coral to the reef using a specially-developed marine epoxy. In spite of the volunteer labor, the repair bill will likely run into the millions of dollars. They need money for equipment and supplies for the reef restoration.

Word of mouth is crucial for any author to succeed. If you enjoyed this book, please consider leaving a review at Amazon even if it's only a line of two; it would make all the difference and would be very much appreciated.

Say Hello!

Eric talks about adventure and taking time to be creative, along with diving and writing, on his blog at www.booksbyeric.com. He would love it if you dropped by to say hello.

You can also follow him on Twitter, get in touch on Facebook or through Google+. Lastly, you can always send him an email: eric@booksbyeric.com

About the Author

Life is an adventure for Eric Douglas, above and below the water and wherever in the world he ends up. Eric received a degree in journalism from Marshall University. After working in local newspapers, honing his skills as a story teller, and following a stint as a freelance journalist in the former Soviet Union, he became a dive instructor. The ocean and diving have factored into all of his fiction works since then.

As a documentarian, Eric has worked in Russia, Honduras, and most recently in his home state of West Virginia, featuring the oral histories of West Virginia war veterans in the documentary *West Virginia Voices of War* and the companion book *Common Valor*.

Visit his website at: www.booksbyeric.com.

Mike Scott Adventures
Cayman Cowboys
Flooding Hollywood
Guardians' Keep
Wreck of the Huron
Heart of the Maya

Children's Books
The Sea Turtle Rescue
Swimming with Sharks

Withrow Key Short Stories
The complete Withrow Key Collection: Tales from Withrow Key
Going Down with the Ship
Bait and Switch
Put It Back
Frog Head Key
Queen Conch
Sea Monster
Caesar's Gold

Life Under the Sea

Other books by Eric Douglas:
River Town
Non-fiction
Keep on, Keepin' on: A Breast Cancer Survivor Story
Common Valor: Companion to the multimedia documentary West Virginia
Voices of War
Russia: The New Age
Scuba Diving Safety

If you would like to receive an email from Eric when his next book is released, sign up here. Your email address will never be shared and you can unsubscribe at any time.

Made in the USA
Charleston, SC
10 May 2015